The crowd dispersed slowly, like the shifting sand following a wave.

Mrs. Beabots was the last to leave the room, and then it was just Katia standing across from Austin in the front parlor of the house she grew up in.

"Hello, Austin."

"Katia."

She thought her heart would hammer a hole right through her chest, but she didn't dare let him know how much he affected her. She couldn't decide whether to rush to him and ask his forgiveness on the spot. She felt like she'd turned to stone. She couldn't think or move.

She was filled with blistering guilt.

"Austin, I'm so—"

His hands shot up to silence her. "Katia, leave. Now."

"But, Austin, I want to talk to you."

He shook his head. "Leave. It's what you do best."

Dear Reader,

For those of you who are just discovering the Shores of Indian Lake, *Katia's Promise* is the fourth book in the series. Although Katia's story was the fourth one to be written, it was the vision of beautiful, guilt-ridden Katia returning to Indian Lake after nearly twenty years of living in Chicago that sparked the entire series. I had a vision of Katia standing under a streetlight across from an elegant home, daring herself to go in and confront the man she'd left brokenhearted when she was sixteen. I wanted a heroine who knew she'd "done wrong by him."

Austin McCreary has never forgiven Katia. When she seems to blow into Indian Lake like a gale-force wind and crashes a presentation he's giving in his home, he's not happy to see her.

I hope you enjoy Katia's story as much as I did when I finally put her stormy romance with Austin on paper.

I would love to hear if there's a character you've seen mentioned in Indian Lake whose story you'd like to read. You can contact me at cathlanigan1@gmail.com or my website at catherinelanigan.com. You can find me on Facebook, Twitter, Pinterest and LinkedIn.

Catherine Lanigan

HEARTWARMING

Katia's Promise

—

Catherine Lanigan

HARLEQUIN® HEARTWARMING™

Recycling programs
for this product may
not exist in your area.

ISBN-13: 978-0-373-36726-9

Katia's Promise

Copyright © 2015 by Catherine Lanigan

Printed in U.S.A.

Catherine Lanigan knew she was born to storytelling at a very young age when she told stories to her younger brothers and sister to entertain them. After years of encouragement from family and high school teachers, Catherine was shocked and brokenhearted when her freshman college creative-writing professor told her that she had "no writing talent whatsoever" and that she would never earn a dime as a writer. He promised her that he would get her through his demanding class with a B grade so as not to destroy her high grade point average, *if* Catherine would promise never to write again.

For fourteen years she did not write until she was encouraged by a television journalist to give her dream a shot. She wrote a 600-page historical romantic spy-thriller set against World War I. The journalist sent the manuscript to his agent who then garnered bids from two publishers. That was nearly forty published novels, nonfiction books and anthologies ago.

Books by Catherine Lanigan

Harlequin Heartwarming

Heart's Desire
Love Shadows
A Fine Year for Love

MIRA

Dangerous Love
Elusive Love
Tender Malice
In Love's Shadow
Legend Makers
California Moon

Silhouette Desire

The Texan
Montana Bride

Visit the Author Profile page
at Harlequin.com for more titles.

This book is dedicated to my husband, Jed Nolan,
with all my love forever.

Acknowledgments

I don't know how many times my editors have had
to pull their hair out over my manuscripts until,
together, we finally create a jewel, but I'm hoping
no one runs to a wig store on my account. Each
time I sit down to the computer I say a prayer of
thanksgiving for everyone at Heartwarming.

To my editor, Claire Caldwell, believe me,
there aren't enough words in this clunky English
language to express my sincere gratitude
for your brilliant guidance and creativity.

Many thanks to Victoria Curran for expecting
superior storytelling out of me and all the authors.
I also appreciate all you do out there in the real
world to promote the line and the authors, and the
push to get our books into more retail venues.

To all the Heartwarming staff,
you are extraordinarily talented individuals,
and it shows. From our unique and compelling
covers to the cover copy to the daunting hours
of promotion on social media it takes to
make our presence known, thank you.

To Dianne Moggy—as always,
I send you my sincere gratitude and affection.

CHAPTER ONE

GOLDEN AND BRONZE autumn sunset beams shot through the wooden slats on Katia's high-rise apartment windows. She padded across the beige carpet in bare feet, rushing from the bathroom to the bedroom. She was late for her own party.

She'd spiraled a navy towel around her hair, then spritzed herself with jasmine-and-almond-scented body spray. Now, standing in front of her closet, she pulled out the black silk and lace sheath dress she'd recently bought at her favorite resale shop on the far North Side. The dress had obviously never been worn. Like most of the dresses at Sonja's Secrets, this one had probably belonged to an affluent woman from Wilmette or Kenilworth who shopped out of boredom and not need. Katia hadn't had time to be bored since she was very young. Ten years ago, she was too busy building her résumé and her reputation in the insurance business to shop, go to the movies or do anything other than work. Then she'd turned thirty, landed a job at Carter and Associates with Jack Carter, and in her four years there, she'd become a manager. She'd won confidence and approval.

She was on top of the world.

Katia zipped up the dress and turned to check herself in the full-length mirror on the back of the bedroom door. She smiled. The dress fit like a dream and showed off her slender figure, and the well-placed darts accentuated her waist. Katia only had two rules when it came to diet and exercise: no French fries, and she walked the twenty-one blocks to and from work every day. Life already had enough rules to follow, she thought.

Katia unfurled the towel and shook out her messy mane of coppery hair. She quickly applied black eyeliner to make the dark green of her eyes pop. She swooped on blusher and then uncapped a brand-new flame-red lipstick. The salesgirl at Macy's had claimed it was such a powerful red, it would change her life.

Just then, Katia smelled something burning in the kitchen. *The turnovers!*

Tossing the lipstick onto her dresser, Katia raced, still barefoot, into the kitchen. The timer was chirping, and there was a thin stream of brown smoke coming from the oven. Using an orange pumpkin-shaped pot holder, she opened the oven and pulled out the cookie sheet of feta cheese, spinach and bacon phyllo dough appetizers.

Katia looked over the tray of golden crisp finger foods. Only one victim. *I'm saved*, she thought.

As she turned off the oven, the intercom rang. It was Joey, the doorman. "Miss Stanislaus. Your guests are arriving. In droves, I might add. Should I send them up?"

"Yes, Joey. Thanks."

Katia hung up and quickly moved the hot appetizers onto a tiered serving stand. She took the stand into the dining nook, placed it strategically on the table and surveyed her work.

Katia's apartment was small, but it had a large enough dining and living area that she could comfortably host small parties, like the engagement party she was throwing tonight for her coworker Tina and her fiancé, Allen. The kitchen was minuscule, but since Katia didn't cook—except for when she had company—she didn't mind. The bathroom was more of an alcove than a room, and the only saving grace in her bedroom was the walk-in closet, which housed the bounty of her bargain-hunting addiction.

The building had been constructed in the late 1950s and wasn't very aesthetically pleasing. What it had going for it was great access to her work, security and a massive window that looked out over Chicago. Many was the night that Katia lived to see the lights glittering beneath her, as if she was walking on stars.

Katia smoothed the white cotton tablecloth she'd bought at an outlet store—yet another great bargain—and straightened the fruit platter of grapes, pears, melon wrapped in prosciutto, pineapple chunks speared with maraschino cherries, apples for dipping in caramel sauce and twin mounds of strawberries with chocolate fudge. She'd displayed an array of specialty cheeses on a slab of rough-edged marble she'd found at a granite and marble boneyard. She had four kinds of crackers and three bread selections.

She crossed to the antique marble-topped buffet on the wall next to the boring, mantel-less fireplace. This was the most important element of all—the bar.

Recently, Katia had discovered Crenshaw Vineyards while passing through her hometown, Indian Lake, on a business trip. She'd gone back four times, and now her wine rack and portable wine cooler were stocked with some of the best wines Katia had ever tasted. Katia had bought discount wineglasses and garage sale decanters, and she'd trawled eBay for the best deals on bar paraphernalia. But she never scrimped on the food and wine that she served to her guests.

Katia loved giving parties, and though she couldn't afford florists, live music, caterers or even a bartender, she enjoyed making holidays and special events even more exceptional for her friends and coworkers. She wanted them to have happy memories.

"I want them to remember me," Katia murmured as the doorbell rang.

Putting her hand on the doorknob, Katia scanned the room one more time. She couldn't remember if she'd dusted the glass shelf in the bathroom or if she'd lit the scented candle in the kitchen.

There was a knock.

It was too late now for a last-minute check. Katia felt her heart pound ever so slightly, as it always did before an important meeting or a special event, then she whisked open the door.

"Hi, guys!" She beamed at Tina Goodman, her assistant at Carter and Associates, and Allen Hampton, the football coach for St. Michael's High School. "If it isn't the bride and groom!" The second the words were out of her mouth, Katia realized she still wasn't wearing any shoes. She'd been so immersed in the food and decor, she'd forgotten to finish dressing. It wasn't like her to be so scatterbrained, but she'd been noticing herself slipping up more often lately.

Allen—lean, blond and California handsome—kissed Katia's cheek. "You look gorgeous, as always," he said, winking at Tina and pulling her close with a possessive arm.

Katia smiled demurely. "But not as beautiful as the bride." She squeezed Tina's hand.

"Very diplomatic, both of you," Tina teased. She gave Katia a quizzical look. "You're shorter."

"Uh! Didn't have a chance to grab my shoes. Come in before the others get up here. I have to finish dressing."

"We're not early, are we?" Allen asked as Katia ushered them inside.

"No, no. It's just me. I got behind somehow."

Tina shook her head. "That's hard for me to imagine." She turned to Allen. "We call her Miss Excel at work. Because she's so organized, we figure even her leg waxings are plugged into a spreadsheet."

"I'm not that bad," Katia replied defensively, showing them into the living room. "Now, if you'll excuse me for a minute, I have to get my shoes."

Allen grinned playfully and winked again at Tina. "Maybe some earrings, too, while you're in there?"

Tina elbowed him and giggled.

Katia rushed to the bedroom, stuck her feet into a new pair of black Stuart Weitzman pumps and put on a pair of dangling emerald earrings and a bracelet to match. The ringing doorbell kept her from double-checking her reflection in the mirror.

On her way through the living room, she saw that Tina and Allen had found the wine bar and Allen was opening a bottle of Crenshaw Cabernet. "Thanks, guys. Oh, and open some pinot grigio while you're at it, please?"

Katia answered the door. Filling the entrance were four couples and a single man, who stood inches taller than everyone else. His charisma dwarfed the group even more. Jack Carter.

"Welcome!" Katia beamed amid hugs and well wishes as her friends moved into the apartment. Jack was last. He bent and placed his hand on her shoulder and started to kiss her cheek, then abruptly pulled back. He smiled awkwardly, as if suddenly remembering she was his employee. He was the boss. "Thanks for inviting me, Katia."

Jack had ironclad rules when it came to office romances. He forbade his employees from dating each other, and under no circumstances could anyone at Carter and Associates date a current or prospective client. Katia thought the rule was wise and necessary, considering the nature of their business. After all these years, however, Katia realized that the long hours and weekends she put in kept her single with a capital *S*.

Katia had very little time for dating, and even when she was at parties or functions, she was always scanning the crowds for new clients.

Katia was perpetually working the room. The company benefited from her dedication, but as she watched her friends gather in her living room, it struck her that all of her friends had paired up in the past few years. Tina was the only one who hadn't gotten married yet, and this was her engagement party.

Only Katia and Jack were left.

She smiled at Jack and lifted her arm to usher him inside. "It wouldn't be an office party without you," she told him.

She glanced down the hall and looked back at Jack curiously. "Barry and Ava aren't with you?"

Barry was Jack's partner and brother-in-law. Jack's sister, Ava, loved parties and never missed one of Katia's gatherings. Ava had once told Katia that she secretly hoped Jack and Katia would pair up someday. As if that would ever happen.

Jack slapped his forehead. "Sorry, I forgot to tell you. The baby got sick at the last minute. Fever, and Ava didn't dare ask our mother to babysit." He rolled his eyes. "She has tickets to the ballet tonight." He wagged his finger. "Never mess with my mother's ballet plans. Anyway, Barry didn't feel quite right coming without Ava. He said he'd see you at the office on Monday."

"Sure," Katia replied dully, truly disappointed that she would miss seeing Ava. Ava was always so much fun, and before the baby had arrived six months ago, she was always up for resale shopping with Katia. Since little Kaylee had arrived, Ava had nearly dropped out of Katia's life. She still called and texted, but it just wasn't the same.

It wasn't only Ava's baby that had shaken up Katia's life. Katia had felt subtle changes at work, too: a lost client she'd believed was a slam dunk, a corporate takeover that had caused them to lose a large account, Barry spending countless hours building a new website, new furrows across Jack's brow.

"Katia!" Allen shouted. "Did you make these?" He held up one of her little turnovers. "With the wine—superb!"

"Thanks," she replied, feeling uplifted by the compliment. She crossed to the bar and stood next to Jack, who had just poured a glass of red wine.

Katia took a glass for herself, a burgundy balloon she'd found at a closeout at Macy's, and
filled it slowly.

Jack took a sip and his eyes grew wide. "This
is incredible. What is it?" He read the label on
the bottle. "Crenshaw. Never heard of it."

"You wouldn't have. It's a secret discovery
of mine."

"I want some," he said in that firm, authori-
tative voice he used when issuing commands at
work. "Can you get me a case?"

"Sure. I've made friends with the owner. Actually, Liz and I have started emailing back and
forth. I'll get on it right away."

Jack flashed his mind-blowing, bone-melting
smile at Katia, and she wondered if she'd ever
learn how not to respond to it.

"Katia, you're the best."

"Thanks," she replied feeling just the teensi-
est bit light-headed. She put down her glass. "I
should see to dinner. Would you excuse me?"

"Can I help?" he offered with yet another
earth-shattering smile. "I admit I'm not much
good around food, other than the consump-
tion of it, but I can lift heavy objects. Turkeys.
Prime-rib roast." He chuckled easily.

God, it would be so easy to fall for Jack.

"Thanks, but we're having shrimp creole.
I think I can manage." Teetering in her high

heels, Katia made it to the kitchen, where she grabbed onto the edge of the sink for stability.

Her heart was hammering, and she'd broken out in a cold sweat.

What was the matter with her? She'd worked with handsome Jack Carter for years. Day in, day out. Evenings. Weekends. She'd never reacted like this before.

Katia looked down at her hands as she let go of the sink. *Shaking? I'm shaking?*

Suddenly, she couldn't catch her breath. She felt clammy and nauseous.

Tina walked into the kitchen, took one look at Katia and said, "Do you have any paper bags?"

Katia shook her head. "No, why?"

"You're hyperventilating."

"How do you know?"

"I've been there. You have to breathe your own air. I need a little brown bag."

"Bloomingdales?" Katia forced a smile. "Corner cabinet. Next to the cookie sheets."

Tina shot to the cabinet, withdrew a small paper shopping bag and then clamped it over Katia's mouth. "Now breathe. Slowly. In and out. That's a girl."

Katia didn't know what was happening, but the bilious taste in her throat had subsided, her stomach no longer rumbled and her head cleared. The ground under her feet was solid again. Tina had miraculously infused marrow back into her bones.

Katia took the bag away from her face. "Thank you, Tina. I don't know what that was. I thought I was going to die. Or at least pass out. That's never happened to me before."

Tina pursed her lips. "You had a panic attack. I get them sometimes."

Katia inhaled deeply and smoothed her hair. "Humph." She pretended confidence she didn't feel. "It's never happened to me."

Tina smirked as she glanced back into the living room and spied Jack talking to Allen. Her eyes tracked back to Katia. "Well, it has now."

Despite her inexplicable anxiety attack, Katia's party was a rousing success. The rice was fluffy, the shrimp tender and not overcooked and her homemade French bread and herb butter was gone before she could dish up seconds for Jack and Allen. While the candles flickered merrily and she served dessert with Tina's help, everyone engaged in lively and thought-provoking conversations about the new play at the Oriental as well as city politics.

All in all, it was the kind of evening Katia had hoped it would be. It reminded her of a time, long ago, when she'd watched intelligent and interesting people gather around a glittering dinner table at Hanna McCreary's mansion.

Katia never forgot those conversations, nor the fact that the guests had never wanted to leave Hanna's house before midnight. Even as a little girl, Katia had absorbed every nuance of Hanna's talent for party giving. Tonight, her studies had paid off.

It was odd, Katia mused, as she dipped her spoon into the chocolate mousse, that Hanna should pop into her mind like that. She hadn't thought of Hanna in a long time, though she had been Katia's mentor in many ways.

Was it possible that these old memories had something to do with her earlier panic attack?

CHAPTER TWO

WITH HER HEAD propped against three down pillows, Katia sat in bed and turned on her iPad. Her guests were gone and the kitchen was clean. With the sound of the dishwasher running in the background, Katia checked her emails. She clicked through the usual sale announcements from her favorite stores and a reminder about her dentist appointment later that week, then read a note from Ava apologizing for missing the party. Katia quickly answered Ava and promised to bring some of her chocolate mousse to the office for Barry to bring home. At least they'd get a taste of the party.

Because Katia had promised Jack that she would order a case of Crenshaw cabernet for him, she banged out a quick email to Liz Crenshaw. She'd been getting closer with Liz since her last trip through Indian Lake. Katia admired her drive and ambition, and she was impressed by Liz's plans to expand her vineyard. Katia was also a very good customer, which had helped spark their friendship. She'd promised Liz she would recommend Crenshaw wines to all her friends. Since the wines were excellent and a good price, Katia didn't have much trouble finding enthusiastic new customers for Liz.

Before typing out her order, Katia asked about Liz's grandfather's health. Sam had undergone open heart surgery just over a month ago, and she knew Liz had been spending a lot of time caring for him. Then she asked about the case of wine and requested that Liz set aside a half dozen bottles so she could restock her bar after tonight's party.

Katia glanced at her digital alarm clock and was surprised it was not even ten o'clock. She was exhausted, and Jack had told her to "get some rest." He'd mentioned something about being sharp for their Monday meeting.

Katia didn't have the slightest idea what he'd meant by that, but he had seemed a bit preoccupied during dinner. The more she thought about it, the more she felt dread creeping up on her like a snake.

If there was something amiss with the company, Katia hoped Jack and Barry had enough confidence in her skills and professionalism to trust her with that information. She'd taken it as a good sign that Jack had attended the party for Tina. Her assistant was hardworking, intelligent and dedicated to the company. Katia believed that Jack recognized her own loyalty to Carter and Associates, and knew that she'd always been focused on becoming a partner. Insurance was one of the few businesses that still rewarded loyalty, longevity and impressively long client lists.

Katia had always intended to be nothing short of a stellar employee for Jack.

That was another reason she didn't understand her panic attack. She'd been in a gazillion situations with Jack that many women would construe as romantic, yet they'd all been for work. They'd sailed into the sunset on Lake Michigan with clients, sipped French champagne on the lawn of a Lake Forest estate and danced to harp music at Christmas high tea at the Drake Hotel. Yet every moment had been strictly professional, in conjunction with Katia's efforts to sign new clients.

Jack stuck to his rules like superglue. He'd never once acted inappropriately; never held her hand or gazed at her a fraction of a second too long.

Over the years, Katia had come to understand that Jack wasn't into her. Period. And that had been okay.

Until tonight.

Tonight, Katia's psyche, if not her conscious mind, had suddenly realized that Tina was the last of her friends to pair off. Everyone was married. Except Katia.

She didn't have weekend lunches or theater matinees with her girlfriends anymore. And when they did manage to get together, half of them had to rush home to kids. Or, like Ava, they had to break dates because of a sick child.

Katia's iPad dinged with a new email. Katia smiled as she opened the note from Liz.

Hi, Katia,

I'm so happy your friends like our wine so much and that you are true to your word about being my Chicago advertising advocate. I will be happy to put a case aside for you as well as the extra bottles. You can pick them up on your next trip through town. When do you think that will be? I've come to look forward to your visits, and though I don't email on a daily basis, I'm apparently falling into the habit.

We've been busy with the harvest, but for me, there's been a big change. Since I saw you only two weeks ago, Gabe and I got engaged! Because you two knew each other in high school, sharing the news with you was fine with him.

Katia groaned. "Not you, too! Is this some conspiracy?" She exhaled deeply, hoping to rid her cells of her growing envy. She read further.

Honestly, I've never been into the white-dress thing, though nearly all my girlfriends are. Frankly, Gabe and I are talking about eloping. Or a seriously small wedding. Don't say a word—not that you know that many people here anymore! We just don't see any point in waiting another week, to be honest. Who knows, by the time you come through Indian Lake again, I may be married!

And thank you for asking about my grandfather's health. He's doing amazingly well. I can't believe it, to be honest.

The reason we're still up is because we just got back from driving an order into town. It was last minute and our customer can be rather demanding when he wants to be. Actually, it's pretty exciting for us in Indian Lake. Austin Mc-Creary—you probably wouldn't have known him when you lived here since I think he's quite a few years older than us. But anyway, we're excited because he decided to build a car museum on the south side of town. He's giving a big show-and-tell for the City Council, the Mayor and the Northwest Indiana Tourism Board members and officers. Should be around fifty people. Actually, I'm going to bartend for him, which is another chance to get our wines advertised and "out there." But Grandpa is fine. He'll be so pleased when I tell him that our wines were such a hit at your party.

Let me know when you'll be coming through town. I don't want to miss you!
Fondly,
Liz

Katia threw back the covers and shot out of bed as if she'd been set on fire. She raked her fingers through her long hair and pulled it tightly away from her face. Any thoughts of sleep were distant.

"This isn't happening. *Austin?*"

Katia paced at the end of her bed and then left the bedroom. She went straight to the kitchen and poured a tall glass of milk, took out a full bowl of chocolate mousse and sat at her small table. Her mind raced as she shoved the mousse into her mouth.

She'd made four trips through Indian Lake and hadn't once thought about Austin. *Oh, no. Instead, tonight, when I practically felt as if I was having a heart attack...* Now *he comes back to haunt me.*

She knocked back a big slug of milk. *A car museum. Humph. What's that all about, Austin? As if you need a museum.*

Katia finished off the mousse and swallowed the last of the milk. The dishwasher was still running, so she put her dishes in the sink.

Padding quietly into the living room, she

sank onto the sofa. The truth was that Indian
Lake and Austin McCreary were part of her
past. All these years that she'd been in Chicago, working toward her dream of becoming
a partner at Carter and Associates, she'd barely
thought about her childhood. It was her job and
the need to go beyond Chicago to find clients—
not nostalgia—that had led her back to Indian
Lake this summer. She'd stumbled upon Crenshaw Vineyards, and her new friendship with
Liz was the reason she'd returned on several
occasions.

Katia had stuffed her past deep down inside
her, refusing to bring those shadows into the
light. She knew all too well that it could be
dangerous to allow those memories to rise to
the surface.

Katia had grown up in a mansion in Indian Lake filled with elegant antiques. Katia's
mother, Stephania, had been the housekeeper,
but Katia had paid attention to every nuance
of Hanna and Daniel McCreary's lifestyle. Because Stephania had been responsible for over-
seeing the McCrearys' everyday schedule, as
well as holiday events and dinner parties, Katia
had eased into whatever job needed doing, from
sous chef to table decorator to bartender. Before Katia had hit her teens, she'd learned about
wines from Mr. McCreary. Katia had developed

a sharp palate, which she believed was even better than Austin's at the time.

Austin was three years older than Katia. She hadn't seen him since the summer she was sixteen, when she and her mother had left Indian Lake. That was the summer Katia had known for certain that Austin had finally fallen in love with her. She'd been in love with him since the day she and her mother had moved into the McCreary mansion when she was only seven years old.

Katia's parents were immigrants from Russia. Her father had been a mason and tile layer until his death in a truck accident on the South Side of Chicago. Katia's mother, Stephania, spoke very little English and had never worked in her life before her husband's death. A friend from their church had told Stephania she knew of two people looking for a full-time housekeeper. Stephania had applied for both jobs, but Hanna McCreary had wanted a live-in housekeeper, and Stephania couldn't turn down the offer of free room and board for her and Katia.

Daniel McCreary owned a large auto-parts manufacturing plant and a retail store in Indian Lake. That same year, he had signed a very large corporate contract, which required him to spend more hours at the plant and less time at home with his wife and son. Hanna was the president of three charities and overwhelmed with her duties.

Stephania and Katia lived in the rear rooms on the first floor with their own entrance at the back, next to the driveway that led to one of three large old carriage houses. These buildings had been converted into garages to house Daniel's collection of antique cars.

When they were kids, Austin often treated Katia like a pest and did his best to pretend, especially around his school friends, that she wasn't anyone special to him. But in the long summer evenings when the light refused to fade and children's attentions were not easily occupied, Austin had sought Katia out for tennis matches on the family clay courts, a swim in the pool, games of chess or Monopoly when it rained. She was his partner when his mother had forced him to take dancing lessons, and she had held a foil and worn thick cotton armor when he'd learned to fence.

Even then, Katia had known that she was only a substitute playmate for Austin, someone to stand in when his father was too busy to see him, but she didn't care. She thought Austin walked through the stars at night and skated on sunbeams in the day. In her eyes, he could do no wrong. When Austin was with her, he was happy, carefree and inquisitive. She didn't care that he shunned her as a "servant" when he was trying to impress his school friends, though at times, their barbs pierced the edges of her feelings. Katia believed that Austin would be her hero and come to her rescue if she ever truly needed it. She believed they were closer than any two people alive and only she knew the "real" Austin.

When Austin was fifteen and she was twelve, Daniel McCreary died. Gone was the man Austin had revered and tried to emulate. She remembered eavesdropping on dinner conversations where Daniel would herald the accomplishments of his grandfather, Ambrose McCreary, who had been one of the pioneer automobile designers at the turn of the century in Indianapolis. He'd talked to his son about Duesenbergs, Auburn Cords and Studebakers. Names from the past, connoting elegance and innovation. Katia had been enthralled as Daniel had spun his dreams of manufacturing replacement parts for antique cars. Austin had continually nagged his father for more stories about Ambrose and the kind of mind that he'd had. More than once, Katia had heard Austin say, "I should have been born back then. I could have been great like him."

Though she'd understood that Austin was expected to take over his father's manufacturing plant once he finished business college, for Austin, life without his father in it was like sleepwalking.

Daniel's funeral had been on Valentine's Day. Afterward, nearly a hundred people had come to the McCreary mansion for an enormous buffet dinner reception. They'd eaten, drunk, cried, laughed and reminisced.

That night, a blizzard had barreled into Indian Lake, nearly shutting down the interstate. Many guests had been snowbound and talked about sleeping on the library floor until the weather cleared up.

For Austin, it had all been too much. He'd disappeared.

Katia had been frantic until she'd glanced out her bedroom window and seen a faint light glowing in one of the carriage houses. She pulled on her boots and coat, and, taking an envelope from under the sweaters in her dresser drawer, she'd clomped through the new-fallen snow to the carriage house.

She'd found Austin sitting in a blue 1926 Bugatti convertible—Daniel's favorite. Austin had been sobbing his heart out.

Katia was careful not to make any noise as she approached the car. Daniel had never allowed her to look at the cars, much less touch them. Austin, however, had gleefully sneaked her into the carriage houses each time his father had acquired a new beauty. Austin had been all too happy to display his extensive knowledge of the features and history of each car. He'd taken pride in the fact that his father would go to great lengths to find authentic chrome bumpers for his Duesenberg or brass and glass headlamps for a 1920 Stutz Bearcat. Katia had loved the romance of the exquisite cars with their leather seats, velvet upholstered doors and sterling silver flower vases. It was her way of living in another era by literally touching objects from bygone times.

Sometimes Katia would double-dare Austin into sitting in the 1955 Rolls-Royce Silver Cloud. She liked to pretend she was a movie star or a princess in Monaco. Anyone but who she was—the maid's daughter.

Most of the time, Austin obliged her. He'd told her that since she understood his love for antique cars, she had to be his "kindred soul." She hadn't known what that meant at the time, so she'd looked it up in one of the books in Daniel's library. When she'd read the meaning, she'd wondered if this was Austin's way of telling her that she was special to him.

She'd just begun to feel as if they were becoming real friends when Daniel had died.

Katia eased her hand over the side of the

door and opened it from the inside so as not to smudge the polished exterior. Usually, touching the precious car would have been an invasion, but Katia felt that the world had somehow changed.

It was time for Austin to learn that she was more than just the housekeeper's daughter and his stand-in playmate. Austin's eyes were swollen. "Katia. I should have known you would find me."

"I'm not leaving. Even if you ask me," she said, climbing into the passenger seat.

"I won't," he said, wiping his tears on his tweed jacket sleeve. He folded his arms across the steering wheel and then laid his face on them. "I can't believe he's gone. What will I do?"

"What you've always done. You'll grow. Learn and become a man," she said with a tiny shrug.

"I miss him so much already," Austin said. He gulped, sounding to Katia as if he'd swallowed something very large. She understood the feeling intensely.

"I know you do," she said softly, looking at the round dials on the metal dashboard. "That part never goes away."

His face twisted into a grimace of disdain and disbelief. "What do you—" He stopped abruptly. "I'm so sorry, Katia. So sorry. Of course you know how I feel. You know exactly how I feel. None of the people I go to school with have lost their dads. But you have." Tears filled his eyes, yet he studied her as if he was seeing her for the first time. "It's been a while since you talked about your father. Do you still miss him?"

"Every day," she whispered, a flame igniting at the base of her esophagus and flaring up into her throat. "He—he used to call me Katia *lyubov.*"

"Louie bov?"

"*Lyubov.* That's how you say it." She nodded. "It means Katia love."

"He was a sentimental man, then?" Austin asked.

"Yes. He worked hard all his life, but my mother said he had the heart of a poet. She always loved fine things, and he wanted to give them to her—that's why he worked so hard to bring us to America. He told her he would give her the world, but—"

"He died," Austin finished for her. "Just like my dad."

"Yes. Now they're together. Watching over us, my mother says."

"Do you believe her?" Austin asked solemnly.

"I do."

"But how can you know? For sure, I mean. Sometimes I think that whole heaven thing is just another fairy tale."

"You're just angry right now. You don't know what you're saying."

"I *am* angry. My dad wasn't supposed to die. He was too young. We had great plans for after graduation. He told me we were going to go to Germany together and drive the autobahn. I wanted to see how they made German cars. I wanted to take classes over there and learn to fix all kinds of foreign cars."

Katia looked away from him. "Your mother was never going to allow that to happen and you know it."

"My dad could have talked her into it."

"She would never let you be a mechanic. Even I know that! She wants you to be a businessman and get a degree from Harvard."

"Well, it's not what I want. Besides, I don't see any other man of the house around here now, do you?" he asked.

"No."

"See? That's how things have changed. I'll be making the rules now."

Katia chuckled at the lofty tilt to his chin and the smirk on his lips.

She pushed her face up against his. "Don't you ever look at me like that again, Austin Mc-

Creary, or I will never speak to you again. You are not the boss of me and never will be. You got that?"

Austin moved back a few inches. "I just meant that things will be different."

"Yes. They will. But our parents still make the rules. We don't have any power yet."

"Power?"

"That's what my mom says all the time. She must remind me twice a day that I'm only a servant's kid. I have no power. That's why I have to graduate high school and go to college. I think your mother is right about that, too."

"But I don't want to run the family business. I want to work on antique cars."

"Well, I want to be a movie star."

"You're pretty enough," Austin said with a smile that Katia knew she'd remember the rest of her life.

"Austin, I'm not sure what I *actually* want to be. That's just what I want right now. I'll probably change my mind a bunch before I'm even your age. I only know one thing."

"What's that?"

She reached into the pocket of her winter coat and pulled out the envelope that she'd hidden in her drawer for a week. "I want to give you this." She handed it to him.

Austin took the envelope. "What is it?"

"Open it and see."

Carefully, he pulled out a folded piece of red construction paper. It opened into a heart. On it, Katia had glued bits of white lace she'd found in the attic, and she'd written snippets of Russian poems. She'd folded over pale blue pieces of construction paper and glued them to the heart, as well. Each of the folded notes contained dates.

"What is this? July 17? And September 26? I don't understand."

"Those are special days to me. On July 17, the summer I first came to live here, you taught me to ride a bike. On September 26, you finally let me play tennis with two of your friends. You said you needed another person for doubles."

"Yes. Last year. And we beat them," he said.

"Christmas is always a special day here. And so is Halloween. That's why I put those dates down."

Austin looked at her then, and for the first time, Katia was aware of a boy looking at her with love in his eyes. She felt her heart thrum and warmth surged through her. She didn't know if what she was feeling was normal or not, but it was incredibly exciting.

"And today is February 14. Valentine's Day," Austin said, reaching over to touch her hand. "I don't have a card for you. I don't have one for anyone. I guess I didn't think much about it."

"I made the card a while ago."

"Before my father's heart attack."

"Yeah."

"So you didn't give me this just to make me feel better today?"

"No."

"Then, why?"

"I want to be your friend, Austin. Your real friend. Always."

"I'd like that, Katia," he'd said as he gently folded the Valentine, put it in the envelope and slipped it into the breast pocket of his tweed jacket.

"Always…" Katia said out loud, jolting out of her reverie. Of all her memories of Austin, that Valentine's Day was the sweetest. But what happened afterward made it painful to remember, too.

Austin hadn't had a single opportunity to make any rules for himself. That autumn, his mother had shipped him off to New York to attend York Prep School, where he'd remained until his graduation.

With Austin away at school, Katia felt as if she'd been set adrift on an iceberg in the middle of the Black Sea. Katia didn't know whom to blame. At times she felt as if she'd done something wrong, but her love for Austin wouldn't allow her to hide in shame. Other times, she was angry that Hanna would think so ill of her that she couldn't trust Katia and Austin to be alone. Through it all, she was lonely without Austin and she missed him more than she'd thought possible. By the time she was sixteen, they'd truly fallen in love, and the days without him were torturously long and empty. Nothing she did could fill the void. She counted the days until he came home for holidays. She wrote long letters to him and mailed them without Stephania's or Hanna's knowledge.

Though he never wrote back, he called her every Sunday night just after his weekly call to his mother. Katia waited in her bedroom and told her mother that one of her girlfriends was on the phone. Austin had to stand in line for a pay phone in his dorm, with other boys hanging over his shoulder, and the calls were often strained and awkward. Too often, Katia hung up in tears.

When Austin did come home for vacations, Katia made a fool of herself by hanging on to him, begging for kisses and promising to do everything and anything he asked. Then he would leave again for school and the torture would start all over.

Katia was so caught up in her obsession

with Austin that she didn't realize her wise and sharp-eyed mother had seen and heard everything.

Stephania was convinced Katia would get pregnant on Austin's next school break. There was barely enough income to contribute to Katia's upcoming schooling as it was. The cost of a third mouth to feed—not to mention the time and energy required to care for a baby—would diminish any hopes Katia had of attending college, and her future opportunities would dwindle. Stephania told her daughter that her own job in the McCreary household would be on the line if things went too far with Austin. He would come out of the scandal unscathed, while Katia and Stephania would pay the price—financially and emotionally.

Katia tried to convince her mother that she was wrong about her and Austin, but Stephania couldn't be swayed. Before Austin returned home, Stephania announced to Hanna that she wanted to quit. In a matter of days they'd moved to Stephania's cousin's house on the South Side of Chicago.

Katia was devastated. She was impossibly in love with Austin, and she believed in her heart that he loved her back. But the shame she felt when she overheard her mother explain their sudden appearance in Chicago to her cousins was unbearable. Katia would always know that because of her love for Austin, her mother had lost a good income. They'd been forced to take charity from their family.

Yet being without Austin was agonizing, and Katia cried every night for months after the move. Still, she was embarrassed by the way she'd acted around him; when they were together, she couldn't think straight, much less make intelligent decisions. Though Katia knew that she would never have gotten pregnant, she had to admit her mother was right that her relationship with Austin could have compromised her future and well-being.

The only way to cure her addiction to Austin was to never write or call him again. She despised herself for not contacting him, but at the time, she'd felt she had no choice. She had to make a new life and put Austin in the past— forever.

Fortunately, Stephania landed a good-paying job at a luxury hotel in downtown Chicago. She loved her work and often brought Katia to the city to shop and eat in the hotel dining room. Stephania adored Chicago city life, and this was her way of trying to make amends with Katia after taking her away from Indian Lake. Those had been good years, despite Katia's broken heart. Stephania had remained at the hotel until she'd died of cancer nearly ten years ago.

Katia had come a long way since she'd lived in Indian Lake. But thinking of Austin now, she rediscovered a lead coat of guilt she thought she'd long ago discarded.

Katia had broken Austin McCreary's heart, and she'd never apologized, never tried to contact him. Never once had she lifted a finger to do the right thing.

She was the bad guy.

CHAPTER THREE

KATIA WAS WEARING a gray wool pencil skirt, a black turtleneck cashmere sweater and black pumps when she walked into Jack's office on Monday morning. Jack had called her in for a brainstorming meeting with him and Barry. She carried a legal pad, pen and the chocolate mousse for Barry.

"Good morning, gentlemen," she said cheerily, placing the foil-wrapped cake on the credenza behind Barry's chair. "That's for you and Ava."

Barry glared at the wrapped silver lump. "Thanks. What is it?"

Katia's smile dropped from her face. She noticed Jack's head was down as he peered at a report of some kind in front of him. The tension in the room was as thick as February fog and nearly as visible. "Cake. Okay, guys. What's up?"

Barry glanced out the window.

Coward.

Slowly, Jack raised his head, and his dark

eyes settled on her. "Have a seat. Want some coffee?"

"I'm fine," she replied. "Let's get to it. You look like you could use something."

"Something," Jack mumbled.

Katia stared at the partners. She didn't like the way they were avoiding her gaze, and Jack's face almost wore pity. She felt her blood turn to ice. "You're firing me."

Jack folded his hands on his desk. "I think that's a little drastic just yet."

Barry squirmed in his chair. "I had suggested some staff cuts, but Jack disagreed. The problem is that for all intents and purposes, the company is most likely going down."

Katia pressed her fingertips into her temples. "Wait a minute. Back up. Why don't you tell me what's going on? We're supposed to be brainstorming. Maybe I can help."

Barry swiped his face with his palm. "Right now, we're bleeding money. If we cut your salary and lay off a few employees, Jack and I might be able to hang on."

"A couple of the… You mean Tina?" Katia couldn't believe this.

Apparently, whatever mess they were in, Barry's solution was retreat. Well, she'd tried that strategy once in her life and look where it had gotten her. No. Retreat was out of the question. No wonder Jack had wanted her to stay sharp for this meeting. These guys needed a miracle.

Jack leaned forward. "I didn't tell you last night, Katia, but on Friday, Tina handed in her notice. After the wedding, she and Allen are moving to Wisconsin. He got a job as assistant coach at the university."

"But…she didn't say a word to me." Katia felt wounded and slightly betrayed that Tina hadn't confided in her. Clearly, Tina saw their relationship differently than Katia. Tina was Jack's employee and Katia's assistant. They weren't friends, as Katia had assumed. No, Tina had probably read the situation correctly. Katia should have known better than to assume her work relationships were anything more.

Katia's mind kicked into warp speed. She may have been wrong to get so invested in her friendships with colleagues, but if she wanted to keep whatever career she had left, she needed to come up with a brilliant plan to save her job.

"Can I at least say my piece?"

Barry sliced the air with his arm. "I don't see how—"

Jack cut him off. "Go ahead, Katia." He shot Barry a quelling look. Barry frowned but told her to go on. Katia took a deep breath and decided to give it all she had. "Since the first day

I walked into these offices, I knew I was in the right place and that I would help your company grow. I took pride in my work, and I still do. You both know my goal is to eventually become a partner here. I want equal say, equal pay and equal respect. I want to grow old with this company. You two may be the last honest guys in the insurance business, and I swear to you, I have no problem convincing clients of that. I also know I could sell our plans to the devil himself if I had to." She stood up and put a hand on her slim hip. "So out with it. What's going on?"

Jack exhaled and leaned back in his chair. He twirled a ballpoint pen in his fingers. "All right, truth time. You're aware that we've been pushing for new clients. That's why we sent you up to Michigan and Indiana. You brought us three good companies, but it's not enough." Jack paused and glanced at Barry, who gave him a slight nod. "Katia, our expenses are eating us up. Both Barry and I have taken a pay cut. But the corporate taxes doubled this year. We got notice two months ago that our rent has increased by more than half. Sure, we could move—"

"But rents are skyrocketing in Chicago," Barry cut in. "Add to that the mounting cost of benefits and the 401(k) program. It's not what it was when you first signed on."

"That's why Barry came up with the idea to become a web-based business. Our site is really shaping up—I think Barry's done a great job."

Katia smiled at Barry. "It's a good move. It shows we're on top of the times, and it gives us access to people in other states without having to travel. But it's not enough, is it?"

"No," Jack replied.

Katia tried to concentrate. Coming up with a good idea felt like chopping through a jungle with only a butter knife. Then she had it. She pictured a billboard she'd driven by on one of her trips to Indiana. Stillinoyed? it had read.

The billboard was a direct slam against the political system that was strangling Illinois businessmen like Jack and Barry. Katia had read articles about the steady stream of Chicago-area businesses that were relocating to Indiana. The state was trying to entice companies with lower corporate and property taxes, less regulation and more affordable goods and services.

"How far would you be willing to move?" she asked the partners.

Jack stared at her. "What are you talking about?"

"You just said you'd move across town to lower your rent. How about moving a little farther? Say, out of state, to Indiana. I was thinking about Indian Lake, to be specific. It's only an hour away. Great access to the city on the tollway or the interstate. South Shore runs through there. I will bet the rents are a third of what you're paying. We'd have to let the staff here go, but I could hire locals for the office. Barry can stay here and run the online business so he doesn't have to move Ava and the baby. For now anyway. It'll be bare bones, Jack. You and me. We'll run the office and build our clientele from there."

"Pshht." Barry waved off Katia's idea before she had a chance to finish talking. "It'll never work."

"Why not?" Katia demanded.

Barry raised his eyebrows in contempt. "New clients? From Indian Lake? You're out of your mind."

Think, Katia. Think.

"Jack just told you my three clients from Michigan are good ones."

"Not enough," Barry countered. "We have the entire city of Chicago at our fingertips and we're not getting anywhere."

"That's because the companies here want to be with the big brokers. If they're not dealing with Lloyds of London, they're not happy. But if we move out of our box just a bit and concentrate on smaller communities, people and business in middle America, I think they'll want us. They're dying for someone they can trust. That's what they're missing. They need us!" Katia felt adrenaline spiral through her body. At this point in her pitch, she was convinced she could have sold freezers to Alaskans.

"It's too drastic," Barry grumbled.

Jack peered at Katia. "We need drastic. And I like this. Keep talking, Katia." He folded his arms over his chest.

He was challenging her. If she could pull this off, she knew Jack would back her for a partnership. It was a long way to go and there would be a lot of work ahead, but she could do this. "I just got wind of a large account that's coming up."

"How large?" Barry asked, suddenly more curious than condemning.

"Millions, from what I remember."

"Okay, you have my curiosity," Jack said. "Go on."

"I grew up in Indian Lake." She held up a palm to stop their protests before they started. "Trust me, this isn't about childhood nostalgia or anything like that. In fact, I haven't kept in touch with anyone from back then. Austin McCreary is one of the wealthiest men in town—heir to a family fortune. He's the only McCreary remaining now, but his father left him his antique car collection when he died. Tomorrow, Austin is announcing to the city council his intention to build a car museum in Indian Lake. Can you imagine how much that building alone will cost?"

"I can't. Why doesn't the guy just put them in a garage?"

"He has garages. Three of them. Carriage houses, actually, and they were already full of cars when I was a kid. I'll do some checking around and find out what kind of valuation we're talking about. But the way I see it, he'll have to cover the cars and the museum, there will be liability insurance for the museum workers, and he'll need an umbrella liability plan for the visitors."

"What kind of cars?" Jack asked.

"The 1926 Bugatti is my favorite," Katia replied with a smug grin.

Barry whistled appreciatively. "This is for real? Holy cow!"

Jack beamed with confidence, and Katia was struck with the notion that she'd given him back his charisma. "Can you get into that meeting tomorrow?"

"I…I think so."

"Do it," Jack commanded. "I like this idea of yours, Katia. All of it. I don't have a problem moving to a small town if it will save our hides. Keep an eye out for office space while you're there. And get me this guy's business. I don't care what it takes. A guy like that has to have friends, and if he likes us and our products, he'll get them to come on board with us, too."

"Good thinking," Barry said with his first real smile of the day.

Katia should have floated out of Jack's office on a cloud of victory. Instead, as she left the meeting, she realized she'd just slipped a hangman's noose around her throat. Oh, she'd saved the day, all right. But she knew that if there was anyone Austin McCreary would never, ever do business with—it was her.

Katia wished she could rewrite the past, but that was impossible. She would have to figure out another way to change Austin's mind.

CHAPTER FOUR

AUSTIN MCCREARY SHOVED his tennis racket into a battered brown leather cover, zipped it up and waited for Rafe Barzonni to come around to his side of the clay tennis court. Austin had been playing on this court, in his own backyard, since he was five years old. "Great game, Rafe."

"Anytime, man. You still have the best court in the Midwest. Not to mention a killer backhand I'm never going to beat."

"You're just a glutton for punishment."

"Self-inflicted abuse is not my thing, Austin. Seriously, I've seen guys at Wimbledon who look as good as you."

"Ha!" Austin picked up a white hand towel from the wrought iron table and wiped the sweat from his face. His blond hair was dripping wet. "Tournaments are for young kids. Ones with lots of talent and support. I never had either," he said, his voice filling with regret.

Rafe grabbed his own towel. "Sorry, bro. I know you have talent—for a lot of things. You just don't want anyone to know it, that's all."

"You've got that right. Besides, you're just bad enough to make me feel good," Austin bantered back good-naturedly. "Honestly, I appreciate you being able to play this early in the morning. I've got fifty-some odd people due here at one, and I swear, I'd never get through it if I didn't have a chance to work off some steam." Austin slapped Rafe on the shoulder as they walked through the terrace door and into the kitchen.

At the sink, Austin's sixty-one-year-old housekeeper, Daisy Kempshaw, was peeling an apple. Daisy was short, as thin as one of Austin's rackets and capable of taking on both Austin and Rafe in tennis, a shouting match and just about any other confrontation. Daisy approached life on the offensive rather than the defensive. She was rough, scrappy and had the energy of six men.

"No strawberries and cream today," Daisy announced before Austin had a chance to greet her.

"I didn't ask for any," Austin said.

"Wipe your feet, the both of you," Daisy said. "I just mopped." Then she pointed toward the hallway door. "The caterer is here unloading in the dining room. She's taken up all my refrigerator space with her food, and there's no room for you to eat breakfast with all her whatnots strewn across the nook table."

Austin glanced at the round walnut table that sat in a huge beveled glass window area on the far side of the kitchen. It was stacked with boxes of serving pieces, rental glasses, china and linens.

"Good," he muttered. "I didn't want to use mother's good china and silver for this event."

Rafe picked up his small workout bag. "Well, I'm outta here. See you Saturday, Austin. Nine o'clock?"

"Perfect!" Austin shook his friend's hand.

Rafe strode over to the swinging kitchen door and pushed it open.

"Ow!" came a cry from the other side.

"Oh, boy," Rafe said. He stepped back gingerly.

Standing on the other side of the door was Olivia Melton, dressed in dark jeans and a chef's coat, her hair pulled on top of her head in a tight knot. She held a tray of artistically arranged vegetables in one hand and pressed her other hand to her forehead.

"I'm so sorry," Rafe apologized. "Are you hurt badly?"

"I'll live," she said.

Austin raced to the freezer. "Some ice will do the trick."

Olivia shook her head. "No time. I'll be fine."

"I'm really sorry," Rafe repeated. "I didn't know you were there."

Olivia waved him off. "It's okay. I'm just in a hurry. I have work to do and not enough time to do it in."

Rafe glanced at Austin, who shrugged. "Okay. I'll see you, Austin."

When Rafe had closed the front door behind him, Daisy threw Austin a judgmental look. "You better get showered, mister. Your folks will be here in forty-five minutes." She checked the clock that hung over the kitchen sink. "Make that forty-two."

"I'll be ready." He turned to Olivia. "I'm sorry about the accident. Are you sure I can't do anything for you?"

Now Daisy's warning look was aimed at Olivia. "You? Uh, not a thing. I'll have the buffet table set up in twenty minutes and the poached salmon to decorate. I'll put the rest out after your speech."

"And the bartender?" Austin asked.

"Liz is on her way," Daisy assured him, continuing to peel apples for the fruit tray.

"Then, I guess we're ready."

Daisy speared him with another quelling glare. "We will be when you quit sweating on my clean kitchen floor."

"Got it," he said, rushing out of the kitchen and down the hall.

Just as he was about to climb the staircase, he stopped and poked his head into the living room. The noonday sun poured through the windows and illuminated the room with an ethereal glow. Austin and Daisy had moved the furniture to the perimeter, leaving a large open space for the guests to gather around the architect's model of the car museum he intended to build.

The model sat majestically on a round Sheridan table. It was only balsa wood, glue, paper and cardboard at this point, but for Austin, it was real. Chase Tinsdale, the Chicago architect he'd hired, had transformed Austin's vision into matter.

Austin's grandfather, Ambrose, had built the McCreary mansion to be a close, though more modern, replica of the Hermitage, the home of his idol and favorite president, Andrew Jackson. To honor his grandfather, Austin had chosen the same architectural design for the museum.

For three generations, the consensus in Indian Lake was that the McCreary home was the most beautiful in town. The classic lines and elegance befitted the family's name. To fashion the museum after the house was also Austin's attempt at building a family brand.

To cut costs, Chase had eliminated the two

flanking wings on the north and south sides, since the museum would be facing west. There would be three floors, accessible by elevator, and two sets of stairs, though they wouldn't be as fancy as the cantilevered one in Austin's home. Chase had also altered the original design to accommodate an extralarge elevator to move the cars around the building. On the main floor were a small café, a larger restaurant, a gift shop and administrative offices. The inner rotunda was large enough to display four cars. The second and third floors were designated for displaying cars, as well.

Chase had proposed using UV protective glass windows around the building, allowing light in but keeping out the aging rays that, over time, would act like battery acid on historically correct auto paint.

Austin smiled widely. He'd dreamed of this museum since the day his dad died. Finally, his tribute to his father and grandfather would be a reality.

"Austin!" Daisy yelled from the kitchen. "I don't hear that shower running!"

Austin chuckled to himself. No one had ever bossed him around like his housekeeper. "I'm going!"

Austin took the carpeted stairs two at a time, whistling loudly.

KATIA ARRIVED AT the McCreary mansion at one o'clock sharp. She parked the rental car on Maple Avenue, at the far end of a long line of vehicles, all apparently here for the presentation.

Just seeing the house she had once called home caused her chest to tighten and her heart to pound. Her mouth was so dry she felt as if she'd been chewing on cotton balls all morning. She touched her forehead. Sure enough, she was perspiring already.

Katia, what are you doing?

She didn't understand what was happening to her. Faced with the possibility of losing her job, she'd responded with arrogant courage. She'd had to come up with company-saving solutions at the speed of light, and she'd had to pretend she believed in what she was saying.

She'd been scared stiff then, but her show of confidence had served her well, because somehow she'd convinced both Jack and Barry that they'd never heard anything better in their lives. Now she just had to persuade herself.

She smoothed the lapels of her navy wool suit, picked up her matching purse from the seat and got out of the car.

The moment she turned to face the mansion, she froze. The house couldn't have been more imposing if it was Buckingham Palace.

Her reaction was absolutely ridiculous. She

knew every inch of the house, the grounds… even the pool equipment. She should have been comforted by the fact that this was simply a reunion of sorts.

But she didn't feel safe at all. *This has got to be the dumbest thing I've ever come up with.*

She couldn't believe she was back here to see Austin. She had no clue if he was married or had children. Did he have a girlfriend or fiancée now? Did he ever think about her? Katia had always assumed Austin held a grudge against her for cutting him out of her life when she'd moved to Chicago. But maybe she was wrong. Maybe she'd just been the maid's daughter after all— an insignificant blip in his teenage life. Maybe he didn't remember her at all.

Yes, Katia carried a great deal of guilt because she'd never contacted him, but there was a case to be made for the fact that after that summer, she hadn't heard from Austin, either.

Would he greet everyone at the door? And if he did, what was she going to say? She'd thought about sneaking around to the back door and entering through the kitchen. She knew just how to jimmy the latch on the wooden gate to get in. Katia had devised a dozen excuses to give to Austin if he tried to throw her out. She'd settled on the truth.

She would tell him that she'd been passing

through Indian Lake on business over the summer and that Liz had told her about the museum. Since his presentation was open to the public, she had decided to use the opportunity to see him again.

Katia couldn't predict how difficult it was going to be to sell her insurance to Austin. She had tried to factor in every possible angle and outcome of her pitch so that she was somewhat prepared for whatever he threw at her. What she hadn't considered was this sudden panic attack. She knew she could sell her product to just about anyone, but she had to remain in control to do it.

Katia's hands were shaking. This was impossible. She had to act cool, professional and knowledgeable. Fear was not acceptable.

She noticed a black Cadillac Escalade pull up in front of the McCreary house. The doors opened, and six well-dressed men and women got out and went into the house.

Showtime.

She inhaled deeply to steel her nerves, lifted her chin and crossed the street.

Time to face my past.

Katia slipped in the front door behind the group from the Escalade. Austin was already addressing the group. She'd only had twenty-four hours to prepare for crashing his party, but even a lifetime wouldn't have prepared her to see Austin again.

In her mind, Austin had remained eighteen, so this blond, self-assured, handsome, tanned, enthusiastic man who held everyone spellbound was a shock.

Though he wore black pants and a simple white shirt, the way he pointed out the historic details of the Doric columns flanking the entrance and the use of Indiana limestone for the walkways and porches spoke of sophistication and manners that Katia hadn't seen since she'd lived here.

Katia caught Liz Crenshaw's eye and stealthily moved along the back wall to stand next to her.

"Glad you could make it," Liz whispered with a smile.

"Thanks for telling me about it."

Next to Liz was a petite elderly woman wearing a black-and-white print dress. She smiled at Katia, and her clear, cornflower-blue eyes twinkled. Katia recognized her in an instant. "Mrs. Beabots? Is that you?"

Mrs. Beabots tilted her head to the right, stared at Katia and then her smile grew wider. "Katia Stanislaus," she said softly so as not to disrupt Austin's speech. "Why, I'd know you anywhere, my dear. Come give me hug."

Katia had to bend down to embrace the tiny woman. "I didn't expect to see you."

"Maddie and I were the first ones Austin invited!" Mrs. Beabots grabbed the hand of the pretty green-eyed woman next to her. Katia leaned over and shook Maddie's outstretched hand. "Katia. Nice to meet you."

"You, as well," Maddie whispered back.

Mrs. Beabots nodded. "Maddie made the desserts. You'll love them."

"I'm sure I will," Katia said.

"Maddie's almost famous. She owns Cupcakes and Cappuccino in Chicago," Mrs. Beabots said, beaming proudly at Maddie.

Katia's eyes grew round. She'd been to Cupcakes and Cappuccino with Tina. "I love your café," she whispered to Maddie. "We should talk afterward."

Katia turned her attention back to Austin's speech, thinking how fortuitous it was that she'd made friends with Liz. Now she was reunited with Mrs. Beabots, and she'd come face-to-face with a young Chicago entrepreneur who just might be in need of her insurance services.

Austin continued explaining the museum's purpose and its benefit to the community. Katia counted over seventy-five people in the room. She kept her face hidden from Austin's view by ducking behind a tall man in front of her. Fortunately, Austin was so focused on showing off his model and extolling the family history and his grandfather's creativity that his eyes never settled on one particular face.

Behind Austin were three easels with architectural and designer drawings of the museum interior. He pointed out the features of each of the floors, and when he finished, he asked the crowd for questions.

The journalists peppered him with dozens of particulars about construction, costs and opening dates.

The entire room fell silent when a man who introduced himself as the editor of the *Northern Indiana Times* cocked his head and asked, "And who is the backer for this expensive museum?"

Austin pursed his lips in a self-satisfied smile, nearly bordering on a smirk. "I am."

The editor gaped at Austin. "Let me get this straight. You didn't invite us all here today to petition for donations?"

Austin shoved his hands into his pockets. "No, I didn't. As I told you, I intend to pay for the building myself. Eventually, the museum will be my gift to the city."

At the front of the room a young woman asked, "Will you be donating the cars, as well?"

Austin laughed heartily. "I'm afraid I'll be keeping those…at least until my death, which I hope isn't for quite some time. But they will be on loan to the city and housed in the museum. I want younger generations, especially, to understand how thrilling it must have been for the inventors of another age to literally change the way human beings live. Only the airplane and the computer have had as great an impact on our everyday lives as the automobile. I'm proud that my grandfather was a pioneer in the automotive industry over a hundred years ago. This is my way of making certain that his contribution is remembered."

Mrs. Beabots folded her arms over her chest and mumbled something under her breath, though Katia couldn't make out what she said.

Katia was keenly aware that the crowd was hanging on Austin's every word. The reporters took copious notes, and people were filming and taking photos of Austin on their phones. Katia wouldn't be the only one trying to sell Austin insurance. The difference between Katia and other agencies—she hoped—was that she was desperate to save her company, so she would take some risks that others might not. She had already placed inquiries to a dozen companies that she represented to put a package together for Austin that she hoped would make him salivate.

Austin wrapped up his speech and invited everyone to take part in the buffet that had been set out in the dining room. "There's plenty of local Crenshaw Vineyards wine, as well. And we are graced by Liz Crenshaw herself to introduce you to the splendors of their award-winning product."

Austin thrust his arm in Liz's direction to point her out to the guests.

Liz stepped away from the wall and moved forward, stirring the crowd just enough to give Katia a full view of Austin.

Her eyes locked on his, and though he saw her, he didn't seem to recognize her. Or he did, and he was a superb actor.

Austin's hands dropped to his sides. Though he kept a smile clamped on his face, he remained rigid.

The crowd dispersed slowly, like the shifting sand after a wave has rushed onto shore.

Mrs. Beabots was the last to leave the room, and then it was just Katia standing across from Austin in the front parlor of the house she grew up in.

"Hello, Austin."

"Katia."

She thought her heart would hammer a hole right through her chest, but she didn't dare let him know how much he affected her. She couldn't decide whether to smile at him, rush to him and hold his hand or ask his forgiveness on the spot. She felt as if she'd turned to stone. She couldn't think or move.

She was filled with blistering guilt.

"Austin, I'm so—"

His hands shot up to silence her. "Katia, leave. Now."

"But, Austin, I want to talk to you..."

He shook his head. "Leave. It's what you do best."

He spun on his heel and stormed into the hall. Katia followed him out of the front parlor and stepped into the main hallway in time to see him talking to a woman carrying a tray of marinated shrimp. Katia assumed she was his cook or housekeeper.

"Daisy, there is a woman in the living room," Austin was saying. "If she's still there after you put that tray in the dining room, call the cops and have her removed."

"Sure thing," Daisy replied.

Katia watched as Austin raced up the majestic staircase and disappeared.

CHAPTER FIVE

KATIA WAS STUNNED by Austin's anger. If she'd ever doubted that he'd loved her once, she didn't anymore. This degree of hatred could only be balanced by the same degree of love. A long time ago, Austin had believed in her and had finally realized that she loved him.

"But we were only kids..."

Katia's eyes brimmed with tears as she gazed up the empty staircase, knowing Austin had gone to his room. He'd abandoned his guests because of her. He'd told his housekeeper to have her thrown out.

Katia knew she'd be in trouble if she stayed, but Jack's directive wasn't far from her mind. She needed to meet the people in that dining room, needed their expertise and guidance to help her establish Carter and Associates in town. She couldn't let this opportunity pass her by.

Yet her heart went out to Austin. What could she say to him? An apology, after all this time, seemed meaningless. Austin wasn't angry because she'd moved. He was angry because she hadn't come back. And worse, she hadn't come back for him.

Was that what he was saying now? That he thought she'd come back to rekindle their romance? Nothing could have been further from her thoughts. She wasn't in love with Austin. She'd put those feelings away a long time ago. She was here to keep her job and build her future. With Jack.

One day, after she made all that happen, she would move back to Chicago and resume her life. *Yes*, she thought, *I'll go back, and everything will be just as it was.*

Just then, the housekeeper came out of the dining room with an empty bowl. She peered up at Katia. "You're staying, aren't you?"

Katia made the decision on the spot. "Yes," she said. "Are you going to call the police like he asked?"

Daisy shook her head and planted a hand on her hip. "If I had a nickel for every time he told me to do something stupid and I didn't do it—"

"I get it," Katia said, her eyes wandering up the stairs again. "Is he often like this?"

"Angry? No. Shutting himself away? Always."

"Really? But why?"

Daisy's eyes narrowed. "You're new in town, aren't ya?"

"Sort of. Well, yes."

"So you don't know about him?" Daisy pointed to the second floor.

Katia was tempted to share the whole story, but then thought better of it. "What should I know?"

"He likes being alone. A lot. He's a recluse, I'd guess you'd say. And I would know. I've been here for nearly twenty years. I nursed Mrs. Mc-Creary through her grief. Then cancer. I went to Austin's college graduation. Hanna and I were the only ones there. I'm just about the only family he's got left, really."

Katia smiled and thrust her hand out to Daisy. "Then, I'm grateful to you for taking care of him. I'm—"

"Katia," Daisy replied, staring at Katia's hand.

"You recognized me?"

"Not till just a minute ago."

"So he told you about me?" Katia asked, lowering her hand and wondering if she even wanted to hear the truth.

"His mother did. Broke his heart, she told me. You two musta been somethin' back then for him to act like this after all these years. Still," Daisy mused, looking up the stairs, "this is typical Austin behavior. You might as well go in and have somethin' to eat. He won't be back down."

"What? He has guests!"

Daisy shrugged. "Oh, them? They don't care. They probably didn't expect him to hang around after his talk anyway. He doesn't socialize."

Katia was disbelieving at first, but then she glanced into the dining room and saw everyone chatting and eating as if nothing had happened. Daisy certainly knew more about the Austin of today than she did. "So Austin is incommunicado for the rest of the afternoon?"

"He'll be on his phone or laptop until they leave," Daisy told her. "Then he'll go to the plant till late in the evening, as usual."

"Well, thank you, Daisy. I think I will have something to eat. It's a long drive back to Chicago."

"Oh, so that's where you've been?" Daisy probed.

Katia understood in an instant that Daisy was probably as loyal to Austin as she was to Jack. Daisy would relay any information she revealed. Katia chose her words carefully. "For the moment, yes. My insurance firm is relocating here to Indian Lake. That's why I do need to introduce myself to some of the guests. I'm looking to rent office space, hire office personnel, find both myself and my boss places to live. Things like that."

"What about your family?" Daisy asked.

"I'm alone," Katia replied, intending to sound neutral. Instead, the word came out of her mouth with a great deal more feeling than she'd planned. Again, she had no idea why her emotions kept overwhelming her at such inopportune times. It was as if they had a life of their own, and the steel-edged control she'd always maintained had sprung a leak. "What I meant was I'm not married, and I don't have to worry about children and schools and all that."

"I know what you meant," Daisy said. "Housing is hard to find here in Indian Lake. Good luck with that." Without another word, Daisy turned and trounced toward the kitchen.

Glancing up the stairs one last time, Katia felt a strange pull to ignore her company's mission and go straight to Austin's bedroom and demand to speak with him, but she chickened out.

Katia forced herself to move into the dining room. The buffet table was centered with a huge bouquet of sunflowers, bronze chrysanthemums and yellow roses. The guests were laughing and discussing the impact of the car museum on Indian Lake tourism. The tourism board members were tossing around ideas about ad campaigns, and she heard two of the city council members chatting about potential problems with traffic and parking.

"Katia," Liz called from the far side of the room. "Come join us."

Liz was standing with Mrs. Beabots and Maddie next to a dessert table that was laden with dozens of exquisitely iced and decorated cupcakes. Mrs. Beabots sipped a small glass of white wine.

"Those are gorgeous," Katia gushed as she inspected the desserts.

"Thanks," Maddie replied. "I wanted them to be a bit over-the-top for Austin."

Katia's head jerked up. "Why's that?"

"If it weren't for Austin being my first investor, my café here in town would never have existed and I wouldn't have dreamed of building my business into franchises."

Katia was surprised. Austin might be a recluse, but he obviously had a head for business. "He did that?"

Maddie smiled broadly. "He's a strange duck, I'll give him that. He's never set foot in my café, can you believe that? I still bring him seven cupcakes every Friday morning at eight. Just like clockwork. Although I mix up the flavors for him so he can try my new recipes." She rocked back on her heels, seeming both proud and grateful. "He's been a very good friend to me."

"I should say so," Mrs. Beabots added. "I've

known Austin and his family since I was a young girl."

"Really?" Katia and Maddie chirped in unison. Katia swallowed back a guilt-edged lump in her throat. She remembered Mrs. Beabots as the kindly older lady down the street whose gardens she always admired. She also recalled Hanna talking about charity committees she served on with Mrs. Beabots. Since Mrs. Beabots had known the family for decades, she would have heard all about Katia and her former relationship with Austin. Mrs. Beabots could be a very good ally for her.

Liz handed Katia a glass of white wine. "Try this chardonnay, Katia. It's a new reserve for us. Aged eighteen months in French oak barrels. I value your opinion."

Katia sipped the wine and smiled. "It's so buttery and smooth. I love it."

"I thought you would." Liz beamed and then noticed Maddie and Mrs. Beabots staring at her. "What?"

Mrs. Beabots patted Liz's arm. "Katia was just about to tell us why she's come back to Indian Lake. Weren't you, dear?"

Katia nearly choked on the wine. Maybe Mrs. Beabots wouldn't be the best ally after all. She cleared her throat. "I-I'm relocating my company to Indian Lake as soon as I can find an appropriate office."

"That is so cool!" Liz interjected happily.

"How large of a space?" Maddie asked perfunctorily. "Do you plan for many employees? Will they be moving here with you?"

Mrs. Beabots placed her hand on Maddie's cheek and looked at Katia. "She gets excited. Now, Katia, there's a lovely upstairs loft across from the courthouse that had a rental sign in the window. I saw it just last week. Let's see…" She glanced around the room. "Yes. There's Sharon Goodman. I'll introduce you. The space would be perfect for you. It's got a beautiful view and two walls of glass. You'll like that."

Maddie shot a curious look at Mrs. Beabots. "How do you know what she'd like?"

"Why, it's obvious. She's been working in Chicago with all those lights and city amenities. She and her boss will never stand being on the outskirts of town for a minute. They'd go stir-crazy. That intersection is the busiest in the county. It's only a block to the deli. A block and half to Enzo's. The bank is on the corner and—" she stared pointedly at Katia "—it's only six blocks to my house."

"Your house?" Katia asked.

"That's a great idea!" Maddie exclaimed. "Mrs. Beabots has an entire third floor that was renovated into a very nice apartment a year ago. It used to be a ballroom. Luke Bosworth and his two children lived there before he married Sarah Jensen next door."

"Sarah Jensen? Do I know her?" Katia asked Mrs. Beabots.

"She's a bit younger than you, but you might remember her mother, Ann Marie Jensen. She died a couple years ago. Cancer. You might recall that Ann Marie planted the flowers along Maple Avenue. Sarah lives in the family house now with Luke, Annie and Timmy."

A hundred memories of being a little girl flashed through Katia's mind. Walking along this street to go to school, to church or into town with her mother to shop. Happy memories. Loving memories. Suddenly, Katia's life in Chicago dissipated like fog lifting off a hill as it rose out of a valley. She *did* remember Ann Marie kneeling on the November cool earth of the boulevard, planting tulip and iris bulbs. Mrs. Jensen had taught her how to plant a bulb. She'd shown Katia how to place the bulb in the earth with the flat side down and the tiny shoots pointing upward. It hadn't been the kind of information that would change anyone's life, but the kindness, tenderness and concern she'd shown Katia, who had been all too aware that she was only a housekeeper's daughter, had stuck with her.

"I would like to meet Sarah," Katia told Mrs. Beabots. "We have a lot in common, both having lost our mothers."

"Consider it done," Mrs. Beabots assured her. "And I insist you move in with me. I wouldn't have it any other way."

"It sounds lovely…" Katia hesitated.

Maddie nudged Katia with her elbow. "Trust me, there are no high-rises here. No doormen. There aren't any complexes at all, if you remember. That much about Indian Lake hasn't changed. The best apartments are in the houses along Maple Avenue. Mrs. Beabots's is the prettiest and the biggest of all."

Katia's eyes widened. "How big?"

"Very," Mrs. Beabots cut in. "Two bedrooms, large bath, living room and kitchenette. When Luke lived there, I usually cooked for him and the children. Then there are formal gardens in back for reading and contemplating. Lester MacDougal does all the yard work now. Except for the spring planting. I do most of that myself," she said proudly. "I'd be happy to show it to you this afternoon."

"I would love to see it."

Mrs. Beabots clinked her glass against Katia's. "You will find, my dear, that securing office rental in Indian Lake is child's play. Residential housing is nearly impossible. You can walk six blocks, can't you, dear?" Mrs. Beabots asked.

Katia grinned widely. She wasn't sure if her mother was watching over her and putting all these puzzle pieces of her life together, but there was no question that today was fortuitous. This was so far beyond lucky that it frightened her.

Katia raised her glass and saluted Mrs. Beabots. In one fell swoop, she'd gotten a lead on an office space, a potential place to live and, she hoped, a wily but knowledgeable ally in her pursuit of Austin's business. "Oh, I can walk it back and forth all day long," Katia assured her.

"Well, then. Let me introduce you to our mayor, Blair Milo. She's a few years younger than you are, dear, but she's a real dynamo. She will show you the ropes around Indian Lake in a jiffy—the new ones, that is. You should join her on her Fitness Friday jogs."

"The mayor runs?"

"She does it all over the state," Maddie said, biting into a shrimp.

"I think I'm going to like Indian Lake," Katia said.

"I certainly hope so." Mrs. Beabots's gaze drifted toward the empty hallway.

Katia knew Mrs. Beabots was thinking about Austin. She couldn't help wondering just how much Mrs. Beabots knew about their teenage romance. Had Austin ever talked about her after she'd left Indian Lake, or had he kept his feelings to himself?

Apparently, everyone in town knew that Austin was a loner, and they accepted him for it. But he hadn't been like that when she'd known him. Of course, they were just kids then, and their personalities hadn't molded into who they were today.

As much as Mrs. Beabots, Liz and Maddie were enthusiastic about Katia's move and welcoming her to the community, something unsettling continued to plague her.

That something, she knew, was sitting upstairs in the bedroom at the end of the hall.

CHAPTER SIX

AUSTIN FINISHED UP his call to Joe Collier in Phoenix. They had met at York Prep School and had been friends ever since. Joe was a venture capitalist and was constantly on the lookout for new start-ups. For the past fifteen years, Austin had spent the Christmas holidays with Joe and his wife, Vicki. Each time Austin visited, Joe would have a new company he'd be interested in, and he'd try to snare Austin into investing with him or flat-out buying it. Austin always declined the opportunity. It would take a gale-force wind to pry him out of Indian Lake.

Today, a storm had blown into his life, and its name was Katia.

Austin picked up his iPad and stared blankly at his apps, but all he saw was Katia's beautiful face gazing back at him. He'd always thought she was pretty; even when they were kids and then teenagers, she was his dream girl. But the sight of the woman she'd grown into was a shock on about a dozen levels. He couldn't remember what he'd said to her, or how he'd even managed to speak. All he'd felt was an over-powering rage that had threatened to burst out of him. If he'd remained downstairs and confronted her, there was no telling how far that rage would have taken him. He would never be physical, but he feared worse. He was afraid of what he would say to her.

Betrayal like hers was something no man could ever truly conquer. Wars were fought over women who'd wronged men. Austin had loved Katia with all his heart, and she'd left him.

Night after night, in the seventeen years and eight months since she'd left, he'd tried to make sense of it all and had come up dry. He'd never gotten past it. As far as he was concerned, she'd never given him a reason. She and her mother had simply moved away, without notice, on the very day that Katia was supposed to fly to New York for his senior prom.

He would never forget standing at LaGuardia, waiting excitedly with a bouquet of flowers. But Katia hadn't walked off the plane. He'd waited for over half an hour. He'd gone to the ticket counter and asked if they were sure all the passengers had disembarked. The woman had assured him that the plane was not only cleared and cleaned, but ready for a new boarding. After that, he'd raced to a pay phone to call his mother.

Hanna had told him that Stephania had quit her job that morning. Apparently mother and daughter had been planning their departure, since their bags were already packed. They had walked out of the house and out of the McCrearys' lives forever. His mother had railed on and on about their disloyalty, lamenting that she could never trust anyone on her payroll. Hanna had been clearly upset as she'd told him it was obvious that, to Stephania and Katia, the McCrearys had never been more than a paycheck.

Hanna had explained to Austin that he was lucky to find out what kind of person Katia was while he was still young, and not later, when he was "in too deep." After all, he and Katia were just teenagers. Technically, they weren't even dating. He'd asked Katia to his prom, that was all. "Yes, Mom," he'd said, looking down at the wilting daisies. "It's just a prom."

Hanna had told him there would be many other girls in his future and when the right one came along, he would know it.

Austin had thrown Katia's flowers in a nearby trash bin and walked out of LaGuardia determined never to give Katia Stanislaus another thought. He would wipe her out of his mind as easily as she'd erased him.

But Austin didn't forget. What he remembered most was her uncanny ability to sense his moods. Wherever she was in the house or gardens, if he was upset or lonely, she always found him and knew exactly what to say to uplift him. She always put him first. Because he was obsessed with tennis, she urged him to teach her. She'd come close to beating him once too often.

It had always seemed to him that no matter what hobby, sport or academic interest he'd taken up and tried to excel in, Katia had been better. She'd gobbled up life as if she was at a banquet. She had twice the drive to succeed as he did, and she'd told him that she never wanted to settle for an ordinary life. Like her mother, she wanted the best of everything, but Stephania had never had the education to reach her goals. Katia believed that learning something new every day was the key to success.

When Katia had first moved into the mansion, he'd tried to wish her away, but his parents had needed Stephania. Because everyone else had been so busy with their lives and work, Austin had often got stuck with Katia, who'd followed him around like a shadow. She'd been an embarrassment to him for years. Then she'd become his friend. Then he'd wanted more than just friendship. When he'd been about to graduate from York and start his college life, he'd realized that he was in love with her. Austin had actually thought he would ask her to marry him, though they would have had to wait four years until he got his business degree. But that hadn't mattered.

He'd gone to LaGuardia that day hoping that Katia was the kind of girl who would wait.

As he'd driven back to the school that evening, he'd had to hold his hand over his stomach. He'd felt gutted. And it had been Katia, the one person in the world he'd trusted, who'd struck the blow.

Now she was here in his home, rubbing shoulders with the council members. He didn't know how she'd sneaked in without him noticing. Being the snake she was, she had probably learned how to slither, undetected, in and out of places, situations…and hearts.

It hadn't been until his presentation was over that he had seen her. He'd recognized her instantly, of course, but he could barely believe she was here, in his house.

"Why are you here, Katia?" Austin growled at his bedroom walls. He snapped off his iPad and went to the window to stare out onto Maple Avenue.

His guests were leaving. One by one, all the cars and SUVs pulled away from the curb and drove off. He had no idea what they thought about the museum because he had not joined them for the buffet or spent time asking questions.

The bottom line was that Austin was certain that even if there was a dissenting voice, he would turn them around in time.

Focusing on the museum helped clear his mind a little. Over the past four years, he'd worked with the city and county planning commissions to obtain permits and allowances for the museum. Thanks to their guidance, he'd learned very quickly he could not build within the city limits. There would be too many problems with the parking and the placement of the entrance and exits.

Austin had been looking for years for a few acres to buy for his intended museum. He'd come across the ten acres of old cornfield by sheer luck while reading the announcements of sheriff's sales in the newspaper. As it turned out, he was the only bidder on the property. It was too small to attract interest from local farmers or even the corporate farms that were buying up a great deal of the Midwest. This little patch of land had screamed out to Austin that it was meant to belong to him. It was exactly the size he needed, and the location was perfect. Austin hadn't been able to write out the check fast enough.

Austin heard the front door close, then he heard Daisy's voice shout up the stairs. "They're gone now."

Austin peered down at the sidewalk and saw Katia walking with Mrs. Beabots, Liz Crenshaw and Maddie Strong. He couldn't be sure, but if he wasn't mistaken, he also saw Cate Sullivan, the best Realtor in Indian Lake County, shake Katia's hand before walking off.

Real estate? Why would Katia be talking to a Realtor?

Austin watched as the other women hugged each other, waved and went their separate ways. Katia stood with Mrs. Beabots for a moment, waving to Liz, who drove away in her old truck, and then the two women continued along Maple Avenue.

Where are you going, Katia?

He opened the window and stuck his head out so he could get a better view through the autumn trees. Katia was having a lively conversation with Mrs. Beabots, as if they were long-lost friends. *What the...*

Austin spun away from the window and raced out of his room and down the enormous staircase, past a gaping Daisy who was carrying a stack of dirty dishes to the kitchen. He whisked open the front door and rushed to the sidewalk.

They were easily six blocks away, but if Austin's eyes were not deceiving him, Katia and Mrs. Beabots had just crossed Maple Avenue and were headed to Mrs. Beabots's house.

Scratching his head, he slowly pivoted and started back toward his home.

"She's thinkin' of movin' in with the old lady," Daisy said from the doorway. "Of course, if you'd had just an ounce of curiosity and chutzpah, you would have walked right up to her and asked."

Austin glared at Daisy. There were times when Daisy's bossiness was cute and almost welcome. But at this moment, as he struggled with painful memories, Daisy's practical, take-charge pep talk was annoying. "So you recognized her?"

She shook her head. "I never saw her before today. But I know about her. You and your mom told me. After that reaction of yours, I figured it out for myself." She put her hand on her hip. "As if I would call the cops. That's your answer for everything. The trash man is late. There's a Jehovah's Witness at the door. The pool man didn't show up. 'Daisy, call the cops!' If I had a nickel…"

He stuck his hands into his pants' pockets. "I'm pretty predictable, aren't I?"

"Down to the minute. I like that about you." She smiled fondly.

"I just wish I knew what she was doing here. How did she get in? Did you see her come in?"

Daisy shrugged. "I didn't see half of them.

Once I opened the door, it seemed to be a steady stream of folks. I don't know very many of them, except the mayor—I voted for her. Miss Crenshaw and Maddie. Katia seems to know them pretty well."

"Really? They're much younger than Katia. I doubt she would have known them from school. Do you think Katia has been friends with them long?"

"I couldn't tell you, but they seemed awfully close, chatting during lunch and all." She studied Austin. "Aren't you curious where Katia's been since she left?"

He raked a hand through his hair. "You bet I am. And that is the first question I'm going to ask her. Among a thousand—"

"Chicago."

"What?"

"She's been living in Chicago. At least until now. She'll be living here in Indian Lake soon, so you can ask her all the questions you want."

Austin was aghast. How was it possible that his housekeeper, who had never met Katia before today, already knew more about her than he did? Austin chided himself. Daisy was right. If he'd had the pluck to face Katia down, he would have found out all these things and possibly more. But he'd retreated; at least, that was what it would look like to Katia and the rest of the townspeople.

There goes Austin McCreary, slipping into his shell again.

For years, Austin had used his reputation as a recluse to serve his own purposes. Austin didn't like people poking into his business or his personal life and asking a lot of questions he didn't want to answer.

The underlying problem was that Austin himself didn't have the one answer he needed. Had Katia ever loved him, and if she had, why would she have left?

Austin felt that his adult life had begun that day at LaGuardia. He'd been abandoned, and he'd felt adrift all this time. She'd left a dull ache in his heart that had never completely gone away. It was his pain that told him he'd found true love with Katia. She hadn't been just a high school romance. What they'd had was real and he knew he'd never find it with anyone else.

He didn't know how to respond to the simplest questions, the kind people ask at parties and gatherings, because they always brought back memories of Katia and the plans they'd made for a future together. "Are you married? Do you have children? How's your business?"

Though he replied with platitudes, the true answers were troubling, even to him. "I'm not married. She left me. I don't want children except with Katia, but I can't forgive her for leaving me. I hate my business. Running my father's company is boring and unfulfilling."

In truth, Austin felt as if he was sleepwalking through his life. Being numb to his heartbreak was his only coping skill.

But today, Katia had come back. He had to give her credit. She didn't slink around town, find a place to live, get a job or whatever it was she was here for and then let him find out she was in town. She'd rushed right in.

She'd come to his house and crashed his party. If he hadn't gotten angry, he might have been able to question her and learn everything he wanted to know. Katia had grit, all right. She had enough for the two of them.

"So are you going to follow her and see where she went?" Daisy asked.

"Isn't that illegal?"

"You could just cruise by Mrs. Beabots's a bit slower than you usually do on your way to the plant," Daisy suggested.

"The plant!" Austin checked his watch. "I'm due there in twenty minutes."

"I know." Daisy reached behind her and grabbed his car keys and his briefcase from the entry table. "I assume you're taking the '89 Corvette?"

"Why would you think that?" he asked.

"Because it's the one you moved out of the carriage house and put in the driveway this morning," Daisy replied in the assuaging tone she used to remind him that she was a better conscience than the one in his head.

"Oh, right." He took the keys and briefcase. "I'll be home at six as usual."

"Dinner will be ready," Daisy replied with a smile. "Steak and butternut squash."

"Great."

He went over to his black convertible, wondering if he should put the top up. If he saw Katia as he passed Mrs. Beabots's house, would he want her to see *him*? Should he wave to her as if nothing had happened? Should he stop and talk to her? Maybe he should apologize about the calling-the-police thing. Was she deeply offended by that, or did she even care? He turned on the ignition and backed out of the drive. Daisy stepped back into the house and shut the front door.

Austin's head was filled with so many questions he thought it would burst.

The heck with it. Probably best to let sleeping dogs...totally alone.

Austin drove down the block, turned left on Iris Avenue and decided to take another route to the plant.

CHAPTER SEVEN

PELTING RAIN NEARLY drowned out the sound of Jack's voice. Katia sat across from him in his office, holding her cell phone on the off chance that Austin would return one of the half dozen calls she'd placed to him in the past twenty-one hours. The only number she had was his landline, which had been printed on a brochure she'd picked up at the museum presentation. Austin didn't have voice mail, but Daisy always answered calls after the fifth ring, giving Austin time to pick up first. Katia had phoned him as she'd driven out of town the night before.

It had taken her hours to get up the nerve to dial his number, but once she'd spoken with Daisy, she realized she was never going to do business with Austin if she didn't take care of their personal matters first.

The second time she'd left a message with Daisy, Katia still had hope that Austin would return her call—out of curiosity, if nothing else. She'd tried a few more times until nine o'clock, which was her personal cutoff for making calls in the evening. Daisy assured her she'd passed on the message, and told Katia she didn't think another one was going to make any difference.

"He doesn't want to talk to me," Katia had replied flatly.

"He didn't say that," Daisy had countered. "But my experience has been that when he waves me away like he's been doing when I tell him it was you, he's not interested."

"Waves you away, huh?" Katia had asked. "With no comment?" Katia remembered the gesture from when they were kids. It was how she'd known she was bugging him. Katia's frustration rose.

"None."

"Thanks so much for your help, Daisy. I'll see you soon," Katia had said.

"Oh, really? And when will that be?" Daisy had probed.

Katia knew that Daisy would inform Austin of her plans. "I should be there by the end of the week, so the movers tell me."

"I hope it goes well for you," Daisy had said before hanging up.

Wrongly, Katia had assumed the news that she was moving to Indian Lake would spark some interest from Austin. But so far, he'd remained silent.

Fine. You want to play hardball, Austin Mc-Creary? Then, you're in for the fight of your life.

Jack clicked his ballpoint pen. It was a nervous habit that Katia had noticed years ago. He seemed both anxious and excited. She smiled broadly.

"It went extremely well," she told her boss before he had a chance to ask. She tapped her phone screen. "I took dozens of shots of the office space I think will be ideal for us."

Jack took the phone and glanced at the photos. "Attractive. Love the walls of windows. Quaint view. How much?"

"Less than a third of what you're paying here."

"What's the catch? Do I have to sign for ten years? A double security fee? Four months' rent in advance?" Jack braced for the particulars.

"Two-year contract. Security deposit is one month's rent and the first and last months' rent in advance. The parking is limited, but we're not selling retail clothing. I'll have a car, but except in bad weather, I'll be walking to work."

"From where?"

"I've already rented a very nice apartment for myself," she said proudly. "A converted ballroom, to be exact. Nearly eighteen hundred square feet. You know how tiny my apartment is. This is just fabulous. I love it. And I adore the landlady. She's an old acquaintance, actually."

"That was fast. I'm impressed. Did you find a condo for me?"

Katia couldn't stifle her laugh. "Sorry, Jack. This is a small town, and there aren't even any apartment buildings, much less condos."

"This is a joke. Where do people live, then?"

"Houses. There are lots of old mansions that have been turned into apartments. I hired a Realtor to work with you. Her name is Cate Sullivan, and she's already sent me some listings. I'll forward them to you."

"So basically, we have a place to work, but I have no place to live." He groaned.

Katia pulled up the first emails from Cate and handed her phone back to him.

"Hey, I love this lake! Can't I find a condo on the lake?"

"Actually, you're in luck. Cate said there are some small older condos available. They're not going to be what you're used to in Chicago—"

"I could go fishing!" He grinned at her, but Katia simply stared back at him, straight-faced. "Okay. So I've never been fishing. But I could learn."

"Sure." Katia pulled a business card out of her skirt pocket. "Give Cate a call. She said the condos always go up for rent this time of year. I figured if you spent the winter on the lake, by spring you'd have a better idea of what you'd like."

Jack interrupted, "And by then we should know if we're going to be staying."

"Jack, the office is a two-year lease. Are we going to do this or not?"

Suddenly, Katia felt the earth shifting again. She'd already called the movers; they were coming in the morning, and she'd given notice to her landlord, who had a new tenant lined up in less than six hours. Katia had never been the kind of person to sit on fences. Once she made a decision, she plunged forward. She'd paid her deposit to Mrs. Beabots. She'd made a call to one of Maddie's friends who owned a car dealership and she had an appointment to look at cars as soon as she arrived in Indian Lake. A more prudent person would have waited for the green light from her boss. Katia realized she was more desperate to save her job than she'd thought. She had a lot riding on her decisions.

She continued to stare at Jack.

Jack's handsome face was set with determination. "We're doing this. Period. We have no choice. How soon will you be up and running for me to transition over?"

"A month, maybe?"

"Six weeks. That takes me through Thanksgiving, and I promised Ava and Barry I'd be here at least for the holiday. Barry says we can close down this office in three weeks. Our lease is up, so no problem there. I'll need to come to Indian Lake and check out that condo. You're in charge of office personnel for now."

"I'm only hiring a receptionist. Until we know where this is going, we need to be as bare bones as possible."

"Done and done." He folded his hands. "So did you hook up with McCreary?"

Katia swallowed hard. She'd been anticipating this question all morning and she still hadn't decided if she would lie, bend the truth, be honest or evade. Now that the moment was here, she figured all of the above into the equation. "I sure did, Jack!" she replied with more enthusiasm than she'd planned. She hoped she didn't sound too phony.

"Excellent. How did the first meeting go?"

She sat back in her chair confidently. "Very well."

"So it's true he's planning this museum thing like you told me?"

"It's incredible," she replied honestly, thinking that telling the truth as much as possible could only serve her well in the future. She felt as if she was tiptoeing across quicksand. If she could just get to the other side of all this, she'd be safe. For the moment anyway. "It's three stories and can house as many as fifty cars."

Jack whistled. "That's a lot of toys!"

"I'm not sure he has that many at the moment."

"He didn't tell you the exact number?" Jack asked incredulously. "That's imperative information. Can you imagine?" Jack swiped his face with his palm. "This guy must be loaded."

"He inherited most of the cars from his great-grandfather on down to his father. They've been in the family a long time," she said, feeling comfortable dispensing the truth once again.

"When's the next meeting?"

Katia instantly felt like one of those clowns at a county fair who got dunked into a pool of water with baseballs. Of course Jack would think she'd set up a second meeting. That was why she'd been calling Austin so much. Of course, Jack would also expect professionalism from her. "Next Monday morning," she lied, promising herself to do her best to make it true.

"Are you insane?"

"Excuse me?"

"This guy just announced his plans for this museum to half of the Midwest. Every broker we know will be calling him. You need to meet with him tomorrow."

"But my movers come tomorrow."

He waved away her concerns. "Have Tina see to the movers. Go home tonight, pack what you need and get back to Indian Lake. There's not a moment to lose." Jack rose from his chair, which was his way of ending a meeting.

Katia took her phone from his desk and left. Jack was right. Austin's business was crucial to her own career, but it was also a necessary part of the plan to save Carter and Associates. Katia had been successful in the first phase of her re-organization plans. She'd cut many of their operating costs, but she hadn't had two seconds to enjoy even a droplet of victory.

Katia knew she had to hustle if she was going to win Austin's business. She just hadn't thought she would have to move quite this fast.

IT WAS AFTER eleven, and Katia still hadn't finished filling all the suitcases, tote bags, shopping bags and several boxes that she would drive to Indian Lake in the morning. She still had to tackle her closet. Though the moving truck was scheduled to arrive on Saturday morning with her furniture, she still needed her personal items, clothes, electronics and business files to tide her over until the weekend.

Tina had promised to be at her apartment at seven in the morning, before the movers arrived at eight. Katia wanted to be on the road shortly after she got the movers situated. Though she'd promised Jack she would wrangle a meeting with Austin at some point the next day, that didn't mean she had to be in Indian Lake at the crack of dawn.

As Katia pulled out another armload of hanging clothes from her closet and dumped them on the bed, she wondered for the first time if there was wisdom in owning so many clothes.

Fortunately, her new apartment had huge closets, which would house every last lace top and pencil skirt. However, she had to consider the cost of boxes and the extra space they'd take up in the moving van.

Wandering to the back of the closet, Katia found plastic zipper cases that contained scarves, gloves and winter hats. She pulled them out and placed them with the other items she would take in her car. Returning to the closet, she looked up and noticed a wooden box she hadn't seen in years. Decades.

It was a box Austin had given her for her twelfth birthday. She hadn't thought of it in ages, and suddenly here it was, as if appearing by fate.

Or dumb luck.

Katia went to the bed, sat down and opened the box. She gasped and felt her heart trip in her chest. Two white origami birds nearly sprang out of the box as if they'd been set free from a cage.

"Austin…" She said his name with the kind of emotion and awe she had once felt. He'd made them for her the day after she'd skinned both knees learning to ride his old bike. She'd only been ten years old, and his racing bike had been too big for her. He'd been patient with her despite his apparent disdain for the job, which had been thrust on him by his father. Katia had fallen after wobbling along Maple Avenue for a block. Katia had not sobbed, but tears had streamed down her cheeks. It was the first time Austin had seen her cry.

The next day, he'd given her the birds as a symbol of her bravery. She'd thought they were lovebirds.

She found other treasures in the box. A tarnished silver locket he'd given her for Christmas the following year. She found movie-ticket stubs, a pin from the county fair and folded notes that he used to slip under her door announcing yet another tennis game that he expected her to play. She found a small notebook in which she'd tallied all their tennis scores. She'd marked how many times he beat her and how many times she'd come close to besting him. She found a key chain that had a little tennis racket…attached to a key.

Katia's hand froze as she held the key up to the light. *Austin's front door key.*

Was it possible that the key still fit? Surely, in all these years, he'd changed the locks.

Or had he? Katia continued to look at the key. Austin was a man of routine. He didn't like change. He clung to the past as if the future would set him on fire. The chances were strong that the key might still work.

She wrapped her fingers around it possessively.

Maybe not so dumb luck.

CHAPTER EIGHT

AFTER HER ARRIVAL in Indian Lake, Katia continued to phone Austin at home, but now her calls simply went unanswered. She guessed Austin had caller ID and that both he and Daisy were ignoring her. By the next day, he'd have her on his blocked-caller list.

There was no other strategy for her to take than the obvious one.

Katia stood at Austin's front door and pressed the bell. She heard the familiar, elegant Westminster chimes play. She'd thought they were lovely when she was a child, but now she found them pretentious.

It was dinnertime, but Katia hoped Austin had not begun eating yet. She had to talk to him about the insurance for his museum. Jack was expecting a great deal from her, and there was no time like the present to get started.

Katia had also chosen to show up now because Maddie Strong had told her that Austin spent his days at the plant and left his office at the same time as his employees, around six. It was now six-thirty, quite dark, and even from the front steps, she could smell something like roast beef and garlic wafting from inside the house.

Katia had walked from Mrs. Beabots's house so that Austin wouldn't see her car pull up. If he'd seen her rental the other day, she didn't want to give away her presence before she had a chance to talk to him. Even if he hadn't seen the car, the Illinois license plate might give her away, especially since she'd told Daisy that she'd been living in Chicago. She knew Austin probably had *that* piece of information by now.

Katia pressed the bell again, but still no one came to the door.

As the chimes faded, Katia's heart began hammering, and she felt short of breath. Her hands were shaking so she closed them into fists to mask her trembling. It wouldn't be good for Austin to know he had the advantage. She was here to get him to talk to her, but every time she considered how to approach the situation, she changed her mind and altered her plan of attack. Her heart felt as if it had started moving up to her throat. She clamped her fist against her chest.

The door swung open with such force, Katia thought she'd be swept inside. "Austin."

His blue eyes slid from her face to her balled

fist over her heart. "Ah. *Mea culpa*. That's a good start," he said. His sarcasm felt sharp enough to slit her skin.

Katia suddenly felt like the most infinitesimal being on earth. Her past—*their* past—came slamming back to her. She had wronged Austin and hurt him so deeply, so terribly, that he'd never gotten over it. That was clear to her now. How could she ever make that up to him? He had good reason to hate her.

"What are you doing here?" he demanded.

"You wouldn't answer my calls." She tried to put a cheery lilt in her voice but failed miserably. "I figured you were trying to ignore me."

"Good assumption," he ground out.

This was going to be more difficult than she'd imagined. If she was even going to broach the insurance subject, she would have to convince him that she was truly sorry and try to regain his trust.

But would he ever believe her?

She looked at him, and as she spoke the words, she knew she'd never felt such remorse. "I'm sorry, Austin. I'm so, so sorry."

"For what? Your telephone harassment?"

"For not going to your prom with you. For not telling you about our move to Chicago. For hurting you the way I did."

Austin rolled his eyes and gripped the door

with white knuckles. "You think I'm *mad* at you?"

"I can see that you are," Katia countered, her voice growing louder.

Daisy came up behind Austin and yanked the door out of his grasp. "You gonna dump your dirty laundry all over the street? Bring it inside. Now. The both of you!"

Austin exhaled and took a step backward so she could enter the house. He wouldn't meet her eyes and stared at the floor, seemingly lost in thought.

Was he remembering that fateful day when she had left him standing at LaGuardia? She knew he'd waited for her there, but she hadn't been on the plane. Now she was here, literally on his doorstep, trying to apologize. Her heart was still in her throat, and she found she was just as speechless as he was.

"We'll go to the living room," Austin said, leading the way.

Katia glanced at Daisy, who jerked her head toward Austin in a gesture of support. Katia twisted her hands, wishing they would stop shaking and that the room would stop tilting.

"May I sit?" she asked feebly, wondering if this time it wasn't just panic—although she was entitled to it—but an actual heart attack. It was probably just as well. Any other woman in her situation would already be dead.

Austin gestured to one of the room's two aqua bergère chairs, and Katia sat. No wonder her prized possessions were her own bergère chairs, she thought. They reminded her of home. Austin's home, rather.

"I didn't think you'd even talk to me," she said.

"I'm not. Technically, Daisy let you in." He stood next to the mantel under the huge oil portrait of his father. "So why not say what it is that you came here to say."

Katia's eyes scanned the room. Oddly, the familiar surroundings gave her the sensation of comfort and calm. She was amazed at how quickly and clearly she remembered everything about her life in this home. Every stick of furniture was exactly the same as when she was a child. If that wasn't enough to dredge up the memories she'd placed in the catacombs of her heart, there was her favorite smell of lemon oil on old wood and that particular spicy, musty fragrance that accompanied old furniture. Perhaps this was where Katia had acquired her love of antiques and all things that spoke of elegance and permanence.

Her heart returned to its normal pace, and her hands were growing steadier by the moment. As she looked up at Austin, she felt her strength return. She wasn't sure if it was adrenaline or just a large dose of indignation, but her panic was receding. "Let me get this straight," she said. "You aren't mad at me?"

"That would imply I have an emotional investment in you," Austin replied, his tone as cool as a glacier.

"How long have you practiced that line?" she countered quickly. Then she saw the wounded look in his eyes. "I'm sorry…again."

"Forget it. You should just go."

"No! Austin. I, uh, came here to talk to you about…" Suddenly, she couldn't remember the first aspect of her sales pitch. She was tongue-tied. "I wanted to talk to you about my business."

"Business?" he spat, as if the word were laden with battery acid.

"I'm in the insurance business. That's why I moved here."

"What kind of insurance?"

"All kinds," she said, not believing she could be messing up this badly. On her way over here, she'd only been thinking about saving her job, but now she realized that this meeting shouldn't be about what she wanted from him. He needed a great deal from her, and it was obvious that he was only interested in talking about his feelings, both past and present, as well as her responsibility for them.

Katia felt every ounce of shame that had weighed on her heart for the past twenty years.

She remembered the way Austin used to look at her with clear, bright and trusting eyes. Now his expression was guarded and closed off, and his eyes held a melancholy that she realized she had put there.

Her heart went out to him, but she wished he would be open-minded enough to see her point of view.

She stood up and faced him, but the moment she was on her feet, she felt shaky and afraid again. "We left because my mother was terrified that I would get pregnant. As the maid's daughter, my future would be ruined. I would never have finished high school and college. You and I were—"

"In love."

"Yes," she admitted, and then stopped abruptly, sinking back into her chair. Had he really said that out loud? Back then, he'd never come out and told her that he loved her. He'd told her that she was pretty, but so had her Sunday-school teachers and Mrs. McCreary's friends. He'd said he liked her. That she was a good tennis partner. But had Austin truly loved her? Was that the source of this antagonism? She knew she'd hurt him;

she'd chalked a lot of it up to his pride. The Mc-
Creary name and reputation.

"We were," he said, his eyes softening. She'd
seen that look before. It was the one he'd given
her when he'd first begun to see her as more
than his pesky shadow. The look was filled with
appreciation and approval. Respect and endear-
ment. But was it love?

"I couldn't call you, Austin. I was too embarrassed. I felt terrible about what happened and
very ashamed. My emotions were all over the
place. I felt it was all my fault that we had to
leave our home and my mother had to quit her
job. I remember walking around my new school
with my head hanging down. I was so guilt ridden, I couldn't make eye contact with anyone.
My mother was so paranoid about us, about
what she thought we would do, that I wanted to
assure her she didn't have to worry. If I'd called
you, we would have been on the phone constantly and that would have caused my mother
even more grief. We might even have tried to
meet up in secret. At the time, I saw no other
way out."

"I'm trying to understand," he said, moving
away from the mantel to sit in the chair next
to hers.

There was a dark cabriole leg table between

the two of them. Just enough distance to keep them from colliding.

He continued. "As I remember, your mother lurked around every corner. I'm not so sure *anything* could have happened. At least not in this house."

"It nearly did at Indian Lake," she reminded him.

"Summer was just coming in," he said, looking down at his hands.

"Sunday. It was a Sunday," she said, the afternoon coming back to her in vivid detail. They'd gone to the beach, lying to their mothers that they were strawberry picking. They'd bought strawberries at a farmhouse on the county road, packed neatly in wooden pint baskets to keep the illusion intact. Katia had forgotten about their eagerness and Austin's kisses.

They'd talked about the future. He'd revealed his dreams, which had little to do with the successful McCreary automotive-parts plant he was destined to run. Austin had hoped to try out for the national tennis championships. His mother had laughed at him and claimed his ideas were ridiculous. She'd scolded him for pursuing "pointless" hobbies. Austin had made matters worse by telling his mother he wanted to work on cars and perfect his mechanic skills instead of attending business college. Hanna had flown into a rage and threatened to disinherit Austin if he turned his back on the family business for his childish pursuits.

"Did you ever think about me, Katia?" Austin asked with trepidation.

Leveling her green eyes on his, she felt the lump in her throat threaten to choke her. Suddenly, she was sixteen again and more in love than she'd thought possible, then or since. Had her feelings for Austin been deep and real? Or had they been only a side effect of growing up, as her mother had constantly told her?

Katia was more confused than ever. Though contrite, she didn't want Austin to think she'd come here just to cleanse her soul, or that she'd been pining away for him since they were teenagers. She'd built a new life filled with friends and success and triumphs. Hadn't she? But if all those things were true, why did she care so much about how he'd react to what she said?

Katia chose to tell him the truth. "I couldn't get you out of my mind. I wanted to call you, Austin. But like I said, it wasn't easy for me. When we first left, we stayed with a cousin. My mother and I were in a tiny room sharing a double bed. We were counting every penny, and she would have known if I made a long-distance call. I wrote letters to you, but I didn't mail them. Frankly, I was afraid to contact you."

"But why?"

"In the beginning, I was hurt and ashamed. It was awful for me not to be with you. Then as time went on, I realized that if I had come back, I would have ended up resenting you because I *did* want a new life for myself. I wanted a real career and my own apartment. I wanted to know what it was like to live on my own and make my own decisions. If I'd stayed here, I would have been your girl. And that's all." Katia was almost in tears. She'd thought the guilt she carried couldn't get any worse. She was wrong. Reliving the past with Austin sitting right next to her was agonizing.

"I guess that says it all," he said. "Being with me wasn't enough."

Katia blinked. A slow burn of anger started low in her belly, but it didn't stay there long. It threatened to engulf her entire body.

"Of all the arrogant—" She shot to her feet and loomed over him with both hands on her hips. "Are you kidding me? Are you actually going to tell me that you expected me to sit here in Indian Lake and wait for you, as if you were a…a soldier off at war? As though you were doing something heroic?" She threw her head back and laughed. "You've really lost it, Austin, if you think a woman with any brains or talent is going to make some guy the center of her universe. It doesn't work that way. Couples are supposed to be partners."

"Yeah?" He bolted to his feet and stood nearly nose to nose with her.

"Like we used to be?" Katia knew this was her chance. "We could be partners now," she said hesitantly. "If you'd let me. I could help you with your insurance."

He rolled his eyes and his cheeks flashed crimson. "That's what you're really here for, then? To sell me something? I knew I couldn't trust you. Serves me right for letting you in."

Katia winced. "I had that coming."

"Is that the *only* reason you wanted to see me, Katia? Truthfully."

"Okay. Truthfully? Yes. And no. I *did* want to apologize. I was sincere about that."

Katia could feel her eyes blazing as she spoke to him. She felt as though every cell in her body was on fire. Was it because she was mad at him? Or because he was so handsome she couldn't look away? It was all she could do to keep from throwing herself into his arms and discovering if his kisses were still the same. He, on the other hand, appeared cool and collected now, as if he didn't have a care in the world. He wasn't fooling her, though. Her being here today was important to him. She just didn't know to what degree.

His blue eyes were earnest as they searched her face, cooling Katia's temper. His voice was calming.

"I always thought our mothers' attitudes were worse than old-fashioned," he said. "My mother harbored many prejudices, and social class was one of them. She used that thinking against me, as well. Your mother wanted a better life for you, as would be expected. Maybe if my mother hadn't been so fearful and had trusted us a little more, she would have realized that marriage to me wouldn't have been a bad thing."

Katia thrust her hands up and shook her head to stop him. "Wait a minute. Who said anything about marriage? I certainly never brought up the subject."

"No, you didn't. I do remember that part correctly," he replied with distinct sadness in his tone. "But I thought about it a lot, actually. Especially once I left Indian Lake for York."

Katia's ire died a quick death. "You did?" she asked. She felt as if the wind had been knocked out of her. "I had no idea."

"How could you? I was gone for the last three years you were here, and I obviously didn't mention it to you. I'm surprised your mother didn't hustle you out of town sooner than she did."

Katia wondered how so many emotions could have been trapped inside her for so long. Just being here with Austin had reawakened something in her. Though she wasn't quite sure if it was love, nostalgia or simply relief from her guilt, Katia knew that only Austin could have performed this kind of magic.

"Katia. I still have a dozen—no, hundreds—of questions I want to ask you."

Katia felt as if she was being sucked into a whirlwind of emotions she hadn't been prepared for. She needed to breathe and sort out her feelings. One thing was for sure—being with Austin for even a little while was confusing and unsettling.

"Oh, my—I forgot. Your dinner is waiting and I promised Mrs. Beabots I would join her for dinner. I didn't think I would be gone quite this long."

She bent to retrieve her purse from beside the chair.

"Sure. Maybe another time," he said with a melancholy tone.

Katia realized that, to Austin, this must feel as though she was walking out of his life... again.

She had to stop that kind of reaction from

taking hold. "Great!" she said brightly. "I understand you play tennis with Rafe Barzonni quite often. How would you two feel if I joined you sometime?"

"You still play?" He seemed surprised.

"I joined a tennis club right out of high school. I bet I can beat you now," she teased with enough challenge in her eyes to elicit a raised eyebrow from him.

"We're supposed to play on Sunday afternoon."

"Oh, not till then?" She looked at him with the full force of her gaze. "I was thinking I'd like to see you tomorrow."

"I'll be at the plant all day. I don't see how..."

She tilted her head to the side. "I'll be scouring antiques shops for office furniture. Maybe I'll stop by."

Austin turned and started toward the hall. "Okay, fine."

She followed him to the front door. She wanted to kiss his cheek, but his cool gaze kept her at arm's length. "Thanks for seeing me tonight, Austin. I don't think I could have moved to Indian Lake knowing that my friend wasn't my friend anymore."

"Sure." He made no move to hug her or kiss her or even shake her hand. Katia didn't know if that was just his way now, or if she should read more into it.

She walked away feeling a bit hollow. Austin didn't seem at all relieved by their conversation. Was he still angry? Or was he having a hard time trusting her still?

Neither option was good for her.

AUSTIN WATCHED KATIA leave, and slowly shut the door. He walked back into the living room and looked down at the two chairs where they'd been sitting.

Her perfume still lingered in the air, and for just a brief moment, he chided himself for not taking her into his arms and kissing her.

Better to keep her as an acquaintance, he reminded himself. Katia had betrayed him.

Austin had waited so many years to finally point the finger at Katia and accuse her of the heinous crime she'd committed, but now he didn't know how he felt. One minute he wanted to fold her into his arms, and the next he truly wanted to throw her out. Maybe Stephania and his mother had been right all along. Maybe he and Katia were wrong for each other. He'd been born into a different social world than she had, and it had separated them in the past. But this was now. The playing court was level.

Katia would have to earn her way back to his friendship. Romance was strictly out of the question. He'd been burned once. He didn't plan on a second time.

If he wanted to protect his heart, he should never see her again.

CHAPTER NINE

JACK HAD GIVEN Katia a tight budget to furnish the new office, so she knew she'd have to be both fiscally and artistically creative. Because every car passing through the busiest intersection in the county would be able to see into Carter and Associates, she wanted to achieve the maximum effect with furnishings and signage.

The loft had antique light maple floors that looked contemporary against the old redbrick walls. The space was completely open, with only a large storage area and small bathroom in the back, but Katia knew they would need at least one enclosed office for private meetings with clients. Luckily, Mrs. Beabots had introduced her to Sarah and Luke Bosworth, and Katia had hired Luke's company to build walls and a door, and if they could afford it, she wanted to add an etched-glass window she'd designed herself. Luke had promised to work up a quote once he got the prices on the materials.

In the meantime, she had made calls to the

local antiques stores and sourced several desks, chairs, tables and lamps. She'd found that used furniture was a higher value than the cheap, prefab box-store variety. Even if some pieces cost more at the outset, they were usually much better quality and lasted longer.

Katia knew Indian Lake was the kind of town where she and Jack would have to get to know the local retailers on a first-name basis. Katia had always prided herself on her ability to bargain hunt, and this expedition was going to test her skills to the max.

She had hoped Jack and Barry would move some of the office furniture from Chicago to Indian Lake, but they were only planning to ship the computers and other equipment. The finer pieces of furniture had all been rented, and Barry had paid for all of the bookshelves, file cabinets and his own office furnishings himself. Jack would bring his own desk and two executive chairs, at least, so Katia's budget didn't have to include those items.

She intended to focus on the reception area, which would include the walls of windows. She envisioned two bergère chairs, even if she had to use her own, and fabulous crystal lamps on marble-top tables. In the corners, she would place tall white bird of paradise plants in French jardinières and light them from below with halogen lamps. She wanted the area to shout "security." After all, that's what they were selling.

To keep costs low, she'd hired someone to paint *Carter and Associates* in bright gold letters across the window that faced Main Street, with their phone number and website written below. Jack had mumbled his disapproval, but he'd acquiesced when she explained that the painter cost them one-tenth the price of a sign.

As Katia stood in the empty loft overlooking the traffic, her cell phone rang.

"Jack," she said. "Why don't you just put me on permanent hold? You'll save time dialing my number all the time." This was his fifth phone call of the morning.

Katia's to-do list was a mile long—no, two miles long—and each of his calls felt increasingly unnecessary. Didn't he trust her to do the job correctly? Or was it just that he missed having her in the office? How many times had Tina teased her that she was Jack's "office wife" and that he couldn't live without her? This was the first time Katia had actually been away from the office for longer than a couple days. Her sales trips were mostly overnighters. Now she was truly away from Jack.

Even when she'd taken a vacation, it had never been more than an extra Friday for a long weekend, which she usually spent shopping with a friend from work or going to a play. Katia's focus had always been her job and her career.

"You're on speed dial," Jack retorted. "I just talked to the movers here, and I'm having Tina pack up as much as she can to get it sent over to you."

"Jack..." She sighed deeply, wondering what planet he lived on. It certainly wasn't earth. "I just got here. I won't even have my own furniture here till Saturday. I'm sleeping in my landlady's guest room right now. Plus, I don't have the specs for your office build-out yet."

"That's fine. Just put this stuff where you can. We're having to get out of here sooner than we thought."

Katia's whirring mind stopped cold. Something wasn't right. Jack was a thorough man and meticulous about everything regarding his business. Barry, on the other hand...

"What did Barry do?"

"Oh, you're good. Nothing gets past you, does it? That's why I like having you around." He paused and then rushed on. "Turns out Barry thought he'd save us another five grand, which he did. But the caveat is that we have to clear out of this building by the end of next week. We can do that, but we're scrambling. Rather than move the computers, phones and stuff to my condo, I'll just have them shipped there."

"Fine. So, Jack, this would mean that you'd be coming here sooner than you thought?"

"It does. I have a call in to Cate Sullivan, but could you nudge her a bit from your end, as well? She can email me photos and specs of those lake condos."

Katia crossed her fingers. From her conversations with Maddie, who was building a house on the lake with her fiancé, Nate, Katia was aware that any condo up for rental there would be take it or leave it. They tended to get snatched up fast. "I'll do it as soon as we're off the phone."

"Thanks. And good luck with the furniture shopping."

"As soon as the painter arrives, I'm off."

"What? You're leaving a workman at the office with no supervision?"

Katia chuckled. Jack was going to have culture shock when he arrived in Indian Lake. Not only was there nothing to steal in the office, but the painter was none other than Isabelle Hawks, Maddie and Liz's friend. Isabelle had jumped at the job, telling Katia the extra cash would help her pay the entrance fee for a gallery showing and possible award in Phoenix. Over the summer, Isabelle had created a new series of aquatic fantasy acrylics, and she was ready to exhibit them. Katia was delighted that Carter and Associates was already helping an Indian Lake resident.

"It's not a problem. The artist is a friend of a friend."

"Oh," Jack replied with the edge of humility she'd always admired in him. "Okay. Well, you've got that handled. Let me know how the bargain hunting goes."

"Believe me, I will," she said.

As she hung up, the bell rang in the downstairs hall. It was Isabelle, and Katia buzzed her up.

Isabelle's pretty heart-shaped face was filled with delight as she walked up the stairs carrying a box of brushes, rags, stencils and a can of paint. "You must be Katia," she said with a bright smile.

"I am. Here, let me help you." Katia took the can of paint and held the door for Isabelle.

Isabelle stepped into the office and looked around. "Wow. This is gorgeous, and it's huge! What a wonderful place to work." She headed straight for the window. "The view is fantastic, and the courthouse is so majestic from here."

Katia stood next to her. "I've always loved that clock tower. Now with all the pear trees lining the street and the flower planters, it's just…"

"Idyllic," Isabelle said, taking two steps back and turning to glance out the west-facing window. She walked down the length of it and came back, then she went to the middle of the room and sat down, still looking at the windows.

Katia kept her silence, thinking that she had certainly hired the right person. Isabelle was taking account of the view from all angles. She was considering the workers at their desks and the clients who would sit in the reception area.

"I circled the building for the past half hour, approaching it from each direction, to get a sense of what passing drivers would see. This is definitely the best office space in town, and I'm so glad you have it. Short of a lit sign in Times Square, it doesn't get any better. But to do this right, I want to use a block lettering that won't cut out a lot of your view. I'll put *Insurance* and the phone number in block on the west window.

Katia knew to keep her poker face when bargaining, and she guessed this was Isabelle's way of increasing the fee. "How much extra will that cost?"

"Nothing," Isabelle replied lightly. "I want this to be perfect for you, being Mrs. Beabots's friend. Everyone in town will know I painted it, so I promise it will be beautiful and just what you want. I can sketch out the letters to show your boss," she offered.

"Excellent idea," Katia said. "I'll text a photo to Jack. If he approves, we'll do it."

Within moments of sending Jack the font sketches, Katia received his reply with the go-ahead.

"Fantastic," Isabelle said, pulling a paint-splashed white smock out of her supply box. "I'll just get to work, then."

"I have to leave you alone for a few hours. I'm off to find some chairs and desks. For the office," Katia explained, retrieving her purse and keys from the corner near the windows.

She checked her phone. Low battery, just as she thought. Too many calls from Jack. She'd have to recharge in the car.

Katia turned to wave to Isabelle, who was staring at the brick wall.

"What are you putting up there?" Isabelle asked.

"I hadn't gotten that far."

"If I showed you some of my paintings and you liked a few, would you be willing to display them?"

Katia was intrigued. She hadn't thought of showcasing local artists, but suddenly she found she liked the idea a lot. "What kind of paintings?"

"Acrylics and oils, mostly. Many are landscapes, and like I said, I have my new fantasy series. I can't paint enough of those ones."

"I like this idea. Should I come to your place to see them?"

"Sure. If you don't mind. Though I have to warn you that my apartment is very cramped. The money I save by renting such a small space helps me buy more canvases."

Katia knew she was standing in front of a genuine artist. This woman was as much about her art as Katia had always been about her career. Katia felt she understood Isabelle completely. "You tell me what's convenient for you, and we'll set a meeting."

"Monday is the best for me right now. The Lodge will be closing for the season right after Halloween. Then I'll have a great deal of free time."

"Okay, Monday it is. We'll talk about a time when I get back. How's that sound?"

Isabelle beamed. "Perfect."

THE McCREARY AUTO-PARTS plant was housed in a hangar-like building that resembled another half dozen manufacturing plants around Indian Lake. There was nothing distinctive about the single metal door, the fading summer flowers around the flagpole or even the corporate logo on the small, dark wood sign out front. To an outsider, it was just another factory. To Katia, it was Mecca. Or at least it had the potential to be.

To Katia, the plant was a perfect place to lay the groundwork for the insurance package she intended to sell him.

She didn't have his cell phone number, but she'd told him she was visiting, so obviously he wasn't too concerned about her calling ahead.

She entered the company's reception area and was jolted into the past. If there had been any renovations, they certainly hadn't started here, where first impressions were so important.

The space was not much larger than an average bedroom and was divided in half by a long counter faced with cheap 1970s paneling. Behind the counter was a bleached-blond woman in her midsixties who wore stop-sign red lipstick, rhinestone-encrusted reading glasses and enough black eyeliner to make a raccoon envious. She looked up, gave Katia a once-over and apparently found her pleasing because she broke into a broad smile that rivaled the fluorescent light overhead. "Well, hello, dear! How can I help you?"

"My name is Katia Stanislaus. I'm here to see Austin. Is he busy?"

"Busy? He's always busy." She chuckled, making her very heavy jowls shake. "Is he expecting you?" She peered at an appointment book in front of her. "I don't see your name down here."

"He didn't schedule a time. It's not a formal visit."

"Oh?" She shot Katia a curious glance over the top of her glasses. "He didn't tell me, either."

"I'm an old friend."

"I'm Midge," the receptionist said, reaching for the telephone. "I'll let him know you're here." Midge rang Austin's office, but there was no answer. She hung up and checked the clock hanging on the paneled wall behind her. "I know where he is. Follow me."

Midge rose slowly from her chair and went to a door marked Employees Only.

Katia remembered that this door led to the management and billing offices, but she was surprised to see that the hallway of offices was gone. They were standing in the middle of an open area with a concrete floor, high ceilings, a metal roof and metal walls. To the right were three double-wide garage doors, two of which were open. A pickup truck was parked just inside one door, and another car was up on a lift. To Katia's left were shelves filled with motor oil, solvents, auto paint, antifreeze and mechanics' tools. Under the car on the lift, two men were discussing a problem with the catalytic converter, a connecting pipe and the need for a new muffler. Two legs and part of a mechanics' dolly stuck out from under the pickup.

Katia may have been standing in a garage, but she knew this space was something else. It was one of Austin's childhood dreams.

"Mr. McCreary," Midge shouted over the din of air tools and male conversations.

"Yeah?" came Austin's voice. "Darn!" he yelped.

"You okay, Austin?" one of the men under the raised car answered back.

"Fine, fine. I just dropped the screw I was using. I'll find it."

Midge put her hand on her hip. "Visitor to see you, Mr. McCreary."

"Tell them I'm busy," Austin answered.

Midge started to reply, but Katia grabbed her arm and put her finger to her lips. Midge smiled knowingly and nodded, apparently quite pleased to be included in Katia's game. Katia walked over to the car, her high heels clicking on the concrete. The *tap-tap-tap* was distinct enough to be heard above the tools and laughter. The men grew silent and turned toward Katia.

She stopped at Austin's car, scrunched down on her heels and peered under the car. "Hi, Austin."

His face was smeared with black grease, but even in the dim light his blue eyes shone out at her like two bright beams. A work light glowed around his head like a halo. Had he been this handsome yesterday?

"You're here," he said, his tone a mix of disbelief and delight.

"I am." The garage felt eerily silent. "Is this a bad time?"

"No." He smiled, but didn't make a move to come out from under the car.

"You like it under there, do you?"

"You, of all people, should know that I do."

She crooked her neck to the left. "I see that. But it would be easier for me if we continued our conversation in a more, um, upright position."

"Oh, sorry." Immediately, Austin wheeled himself out from under the car and stood up.

His hair was messy and his clothes were filthy, yet seeing him still made her heart trip. His eyes held a wariness that she should have expected, though she had hoped he would have shown a hint of excitement at seeing her. She'd hoped for too much. He wiped his hands on his overalls, then looked at them. "I guess I should clean up before I show you around."

"Brilliant," she said as he reached for her arm, which she jerked away from him. Austin grinned and quickly turned to the two men under the lift. "Pete, can you finish this up for me? I'll be a while and I promised Tom he'd have the car by end of day."

"Sure, Austin," replied the taller of the two

men, who wore a Cubs baseball cap. "Tom told me to thank you. His wife is very appreciative, as well."

Austin picked up a rag and wiped his greasy hands again. "Pete, you know I empathize with him. Tough break. It's the least I can do."

Austin began to lead Katia back toward the door to reception.

"What kind of tough break did Tom have?" she asked him.

"Oh, his wife just got laid off from the bookbinding company, but they just bought a new house because she's pregnant."

"What kind of job did she have?" Katia asked.

"Executive secretary, I think. She was the boss's right hand. But some ax-man from corporate came down, and she was one of the ones to go."

Katia stopped in her tracks. "Really? Just a minute."

Katia ran back across the garage to the lift where Pete was still working. She pulled a piece of paper and a pen out of her purse and jotted down her number.

"You don't know me," she said, handing the paper to Pete, "but my name is Katia Stanislaus and I'm a friend of Mr. McCreary's. He told me about Tom's wife. My company just moved to Indian Lake, and I need an assistant. Could you give her my number? Maybe we can work something out."

"Sure, I'll do it right away."

She thanked him and rejoined Austin. He looked at her quizzically. "What was that all about? Fraternizing with my staff already?"

"Just a thought I had. I'll let you know if it works out."

He glanced down at his dirty overalls. "I'd better change."

Austin took her through another doorway into his private office, which had an en suite bathroom.

"I won't be long," he told her. "You can wait in here." He headed into the bathroom and shut the door.

This office had once been Daniel's domain, but the old paneling had been replaced with gray-blue paint, and all the molding was now glossy white, giving the room a fresh and airy feel. Charcoal industrial carpet covered the floor. Daniel's old walnut desk sat in the middle of the room, and a wide window faced the street. The two wing chairs opposite the desk had once sat in the library in Austin's home. Photographs of the McCrearys' antique cars and of Austin playing tennis decorated the walls. In many of the pictures, he was holding a trophy.

"You like those?" Austin asked.

Katia had had her back to him as he entered the room, and his voice startled her. She turned around to face him.

"That's pretty impressive, Austin. I'm really happy that you decided to keep playing tennis."

"Thanks to you," he said quietly.

"What have I got to do with any of that?" She gestured at the trophy photos.

"You were the only person in my life who encouraged me to keep pushing myself with tennis. Who knows what limits I might have reached if I'd listened to you earlier or defied my mother or both."

"You were really good, Austin. Really good."

"I still am." He smiled, tilting his head. He came around to the side of his desk. "That's not why you're here, though. Would you like to see the changes I've made at the plant?"

"You ripped out the offices, I saw. Don't you still need them?"

"I moved the offices to the new addition. We also added four new docking bays and loading areas. It's great—the break room is gigantic, and I put in vending machines."

"And you built yourself a playroom," Katia teased. Funny, how his smile made her heart light up. As a child, Austin had been morose most of the time. And lonely. She'd been the one to break through his self-imposed prison back then. Could she do it again?

"Yes, I built the garage for myself, but I also did it for the guys who work for me," Austin said. "When they have car trouble, I fix their cars free of charge. They pay wholesale for the parts we need, but I do the work or teach them how to fix the problems themselves. Saves them some money."

Katia scrutinized him. When had he become so generous? Not that he'd been unkind to people before... But when she had stood outside the school with a car wash poster to raise money for the new gymnasium, Austin had been playing tennis. When she'd helped her mother at the St. Mark's pancake breakfasts, she'd served Austin. Her view of the adult Austin was changing faster than the twist of a kaleidoscope. This Austin felt responsible for his employees. She valued that in her clients.

"Sounds as though you care about your people a great deal," she said.

"I suppose I do."

"Austin, I have to ask. Have you adequately insured the plant here? Covered all your bases, including personal injury coverage for accidents on the job?"

His smile dimmed. "I believe so..."

Her spine straightened as she readied herself

for her pitch. "I was also thinking that with your new museum, you're going to need an extensive insurance package for construction, liability and future employees. I'd like to put something together for you to look at."

Her mouth went dry. He was staring at her with a gaze so steady and hard, it could shatter glass.

"You'd like to put something together."

She was finding it hard to catch her breath. She refused to think about the possibility of a panic attack. Not here. Not with Austin.

She tried to force her voice to be light. "I'm very good at my job, Austin. I'd like to dazzle you with my expertise. If you'd let me."

He inhaled and held it. Katia remembered this move. He only did that when he was really angry and trying to control an outburst. His cheeks weren't flaming red as they used to get when he was young. Maybe he'd conquered that one.

"I haven't gotten that far," he replied, his tone flat and devoid of emotion.

She felt the distance between them growing. She was familiar with the cues executives gave to signal the end of a meeting. That was what this was. He was giving her the brush-off.

"Well, think about it," she said. "I've got another meeting in twenty minutes downtown. Can I call you?"

"Sure." His phone rang, and he looked at the caller ID. "Later," he said, then answered his call.

Katia turned and headed for the door. Her meeting couldn't have gone worse if she'd purposefully scripted her failure.

CHAPTER TEN

INDIAN-SUMMER AFTERNOONS in Indian Lake were as beautiful as a poet's dream. Sun gilded the trees and warm, dry breezes blew through town, rustling leaves that would soon cover the roads and sidewalks. The stores were already decorated for Halloween, and in many shop windows banners announced the Indian Lake High School Homecoming football game and dance.

Austin drove his '89 Corvette convertible down Main Street toward Maple Avenue. He stopped at a red light and glanced at the county courthouse clock tower. Then he looked to the left. On the upper floor of the vacant loft he saw *Carter and Associates* painted in gold.

He shook his head. *What idiot thought of that sign? It doesn't even say what Carter and his associates do.*

The light changed, and Austin turned left. His eyes slid over to his side-view mirror and he saw the word *Insurance* on the loft's other window and a phone number glinting in gold letters in the setting sun's light. "I take it back. Clever," he grumbled, continuing down Maple Avenue.

Austin loved Maple Avenue in the fall. Gone were Ann Marie Jensen's beloved spring tulips and daffodils, but in their place were black-eyed Susans and intriguing grasses that waved in the wind when he passed, making him smile. Few people other than Ann Marie, who'd died a few years ago, knew that he had helped fund nearly all of her horticultural projects. In fact, she was the one person he'd never in his life said no to.

Ann Marie would bake him something sweet, gooey and delicious, and after she'd delivered her "bribe," she would ask for money for one beautification project or another. Sometimes the project was a person, like Lester MacDougal. Lester had walked all the way from Kentucky to escape a violent and brutal father. He'd stopped in Indian Lake when he had seen Ann Marie planting her spring bulbs along Maple Avenue. At Ann Marie's bidding, Austin, Sarah Jensen and Maddie Strong had pitched in to help him, and now Lester operated a fairly successful landscaping business. During the winter and whenever Lester needed a bit of extra cash, Austin hired him to detail his cars.

Austin never regretted fulfilling any of Ann Marie's requests. He wished she was still alive so that he could talk to her like he used to after his own mother died. Ann Marie had become both a friend and a maternal figure for him. They'd kept their friendship a secret from most of the town. Daisy knew about Ann Marie's visits, but that was all.

Although he'd sworn Daisy to secrecy about all his private matters, she had told him long ago that she was a "practical" woman and that she knew "which side of the slice her bread was buttered." As long as she had her job, she'd keep her mouth shut. After that, he shuddered to think about what would happen. This "practical" understanding would keep Daisy employed until her death, most likely. Not that Austin had any great secrets. He simply didn't like nosy neighbors.

Austin approached Ann Marie's old house, which Sarah owned and lived in with her new husband, Luke, and his two children. Austin supposed he should be more of a neighbor himself and send them a card or flowers or something. He wasn't quite sure what the etiquette was in this situation.

Mrs. Beabots's house was next door, and in the driveway was a silver Honda with an Illinois license plate. It was the car that Katia had rented for her move to Indian Lake.

As he drove past the house, his thoughts were conflicted. He'd been angered and surprisingly hurt when Katia brought up the subject of selling him insurance. The idea that she wanted him only as a client, another dollar in her pocket, goaded him. He felt used and dismissed; it reminded him of the seemingly friendly people he'd met at a tennis club in Indianapolis during his tournament days, who didn't support the sport at all and only wanted to sign him up for their pyramid schemes. Austin also felt a bit foolish. Apparently, Katia had returned to Indian Lake for her business. He'd wanted to be the one and only reason she would come back. What an arrogant idiot he was.

Austin stepped on the gas and sped toward his house. He went down to the end of the boulevard where there was a break, turned left and cruised up the half block to his house. He drove up the drive and into the second carriage house, where he always parked the Corvette.

He got out of the car, admiring the 1965 Aston Martin parked next to it. His father had bought the Aston from a collector in Scottsdale the year before he died. Austin seldom looked at the car without thinking fondly of his father.

From a long ceiling beam, Austin had hung several used parachutes he'd bought out at the skydiving school at the Indian Lake Airport. The parachute material was light and didn't scratch the cars, and they served as the perfect dust covers for his prized automobiles.

He billowed a parachute around the Aston Martin and another one around the Corvette. Austin had intended to replace a taillight in the Aston Martin that morning, but he'd taken a longer swim than he'd intended. There were only a few more days left of this glorious weather, and soon it would be time to drain the pool and winterize it.

Austin went into the house through the back door. The kitchen smelled of cinnamon and cloves, and Daisy was pulling a baked chicken out of the oven.

"Are you in for the night?" he asked her. "Can I put the alarm on?"

"Yes!" she said.

Austin punched out his security code and walked over to Daisy. "What smells so good, besides the chicken?" he asked.

Daisy harrumphed. "Not pumpkin pie, if that's what you mean. But close. Baked butternut squash."

He hooked his navy sweater over his arm. "Aw. I was hoping…"

Daisy swatted at him. "You and your sweets. I'm saving you from diabetes. Your mail is on your desk. Dinner will be ready in ten minutes.

And Mr. Nate called. He wants you to call him back."

"Thanks," Austin replied as Daisy took a large casserole out of the oven. She lifted the lid. The mashed squash was covered with marshmallows. He grinned. "You do love me after all."

Daisy frowned and shooed him away. "The recipe called for it. I was just following orders." She turned away and smiled to herself.

Austin went into his office, picked up his mail and flipped through it. After the usual utility bills, he found a letter from the Indian Lake County Council. He assumed it was a thank-you letter for the luncheon and his announcement about the museum. And he was right...until he got to the last paragraph.

As you move forward, Mr. McCreary, we will also need proof of your insurance for the building and the liability umbrella insurance for the workers on site. Later, you will need to provide proof of liability insurance for visitors, maintenance workers, your employees and all volunteers on the premises.

He put the letter down, then sat in his chair. Drumming his fingers on the desk, he went over every detail of his architectural meetings with Chase. They'd secured their building permits and plumbing permits. Parking-area specs were exact. They must have placed nearly a hundred building material orders already. He had insurance on the cars...

Austin shoved his fingers in his hair and groaned. Daisy appeared in the doorway. "What's wrong?"

"I can't believe I forgot something."

Daisy smiled perceptively. "I do that all the time."

"Well, I don't," he replied with a worried frown.

"Wanna bet?"

AUSTIN FINISHED THE last of his dinner and was pouring himself a glass of Madeira port when the telephone rang. Daisy was cleaning dishes in the kitchen, so he went to the library and picked up the phone.

"Austin," Katia said. "I hope I didn't interrupt your dinner again."

"I just finished."

"I—I bet it was good. Daisy is a very good cook."

"She is." He sipped his port.

"I just made scallops and linguine for Mrs. Beabots and myself..." She laughed awkwardly.

"Katia," he said, pausing to look at the clock

on the mantel. It was almost seven-thirty. "I'm going to take a wild guess that you didn't call to talk to me about recipes."

"I didn't." He heard her take a deep breath. "Your plant renovations are amazing."

"Told you," he said proudly.

"Austin, I hope I wasn't too presumptuous in inquiring about your insurance. My work has consumed me too much, it seems."

Austin felt a prickle of suspicion at the back of his neck. Just how much of her apparent friendliness was heartfelt and how much was business driven? Was he just another client to her? He needed to tread lightly. Very lightly, where Katia was concerned.

"I guess I hogged the conversation all afternoon. I didn't ask you a single thing about yourself. What a pighead I can be sometimes. Comes from being alone too much." He cringed. Why had he said that? He didn't feel bad about living alone, and in fact he liked it just fine. He studied the top of his burled-wood desk. He had a million questions he wanted to ask her. Was she married? Divorced? Children? Boyfriend? Was she happy? Did she suffer after leaving him as much as he had when she left?

"Austin?" Katia said. He'd been silent a moment too long.

"Why are you moving here?" he blurted out.

"You said yesterday that you wanted to apologize to me, and you did that. You've done that. So why not just go back to Chicago?"

"You're right, Austin. We have a great deal to talk about, don't we? My company is relocating to Indiana because it's gotten too tough in Illinois with all the taxes and costs going up. Well, you understand that, I'm sure."

"I certainly do.

"One of my bosses is convinced that the internet is the way to build business these days, and I agree with him, to a point. My other boss thinks more like I do—that it's the one-on-one, personal relationship with clients that's most important."

Austin was sure he wasn't the first person to get this speech from Katia. She probably repeated it to every prospective client.

Maybe she had done some investigations into what he would need for the museum. It made sense. She'd always been smart as a whip. Something told him she never passed up an opportunity when it came to her career. It was his bet she was about to give him her best serve. He stood, ready to deliver his backhand.

"Austin, I've taken the liberty of putting together some suggestions for you and the museum. This is just a stepping-off point, mind you, since you'd have to give me exact figures for the automobile values." She laughed lightly.

Austin put his palm to his forehead as he remembered how much he'd always liked her laugh. It was lyrical and sounded like music to him. Katia had a lovely voice, he had to give her that. No wonder she did well in sales.

Katia continued. "I know it's too late to discuss it this week, and I have my movers coming on Saturday. Would it be possible for me to visit with you on Monday?"

His heart sank. So this *was* all about business. Was anything she'd said to him sincere? Her apology, her reminiscences…were they just part of her campaign to win his account? Austin started to answer, but his anger caused his tongue to stick in his dry mouth. "I'm not sure—"

"Maybe another day would be better. I'm flexible," she offered.

"Not Monday. Not any day. I'm not interested, Katia," he finally managed. Austin was surprised at how cordial he was. He'd wanted to blast her and call her out for being conniving. Perhaps it was his upbringing that caused him to dismiss her instead, as if she were nothing more than a telephone solicitor, or if wisdom had overridden his anger and hurt.

"Austin, I have the very best product. I thought that since we were friends you'd—"

"Friends?" Now he raised his voice. "You *never* intended to be my friend, Katia. You came here to get my money. To increase your monthly quota. You thought you'd get to me by apologizing for the past, and I fell for it. I've gotta hand it to you, Katia, you're really good. Sociopath good. I bet you don't have the first ounce of remorse for what you're doing. Thanks, but no thanks!"

He slammed the receiver down.

CHAPTER ELEVEN

KATIA STARED AT her cell phone, wondering if she'd lost the connection or if Austin had cut her off. She guessed it was the latter. Her heart was pounding again, and her hand was shaking. She still didn't quite believe what he'd said. How was it possible that they'd slid from bonding into a free fall back to enemy territory? What had she said? What had she done?

Was Austin so paranoid that he saw her as a con artist or a manipulator? If she was honest with herself, she could see why he might think that; in a way, she *was* using him to secure her job.

Katia was light-headed and out of breath. Though she had very few belongings in her apartment, she remembered that Tina had stuck a pack of brown paper lunch bags in one of her boxes. She rooted around for them, opened one and held it to her face.

Breathing slowly, Katia reminded herself that she was not a vixen or a user. She was concentrating on her own survival. True, she had to land Austin's account to keep her job. That was the prickly part of the equation. And Austin had every right not to trust her or want to do business with her.

If she thought she was the bad guy before, she was really stepping into dangerous territory now. Her choices were glaringly apparent. If she was truly Austin's friend, she would walk away and never mention her insurance proposal again.

But if she did that, she'd lose everything she'd ever worked for and held dear. Katia had no family left, other than her few cousins in South Chicago, and her career was everything to her. She wanted to be Jack's savior. She desperately wanted to be the one to save his company, or at least put it back on track. Katia was sure that once Jack arrived in the new office and threw himself into carrying out their vision, they would find a way to grow Carter and Associates.

For now, they needed to survive. In the process of packing up the Chicago office, she'd accidentally picked up a pile of overdue bills and unpaid tax notices. There was no question that Jack and Barry had been so eager to move forward with Katia's idea because if they didn't do something drastic, they'd go under.

Katia knew she had to make her own dras-

tic move with Austin or the company would be
dead in the water before they were even afloat.

Katia put the brown bag down. Her heart rate
had returned to normal. She didn't know how
she'd done it, but she'd beat back her fears and
anxiety one more time.

She was determined to find a way to get
through to Austin McCreary, even if it meant
their relationship would only ever be professional.

*This isn't over, Austin. I need you, and you're
going to help me.*

Although she knew Austin would still be
fuming, Katia believed the best approach in
this kind of situation was to address the problem, put out the fire and make amends. There
was no time like the present.

Katia started down the stairs and was about to
leave Mrs. Beabots's house by the back door, but
she noticed the older woman in the kitchen as
she passed, dressed in a white terry-cloth robe
with a Ritz-Carlton logo on the lapel.

"Oh, hello, dear. I'm making hot chocolate.
Seems like a perfect night for it." She glanced
at the purse and business portfolio Katia was
holding. "Are you going out?"

"I am. I don't know how long I'll be, so I'll
take you up on that hot chocolate later."

"Anytime, dear," Mrs. Beabots said. "And

give Austin my regards when you see him." She poured the cocoa into a large mug and placed a jumbo marshmallow on top.

"How did you know—"

Mrs. Beabots's wily smile was hard to mask, though she kept her head down as she lifted the silver tray. "Just a wild guess."

"It was not," Katia countered.

"I know. Have a good time, dear. See you in the morning."

Mrs. Beabots moved toward the front parlor, where she often listened to light classical music and watched the residents of Indian Lake go by in the evening. Tonight, many people would be out decorating their houses for Halloween.

"Here, let me carry that tray for you," Katia said. "I'll let myself out by the front door."

"Thank you so much. Please feel free to use the front door whenever you like. I don't mind your presence in my part of the house. Actually, I got quite used to others coming and going when Luke's children were living here. It's always amazed me how children can be in a dozen places all at once. They just move so quickly."

"I suppose that's true. I don't have much experience with kids."

They entered the parlor, and Mrs. Beabots sat in her favorite Victorian chair. "Never had any myself. That's why I've pretended to adopt so many of the young girls in Sarah's circle. You better watch out. I just may adopt you, as well," she said cheerily.

"It would be my honor," Katia replied, placing the tray on the table next to Mrs. Beabots. "Do you need anything else while I'm here?"

"You run along. I'll be fine."

Katia said her goodbyes and let herself out. She wondered if Mrs. Beabots would be so friendly to her if she knew how devious she was going to be with one of her oldest friends.

KATIA RANG AUSTIN'S DOORBELL, and when there was no answer, she pressed it again. The last time she'd come here, it had taken two rings. She wasn't about to phone him, because he would only ignore her call. He did that a lot, she thought to her embarrassment.

Katia felt like a fool as she glanced down at the folder containing her well-researched quotes and comparisons. She had to prove to Austin that he needed her services.

I'm helping him. That's what I'm doing, she thought to encourage herself. She pressed the doorbell again.

When there was still no answer, she took a few steps back. There were plenty of lights burning on both the first and second floors. Now she felt a bolt of anger strike her, laced with fear. She'd apologized for her behavior in the past, and she'd meant it; what more did he want? Surely they could put aside their personal issues and do business like two adults. At least she hoped so. Her career was counting on it.

"You can't ignore me, Austin," she growled.

Reaching into her purse, she withdrew the tennis racket key chain that still held the key to Austin's house. Her former home.

What am I thinking?

She was anxious to talk to him. She couldn't leave things as they were. She had to take drastic measures.

You really are desperate, Katia. She wiped the perspiration from her forehead. She turned around and started to walk away. Then she stopped and went back to the door.

With the key still in her hand, she balled her fist and banged on the door. "Austin, are you home?"

She doubted the key would even work, but it was worth a shot. She inserted it into the lock, and it slipped in easily. She turned it.

"No way!" she gasped and pushed the door open. Quickly, she stepped inside. "Austin?" she called loudly as she walked into the living room. "Austin?"

He wasn't in there, and a brief inspection revealed he wasn't in the dining room or library, either.

"Daisy? Are you here?" Katia called from the hallway.

She headed to the kitchen, where the dishwasher was running and the lights were dimmed. Daisy must have retired for the evening. If Austin was at home, he would have to be his room.

Katia went back into the hall and started up the stairs. *If I'm going to do this, I'm going to do this.*

"Austin? Are you up there?" she yelled.

She heard a door slam, then Austin grumbling as he rushed to the top of the stairs.

He was soaking wet, his blond hair dripping water down his face. He held a navy terry-cloth towel around his waist, and his chest heaved as he shouted at her. "Katia! What are you doing in my house?"

Katia had just opened her mouth to respond when the front door banged open and three uniformed men burst into the foyer. Two were city police officers and one wore a Security One uniform.

"Mr. McCreary! Are you all right? We got a call," the taller of the two young policemen said.

"An intruder," the security guy said, staring at Katia with far too much gleam in his eyes to be professional. He pointed a nightstick at her. "Is she the perpetrator?"

Austin glared at Katia and then ran his palm over his soaking hair to move it off his forehead. "Apparently."

Daisy came running into the hallway. She was dressed in gold-and-brown-plaid pajama pants and a gold T-shirt and was carrying a copy of *SAVEUR*. She looked from Katia to towel-draped Austin to the security guard and the two cops. "Who tripped the alarm?" she asked.

"It was me," Katia confessed.

She felt like wringing her hands, but she didn't. She had to stay calm. If she lost her nerve now, she'd never win Austin over and she'd lose her shot at his business. She had to pretend she had every right to be in the house. At the same time, these police were here to potentially arrest her. She had to be convincing. She had to be contrite and sincere.

"It was all my fault, and it was a mistake," she said to the cops. "I'm so sorry. I didn't think there would be an alarm. There didn't used to be an alarm."

"I had it installed after my mother died," Austin said angrily.

"Oh," Katia replied sheepishly, staring at the key in her hand. "I still had my key."

Daisy, the security guy and the two officers

looked at the tiny tennis racket dangling from the key in Katia's hand. The four of them pasted smiles on their faces and exchanged knowing winks.

"Okay, I'll be going, then, Mr. McCreary," the security guard said, sailing toward the front door.

"Sir, are you sure you don't need anything further from us?" the shorter cop asked.

"No," Austin replied reluctantly, though he continued to glare at Katia. "I think I can handle this."

"So you won't be pressing charges, sir?"

"Not this time," Austin said.

"Then, we'll say good-night," the tall policeman said as they both left.

Daisy put her hand on her hip and narrowed her eyes. "Are you going to stand there half-naked all night, letting us admire you, or do you want me to show your visitor to the library? The living room? What?"

Austin glanced down at his towel and spun away from the stairs, stomping to his bedroom and slamming the door.

Daisy smiled at Katia. "He'll be just a few minutes. Would you like some chamomile tea while you wait? I always find it soothing at times like this. I have some killer shortbread to go with it."

Katia exhaled for the first time since she'd entered the house. "Did that all just happen to me?"

Daisy pursed her lips and nodded.

"I'll take the tea. A double, I think."

KATIA SAT IN the library with a warm mug of tea, feeling mortified and desperate. She was not only afraid that she was about to lose Austin as a client, but also that she'd ruined any chance of repairing their relationship. She was miserable and sick inside.

"You deserve the chutzpah-of-the-year award," Austin said, striding into the room carrying a crystal brandy balloon with a small amount of golden liquid inside.

Katia slapped her palm against her cheek. "I'm so sorry. I can't believe I did that."

"Me, neither." He chuckled, sitting down and taking a sip of his drink. "Mind telling me why you wanted to break into my house?"

Katia was confused by Austin's casual demeanor. She was completely mortified and afraid of losing him forever, but clearly, he was amused by her actions. Still, there was no question she owed him an explanation. "I wasn't breaking anything. I just wanted to see you."

"Why?"

"I wanted to…"

She took a long slug of tea to wash away the shame at the back of her throat. "Our conversation ended...abruptly earlier. I didn't think we were done. Austin, I would really like to talk to you about your insurance."

"Hmm. I figured as much," he replied in that robotic, emotionless tone she'd come to despise. He was already telling her he wasn't interested.

"Did you?" In her mind's eye, she saw a graph that revealed her chances of landing Austin's account plummet to zero.

"Let me guess. You're Carter and Associates." He ground out the name. "I saw the sign on the window. Good job."

She smiled. It was a tiny bit of headway, and she'd take it. She needed every positive increment she could get from this conversation.

"Yes, that's us. After I saw your presentation the other day, I took the liberty of putting together a proposal for your museum. This is a huge endeavor, Austin, and I don't want someone who doesn't understand what you're doing to take advantage of you."

His blue eyes locked on to hers, and she felt the full impact of their earnest expression. "And do you understand what I'm doing?" he asked.

Katia did understand. All the memories of Austin, the kisses and secrets they'd shared, and that she'd long ago tried to bury, told her exactly why he was building this museum. "It's your homage to your father."

"And my grandfather and great-grandfather," he said proudly. "Ancestry is important to me, Katia. If it weren't for all their innovations, the daring leaps they took to break new ground in the automotive industry, I wouldn't enjoy the life I have. I owe them."

"Daring leaps?"

He rolled his cognac in his glass. "Yes. Daring. Just like you tonight. My guess is that you'd break just about any rule in the world to get what you wanted."

"Well, not all of them," she teased.

"But you get my point. My great-grandfather designed those first Duesenbergs. They were works of art back then. He was a stylist. A creator. In many ways, I probably idolize him even more than I did my father. I wish I'd have known him. I like to think we would have been good friends."

"I'm sure you would have been, Austin. You're easy to like."

His glance was searing. "I'm far from that. Ask anyone in town."

"They don't know you like I do," she countered. "And I'll take on anyone who says otherwise."

With a lurch, Katia realized she'd said those

exact words years ago, after she'd heard kids mocking Austin behind his back. She'd been fearless as a child. She'd forgotten that.

He laughed and set his cognac on the end table. "You would come to my defense? After how badly I treated you when we were younger?"

"You made up for those days, Austin. And anyway, I knew you wanted to impress your friends so you could fit in."

"Only ten years old, and you were that astute."

She stifled a pleased smile. "Well, maybe. But like I said, that was before—" Katia felt her heart trip and her breath clutch. It was happening again. The panic attack. Why did this always come over her when she started reliving the past or thinking about love? Or about Austin...

"Before what, Katia?" Austin asked. His voice was so warm now it could have melted the polar ice cap.

Katia felt her bones turn to butter. She swallowed hard. "Before we were in love."

"And before we were inseparable. I taught you to play tennis and poker, which my parents never discovered." He chuckled. "We took scuba lessons together from that crazy old guy my mother hired. Remember? He taught us in our pool."

"I never did get to Bermuda," she said wistfully.

"I did. The diving was glorious, but it would have been more fun if you'd been with me."

She closed her eyes. Had he really just said that? "Being here with you right now, in this house, it's as if the years never intervened. Everything seems so different and yet just the same. As though I'm in a time warp."

"Yeah," he replied. "I like that."

Austin's eyes filled with the same emotion and intensity she remembered from that last summer. Only this was now. He rose from his chair and stood over her. He took the mug from her hands and put it on the table. Then he pulled her swiftly to her feet. "You remember what it was like when we were together, don't you, Katia?"

"I do."

"But do you remember all of it?"

His lips were soft when they first met hers. His hands cupped her face and slowly his fingers moved up to her temples, then into her mounds of auburn hair. Her arms were around his neck in a split second, and everything she'd felt for him as at sixteen came whirling back to her with as much force as a tornado.

"Katia," he whispered. "Tell me again why you came here tonight."

Katia hesitated. She hadn't come here for *this*. She had come here to save her job, but she couldn't think anymore. All she could do was feel. She'd traveled to another dimension, one they'd inhabited years ago. She and Austin were alone there, and all they knew was love.

She didn't know how to answer, so she kissed him again. Slowly, he pulled her hands from around his neck and held them each to his lips.

"Why, Katia?" His eyes probed hers so intensely she nearly buckled under their scrutiny.

"I… It was for business. Initially. But…"

Austin grinned wickedly and kissed her forehead, then the tip of her nose and then both her cheeks. "You are so much fun, Katia. That's one thing I've never forgotten." He pulled her to his chest.

"Really? No one has ever said that. They call me a steamroller at work."

"Interesting." He pulled away, but only slightly. "I'll tell you what. I'll look over your proposal if you make me a promise."

She stiffened. It was a reflexive movement, she knew. She didn't like making promises without knowing the details and conditions up front.

He scrunched his arm around her shoulders.

"See that? You distrust me already. If you do that again, I'll start kissing you, and you will have no defenses against me."

"That's pretty arrogant," she quipped. She wasn't about to tell him that he was completely accurate. Just like when they were teenagers, the minute his lips touched hers, she was hooked. *Not good, Katia.* Now he had far too much power over her, and he knew it. First it was her career. Now it was her heart. "So what's the promise?"

"Tell your boss you have to spend all day with me tomorrow checking out the museum site and going over plans."

"Okay…"

"If you're serious about doing business with me, then it's got to be my way. I know what I need, and I will be getting bids from other companies. If you win the bid, you win fair and square."

"Fair and square? No kissing?"

He smiled. "You look disappointed. That's good."

Katia finally pulled herself together and moved out of his embrace. She picked up her briefcase and took out her proposal, placing it on the end table. She smiled and offered her hand. "If I win your account, believe me, it *will* be all fair and all square. And no, Austin, I'm not in the slightest disappointed."

He shook her hand. "We'll see about that."

CHAPTER TWELVE

A BLAST OF crisp Canadian air cleared away the dense fog that hung like ghosts around the fields of dried cornstalks surrounding Austin's museum site. Bulldozers and excavators rumbled over the dark farm soil like lumbering, robotic aliens. Dump trucks stood at the ready, taking in tons of earth to be transported to the east side of the building. In the spring, landscapers would use Bobcats and spades to create magical gardens that Austin told Katia he would expand every year.

Katia shielded her eyes from the late-morning sun. The scarred earth was patterned with dozens of utility flags, stakes, strings, plumbing markers and spray-painted arrows and symbols. Austin stood beside her, his hands on his hips, blond hair blowing in the breeze. His smile radiated satisfaction.

Katia turned to get a better look at him. No, it was more than satisfaction; that was victory she saw in his face. Austin couldn't have been more fulfilled if he'd just won Wimbledon.

"We have to get the basement and substructure in before Thanksgiving," he explained. "The heavy rains should be over now, if my Farmer's Almanac doesn't fail me."

She shot him a dubious glance. "You're not serious."

"No. But my prognosticators aren't any more reliable, I'm afraid. Once the plumbing and the electrical base are in, we'll just work around the weather to the best of our ability. At least that's what the construction general tells me."

"Makes sense. Freezes and snow won't be half as bad as a flash flood would be. A cave-in could be costly."

"But I'll have insurance for that, won't I?" Austin turned to her, his eyes demanding a guarantee.

Katia had indeed factored construction-site misfortunes, accidents and even theft into her proposal. She and Austin had not yet gone over the conditions of the contract or the cost of the package, but she took his question as a promise that she would soon be gaining his business. Normally, when she was about to land a large client, she couldn't wait to text Jack and give him the good news. But today was different.

This wasn't just another client. It was Austin. At this moment, gazing into his searching blue eyes, standing this close to him, all she could do was remember the feel of his lips against hers.

Had it only been last night that he'd demanded to know her real reason for breaking into his house? Even now, as she stood before him at his building site, she still couldn't give him an answer.

She was pretty sure she'd lost her mind. When she'd taken his house key out of the little wooden box back in Chicago, had she intended to go to him and find out if there was anything left between them? Had she intuitively manipulated her own actions to serve an unconscious desire to bring back the feelings she'd once had for him?

Was it possible she'd been kidding herself all these years? Maybe she'd numbed her heart and mind with career narcotic like so many people she knew. Just how seriously lost was she?

It was the greatest irony, Katia thought, that she'd been so shattered, brokenhearted and ashamed when she'd left Indian Lake that she'd promised herself she would never be vulnerable again. She would do everything she could to protect her heart. Perhaps, in a twisted, self-protective move, she'd pursued a life in insurance naively believing that she could find safeguards. What she'd learned instead was that there were absolutely no guarantees in life.

Nothing was safe. Especially not when it came to love.

Once Austin had kissed her and she'd kissed him back, a deluge of emotions had been unleashed. All these years, she would have bet everything she had that her feelings for Austin were only the memories of her youth. Sure, she'd dusted them off from time to time, but they'd always gone back in the vault on the far side of her heart.

She'd discovered last night that they were very real indeed; they'd only been sleeping. And now that her prince had come along to awaken her, she was afraid there was no going back. Even worse, she had no clue how to move forward.

Austin took a step closer, and when he did she could feel his warm breath on her cheek. The October air was cold, and if they stayed out here much longer, her black wool jacket wouldn't be enough to stave off the plummeting temperatures. When Austin peered into her eyes, Katia felt a warmth rising inside her that she hadn't felt in a long time. This wasn't a memory. This was here and now.

He slipped his arm around the back of her waist. "I'll be covered, right?" He pulled her ever so slightly toward him, just enough for their noses to touch.

"Absolutely, Austin," she responded hoarsely. She cleared her throat. "I'll take care of everything for you."

AUSTIN HELD KATIA a bit closer. Then he buried his face in her neck and inhaled the scent of her perfume. The wind whipped long red-gold strands of her hair around his head. For the moment, Austin didn't care if she'd betrayed him or hurt him. She was here now, and for one second, he had her in his arms. It seemed like a dream come true, and as much as he told himself not to trust her, his better judgment dissolved like sugar in water. It didn't matter how long this lasted, only that this moment existed. He knew it was too much to ask of the universe that Katia be his once again. Love didn't work that way. Once you lost it, it was lost forever. Only fools believed otherwise.

Austin wasn't a fool. He was simply reveling in the luxury of the moment, much like cruising down Maple Avenue in his Bentley or his Cornish. It was a glimpse of the fantasy some called heaven, but it wasn't real.

"Austin," Katia said, moving out of his embrace and folding her arms across her chest.

She gave him a warning shake of her head, just as he was contemplating putting a kiss on the side of her throat. He recognized censure when he saw it. She was shrugging him off. Any thoughts he had of intimacy between them shattered like delicate icicles.

She shivered.

"It's getting cold," he mumbled, feeling an inexplicable sadness overtake him.

He slid his eyes away from her and over to the construction site. "Since I haven't even begun my building yet, I can't take you inside, so how about I drive us back to town, and we go to lunch?"

"Lovely," Katia answered much too quickly.

Austin couldn't be sure, but Katia seemed to be relieved that they were leaving. When he put his hand on the small of her back as they walked to his Corvette, she wiggled away from his touch.

He had to be going nuts. There was no mistaking the wistful, nearly dew-eyed look she gave him when she thought he wasn't paying attention. It was the same look he remembered from their youth. Yet outwardly, she appeared to disdain his embrace or even a simple touch. Perhaps she didn't realize how much that hurt him. He might have been a near recluse since Katia had moved away from Indian Lake, but the real truth was, he'd sworn that if his arms couldn't be filled with her, then he would embrace no one.

They had just reached the car when Hal, the construction supervisor, approached. He was wearing jeans, work boots, a down-filled vest and a hard hat. "Austin," he said waving a rolled-up sheaf of blueprints. "We have a problem."

"What is it, Hal?" Austin asked.

The man unfurled the blueprints on the hood of Austin's Corvette. Austin didn't say a word, but Katia raised her eyebrow. Austin remembered when she had teased him mercilessly by putting a butterfly on the hood of one of the McCrearys' prized automobiles. He'd flown into rage because his father had scolded him many times for "ruining" the finish with some thoughtless, though minuscule, action. Her face had filled with pain, and instantly, Austin had known he'd hurt her. The last thing he'd wanted Katia to think was that his cars were more important to him than she was. He'd failed at that. She hadn't spoken to him for days after that incident.

"My supervisor told me that you're planning to have an elevator in this building." Hal's voice broke through Austin's thoughts.

"Two elevators," Austin corrected him. "One for the cars, which is quite large. One for the tourists."

"These basement blueprints don't call for a

space for the mechanisms. Do the elevators go to the basement? They should, but there's no indication of that anywhere here. I have to know the details before they dig tomorrow."

Austin scoured the blueprint and jabbed his finger at the basement floor plan. "You're right. No elevator. But I know I saw it on Chase's drawing. I can only think that somehow you got something preliminary and not the final one. I have no idea how this happened, but you'd better believe I'm going to find out." He was fuming as he took out his smartphone and placed a call.

"Charles. It's Austin. I'm on the job site, and my guys are getting ready to dig tomorrow, and I'm looking at the wrong blueprints. You want to tell me how this happened?"

Austin paused for a minute as he listened to Charles's explanation. Then he walked just far enough away from Katia and Hal so as not to be heard.

KATIA CAUGHT ENOUGH of Austin's phone conversation to understand that Hal's courier was at fault. She shook her head. "If you want a job done—" she grumbled.

"Do it yourself," Hal finished for her.

Austin walked back toward them.

"Please tell me that the rest of the measurements are right because otherwise everything we've done here is worthless. We'll have to start over and that would mean ten days, even two weeks lost—at least," he snapped into the phone. He ran his hand through his hair as he listened. "Okay. Send it now."

Austin jogged back to Hal. "Do you have your cell phone with you?"

"Yeah," Hal said pulling an antiquated flip phone out of his jeans' pocket.

Austin rolled his eyes. "Not that thing. Honestly, Hal, how many times have I begged you to move into the current decade?"

"Look who's talking!" Katia and Hal said in unison. Austin was the quintessential example of a throwback man. Katia had always known that Austin would have been much happier living in 1910.

Austin glared at Katia. "Where's your phone?"

"In my purse. Why?"

"Give it to me," he commanded. "Charles is texting me a photograph of the latest blueprints while one of his junior staff drives a new set of plans out here from Chicago. Now I'll forward his text to Katia's phone. Hal, you use her phone until you get the new blueprints."

"Hey!" Katia protested. "I need my phone. My boss calls me all the time."

Austin threw her a wicked grin. "Well, you won't be able to answer in the next two hours anyway. You'll be having lunch with me, and potential clients take priority over the boss."

"Uh…" Katia looked at Austin and then at Hal, who shrugged. "Okay."

Austin held open the passenger door for Katia and then shut it after she was settled. Hal slapped him on the back as he went around to the driver's side.

Austin got into the car, but Katia continued watching Hal, who looked at Austin with obvious appreciation and respect. Of course Hal would treat his client with respect. But she saw something else, a kinship that told her more about Austin than any online background search.

"So where are we going to eat?" Katia asked when Austin pulled on to the road.

"Chez Daisy," he said, smiling impishly. "I put in a special order for us. Your favorite."

"As if you know," she harrumphed.

"I figured on a cold autumn day you'd be in the mood for butternut-squash ravioli." He glanced at her, and his blue eyes were filled with warmth.

"How in the world did you remember that?"

"Because it was my favorite, too. Although now I like it with a Courton-Charlemagne and maybe some grilled shrimp on the side."

They turned onto Maple Avenue and cruised

up the driveway to the back of the property, where Austin parked inside the closest carriage house. Katia got out of the car and looked around.

"By the way, Austin, when are you going to let me see the rest of your cars?"

"I was just waiting for you to ask," he said, carefully closing the driver's door. "I assumed you would need a full inventory for your price quote."

She tapped her temple. "Most of them I remember from when we were kids. But I double-checked the list you gave out at the presentation. You've added a few to your father's collection."

He moved toward the door. "So how many did you include in the quote?"

"Twenty," she answered. "Based on the architect's drawings and figures, and what I could glean from our conversations."

He opened the back door for her. "You're right on the money. I might change it around a bit as time goes on."

"I've made contingencies for that," she assured him.

Daisy was at the oven and had just hoisted a large casserole dish on to the top of the stove. She closed the oven door with her foot, tossed her mitts on to the counter and said, "I set up in the breakfast alcove just like you asked."

"Thanks, Daisy," Austin replied, holding out his hand to usher Katia to the round table and mahogany Windsor chairs.

The table was set with the same blue-and-white-patterned china she remembered from her childhood. There were chunky blue water glasses, yellow linen napkins and Hanna McCreary's beloved sterling silverware. In the middle of the table was a blue pitcher with sunflowers and bronze mums, and around it were miniature pumpkins. It was just the kind of thing Katia's mother used to do for the family—for her—in this house.

A wave of nostalgia rippled through Katia, causing her to miss her mother more than she had in years. Katia reached out for the chair and used it to steady herself. "The table...is lovely, Daisy."

"Austin got the little pumpkins. He says it's tradition. We do that every October."

Katia's eyes flew to Austin, who was staring at her with so much emotion it nearly hurt her to look at him. She felt her heart flip over, but oddly, she didn't hyperventilate. She felt incredibly calm and reassured, as if everything in the world was as it should be.

But it wasn't. She knew that more than anyone else in this room.

Austin moved behind Katia and put his hand

on her shoulder. He bent over and whispered in her ear. She thought she'd melt right through the floor, his touch was so gentle and affectionate. How was it possible she'd gone all these years and not thought about him? Not tried to get this feeling back? And just exactly what was this warmth and kinship she was experiencing?

With a jolt, Katia realized that long-ago love for Austin had never died. She'd just repressed it, buried it so deep it couldn't hurt her anymore. It was killing her to be with him, trying to work with him and not blurt out what was in her heart, but she knew that would be career suicide. Jack would fire her in an instant if he ever saw the least gesture of intimacy between her and a client. She might be able to meet Austin secretly—a lunch here and there—but anything deeper would be much too dangerous.

"Sit, Katia," he said.

"Oh, sorry." She eased herself into the chair.

Daisy set a plate in front of each of them. "I made my cinnamon-and-clove cream sauce for the ravioli, as well," she said. "I'll bring over some French bread, and I have baked apples for dessert."

Daisy placed a pitcher of water on the table and then left the room.

"You eat like this every day?" Katia asked.

"This is a special occasion. I brown bag it to

the plant during the week. But Daisy likes to cook, and I have to admit my evening meals are delicious. Besides, I'm trying to soften you up," he said, greedily shoving an entire piece of ravioli into his mouth.

Katia opened her purse and withdrew a folder that contained a copy of her proposal. "Now that I've seen the job site and met Hal, I want to say that I'm really impressed."

"You're not serious. We nearly had a disaster!"

"But you didn't. Hal is sharp. And that keen eye of his saved you thousands of dollars. Frankly, I think I can do a bit better on my construction premium for you because of Hal."

Putting his fork down, Austin propped his elbows on the table, folded his hands and rested his chin against them. "How much?"

"In the list of coverages I gave you, one of the first features we cover is products and completed operations. If you can keep your overall costs down—not having to tear down and reconstruct after a mistake, for example—the insurance will be cheaper, as well. On a policy that's as comprehensive as yours, my underwriters have flexibility."

"Flexibility, huh? That's going to be an important factor for me, isn't it?"

"Definitely," she replied, daintily cutting one

of her ravioli in half. "Are you planning to have a sprinkler system on all three floors? I only saw it on the first."

"I should, right?"

"The sprinkler system will drive the fire rate down. Oh, and a high-tech security system will bring the cost of the building's insurance down, too."

"I was planning on a couple guys with AK-47s on night watch," Austin joked as he speared another ravioli. "Seriously, though, I have a tech guy who's bringing me a bid on inside and outside cameras, motion detectors and over a dozen plasma screens for the security room."

"Can I get a copy of that contract when you sign it?"

"Sure, if it helps."

"It does. I've based my figures on a noncombustible building with cement floors and cement roof. Sprinklers, fire alarms and a good security system. You'll need worker's comp for the staff. Liability, bodily injury and property damage. Explosion, collapse and underground coverage. Not to mention flood, earthquake, glass, system breakdown, crime coverage and even advertising liability."

"You've thought of it all. Did you throw in tornado coverage?"

"Yes."

"Good. I'm terrified of tornadoes. They come out of nowhere with virtually no warning, and in seconds, everything I've built could be destroyed."

"Trust me, in this area I always factor in tornado coverage. Hail and lightning are in there, too," she assured him. "Now to the cars."

"Ah." He sipped his water. "The cars."

"I think I've changed my mind on the cars, which will save you some money. I want to change my proposal to a floater policy. This one covers the cars while on display in the museum, and when they're transported to another facility for an event or exhibition, such as the Barrett-Jackson Auction in Scottsdale, which I know you like to do."

Austin nodded agreeably.

"However, Austin," she continued. "There will be no street use. No more driving the cars down Main Street on Cruise Night to show off to the tourists."

Austin's fork clunked as it hit his plate. "What? I love Cruise Night."

"They've all seen your cars, and those that haven't can come to the museum. Drive your Corvette with a sign advertising the museum from now on."

He folded his arms across his chest and

pouted. Katia nearly broke into laughter. He looked like he had when he was ten and didn't get his way. Spoiled brat, she'd called him then.

"How much do I save?"

"Well, if I had my phone, which I don't…" She playfully shoved his forearm. "I could use my calculator and tell you to the exact dollar. But roughly—thousands. Over five thousand annually."

Austin whistled. "Okay. That's a huge saving. No more Cruise Night. I like the idea about the Corvette. Will you drive with me and hold the sign?"

"Austin, be serious," she said. Katia pulled out a new sheet of paper with typed columns of figures. "I've shown you everything I think you should consider in this package. We'll cover the building for four million. If it escalates to more than that, we'll make adjustments. The twenty cars at ten million. The premium for the construction is going to run to twenty thousand. We'll start with that, and then as the building progresses, the other coverages will come into play." She took a deep breath. "In total, my quote for your annual policy is a hundred thousand."

Austin's eyes didn't move from her face. He didn't flinch. He didn't blink. "I've done my homework, too, Katia. I checked into everything you're saying, and I'm very impressed at your thoroughness. I was very surprised to see a two-million-dollar liability limit in your proposal. Most agents started me out at only fifty thousand. Apparently, that was their way of keeping the bid low, which is something I appreciate."

"Do you think my bid is too high?" she asked in a straightforward tone.

"I do. I hadn't planned on an executive umbrella, and you included it."

"I thought you needed it. I still do. I don't want to cut it."

"There's also the small matter of coverage for debris removal after property loss. I realize that can be a costly thing around here. Trees down. Flash floods. Water in the basement. I've been through that kind of thing before. At the same time, I'd like to see a more aggressive approach to saving me money."

Austin scrunched his brows together so that they almost touched. Katia recognized that expression; it meant he was about to explode. She didn't see the telltale crimson cheeks that signaled a true angry burn. Possibly, he'd learned to tame his temper. Maybe he was simply driving a hard bargain. She had to make sure she was reading him correctly.

"Austin, am I to understand that you're peeved at me?"

"Disappointed. I expected you, of all people, to take my finances more seriously."

"I do take them seriously," she replied, trying not to wince at the unexpected pang of knowing she hadn't met his expectations.

This was a business deal like any other, yet she was responding emotionally. Again. There was something truly the matter with her, she decided.

"Austin, I don't mind going back to the computer and revamping my proposal."

"I think that would be wise," he said sternly.

She swallowed hard and tried to hide her discomfort. "I'll do my best," she said diplomatically. "If I talk to my underwriters and promise them some credits, I could get the price down to ninety-eight."

Austin leaned back in his chair and shot her an unyielding gaze. "Ninety."

Katia returned his steady look with one of her own. "Austin, I'm not going to cut your coverage just to save you a dime. I know what you expect—the best. That's what I put together for you. I can go to ninety-four."

"Make it ninety-three five and you've got a deal."

Katia could cut her commission, but it would be worth it. "You'd sign the construction coverage papers today if we agreed?"

"I would."

She extended her hand to him. "Then, shake on it. I trust you."

AUSTIN PEERED AT Katia's hand. *Trust.* It was a very big word, and it meant the world to him. She was going to trust him. But trusting *her* had caused him nothing but heartache. This was a business deal, though. This wasn't his life.

He didn't have to be a genius to figure out that the museum would be a very, very good account for any agent. Since Katia had just moved her company to Indian Lake, signing him as a client wouldn't just be a feather in her cap, but a gold one. There were all kinds of Illinois-based companies moving to Indiana for tax reasons. Austin guessed that Katia and her crew weren't any different.

But once he'd signed on the dotted line, would she give him another thought? Was she only in Indian Lake to score him as a client, or were her intentions something deeper? If she stayed here, he didn't know if he could trust her...not just with his business, but with his heart.

Austin clasped her hand in his with a bit more force than he'd meant to, as if by sheer strength he could root her here permanently.

"Deal," he said. "And after the building is

completed, we'll move forward with the other contracts."

Katia's face illuminated with the brightest smile he'd seen yet. "Austin, thank you. I know you'll be pleased working with our company."

His eyes locked on hers.

"I already am."

CHAPTER THIRTEEN

KATIA SAT IN the backseat of Sarah's flame-red Envoy. Mrs. Beabots was next to her, Timmy and Annie were buckled into the seats behind them and Beau, Sarah's dog, rode shotgun. Katia had made the colossal mistake of telling Mrs. Beabots that she needed decorations for the office to complement the fabulous red-and-gold damask chairs she'd found. Mrs. Beabots had assumed Katia meant fall decorations, not the silk flowers and scented candles she'd wanted to pick up at Celebrations To Go.

Now that Katia had actually signed Austin's first contract, she should have felt that she could take a deep breath, but that was not the case. Though she'd moved her own furniture into Mrs. Beabots's house, she was still scrambling to make the office presentable. In two days, Jack's few pieces of furniture and the computers would arrive, and she had an appointment to interview Tom's wife for the receptionist position. The phones and internet would be installed later that afternoon.

"You're going to love the pumpkin house," Annie said, leaning over the back of Katia's seat. "Theirs is the biggest ever."

"Yeah," Timmy said. "My dad takes our pictures on his iPhone, then he posts them on the internet. That's so my grandma and grandpa can see us all the time. Do you do FaceTime with your kids?"

Katia laughed. "I don't have any children," she said.

"Oh," Timmy said.

Katia caught Sarah's eye in the rearview mirror.

"Miss Katia isn't married, Timmy," Sarah said.

He tapped Katia on the shoulder, and Katia turned to him. "If you want a husband, my dad knows some guys."

Katia burst into laughter, as did Sarah and Mrs. Beabots.

"I'm just fine right now, Timmy," Katia said. "I'll let you know if it becomes a problem."

Annie punched Timmy in the arm. "Miss Katia is a career woman, Timmy. Maybe she doesn't want any kids. Did you ever think of that?"

Timmy slapped both hands over his face and then drew them down slowly, rolling his eyes.

"That's so stupid. She's very pretty. Miss Katia, you like kids, don't you?"

"I do. Very much," Katia replied. It was a rote answer that she'd repeated dozens of times over the past few years. Yet, in a split second, Katia felt her throat close up. Her chest constricted and a deep pressure descended on her lungs.

Not again. Not here. Not now! She didn't have a bag. She hadn't planned to get upset, and she didn't want to spend the afternoon talking about her private emotional issues with two well-meaning but much too insightful children.

"See?" Timmy chortled to Annie.

Sarah slowed the Envoy. They passed a clump of towering maple and oak trees, and the pumpkin farm came into sight.

"There it is!" the kids squealed in unison, practically unbuckling their seat belts before Sarah brought the SUV to a full stop.

There was a two-story "house" made of wood scaffolding, with pumpkins lining each strut, so that the walls looked as if they were made of pumpkins. Scarecrows, corn shocks, hay bales and every conceivable pumpkin and gourd were spread out across a wide, grassy expanse. There was a horse-drawn cart that took visitors through a corn maze. Buyers pulled green wooden wagons among the rows of Cinderella pumpkins, green, white and gray pumpkins, gnarled ones, tall ones, fat ones and hundred-pound ones.

"I'll get us a wagon," Sarah said, holding the door for Beau as he jumped down and waited patiently for Mrs. Beabots to climb out of the SUV.

The older woman straightened her tweed jacket and smoothed her black pants. Beau walked alongside Sarah and Mrs. Beabots toward the line of carts while Timmy and Annie made a mad dash for the pumpkin house.

"Miss Katia! Take a picture of me," Timmy yelled as he ran past.

"I think Timmy has a crush on you," Sarah said to Katia.

Katia watched the little boy dart into the orange structure. "I'm flattered. Are you sure?"

"Pretty sure," Sarah replied. "Both he and Annie are fairly outgoing, but he doesn't get personal with most people. I apologize for him if he said anything to upset you."

Katia touched her forehead nervously. Good. She wasn't sweating. "It's okay."

Sarah grabbed a wagon handle. "Which ones do you want first, Mrs. Beabots?"

"Cinderella first. Then the white ones. They're my favorite. I have the children bring me maple leaves, then we stencil them onto the white pumpkin and cut them out. I put silver glitter on the inside and then use a long-burning votive candle. It's really pretty."

Katia eyed her landlady. "And I would have figured you for a traditionalist. A real jack-o'-lantern person."

"Too boring. Though, I will do a couple for the children this year. I thought I'd have a pumpkin-carving contest. What color pumpkin would you like, Katia?" she asked.

Katia couldn't explain it, but ever since she'd moved back to Indian Lake the simplest questions had seemed monumental. Pumpkin carving. The last time she'd carved a real pumpkin had been with Austin. Her mother had bought two pumpkins at a farm just south of Indian Lake. She and Austin had competed for her mother's peanut-butter cookies at the time. Austin had loved those cookies. She remembered how he'd teased her, and she'd punched his arm and smeared pumpkin guts on his cheek. He hadn't wiped them away; he'd just laughed. He'd growled at her and pretended to be a monster, but she told him she would never be afraid of him. Katia had won the contest, of course, being more artistic than he. He'd drawn a typical jack-o'-lantern, and she'd created a pumpkin diva complete with a pair of her mother's cheap plastic earrings.

Katia supposed that in many ways, she was

much like Mrs. Beabots, thinking outside the box when it came to fun. But Katia hadn't had much "fun" for a long time. She hadn't played with children or ridden in a car with a dog sitting shotgun, and she hadn't visited a pumpkin patch.

This year, the only connotation she had with Halloween was that it was the day of Jack's arrival in Indian Lake. She hadn't thought about decorations or peanut-butter cookies or pumpkin contests.

"So what will it be?" Mrs. Beabots urged.

"Gray," Katia answered. "And I can bring any kind of accessories I want to decorate my pumpkin?"

"Anything you want, dear," Mrs. Beabots said, bending over and picking up a perfect gray pumpkin. "How's this one?"

"Excellent choice." Katia took it from her and investigated the backside. "This will do nicely."

Sarah chose a half a dozen pumpkins of all sizes, colors and shapes, along with a dozen small gourds she would use for centerpieces up until Thanksgiving.

"Thanksgiving?" Katia nearly shrieked. She'd barely unpacked, and it already felt as if autumn was flying past.

"That reminds me," Mrs. Beabots said. "Sarah and I have a proposition for you."

"Actually, we need your help," Sarah interjected.

Katia glanced from Sarah to Mrs. Beabots. Both were looking at her with a bit too much anticipation in their eyes.

"What is it?" She was nearly afraid to ask.

"We're chairing the Christmas Candlelight Tour this year," Sarah said. "We were hoping we could convince you to join the committee."

Katia narrowed her eyes. "I don't remember this event."

"Oh, it's only been in the past ten or twelve years," Mrs. Beabots explained. "The money we raise is for the Heritage Foundation, to preserve the older homes and buildings around town. The first Saturday in December, we have a home tour for residents and tourists. Various committees volunteer to decorate some of Indian Lake's loveliest houses. The florist and tree farms donate pine garlands and wreaths. Other merchants and retailers donate silk flowers, candles and other Christmas decorations. We have live carolers and musicians around town, and some of the homeowners pass out Christmas cookies or treats," Mrs. Beabots said proudly.

"My company is very involved in the tour," Sarah said. "It's great advertising for us, and our designers and assistants enjoy the competition."

"I'm curious. Why do you need me? I'm not a designer."

Sarah stared at the ground sheepishly, and Mrs. Beabots stepped in. "We need you to talk to Austin for us."

Katia rolled her eyes and broke into laughter. "You two are so devious. You didn't need to bring me all the way out here to ask me this."

Mrs. Beabots put a hand on her thin hip. "Pumpkins are required autumn decor in Indian Lake. You have to have some in your office. It's our responsibility as your friends to guide you, dear. This is a small town, and tongues sometimes wag. You want to be accepted and to make the right impression for your business. You have to trust me on this. I was once a businesswoman myself." She leveled her blue eyes on Katia with an unyielding gaze. "The tour is another matter altogether. Will you do it?"

Katia held back a chuckle. This tiny woman had a personality the strength of a gale-force wind. She felt as if the queen had spoken, and there would be some serious repercussions if she didn't join the committee.

"Austin will never agree. I don't remember Hanna opening her house to strangers, and he's even worse about that kind of thing than she was."

"Not anymore, he's not," Sarah said. "He just

hosted that presentation for his museum. For the first time in his life, Austin is about people. Even if he doesn't know it."

Katia was thoughtful for a moment. "There's a lot of truth in that, Sarah."

Mrs. Beabots laid her hand on Katia's forearm. "He'll listen to you. The Heritage Foundation is vital to our community. It makes us unique. Of all the people in town, Austin is probably the most concerned about preserving the past. Especially his own family's past. We thought that if you went with us, we could persuade him. What do you say?"

"Please, Katia?" Sarah said. "The McCreary mansion is the most elegant home in town, and until Austin's presentation a few weeks ago, hardly any of us had ever been inside. Even Maddie, who takes him cupcakes every Friday, had only been in the kitchen or just inside the front door. And Austin was her first investor! We're not saying it's going to be easy. Other than putting a wreath on the front door every year, Austin hasn't decorated since his mother died. But I think we'll raise more money than ever if we can get him to show the house."

Katia had never looked into two more beseeching faces than her friends' at this moment. She knew this kind of charity played right to

Austin's interests. He adored old homes, old cars and the history of it all.

Katia remembered how his mother used to decorate the house for the holidays. It had been nothing short of magnificent. Hanna used to hire extra people to hang ornaments and garlands, arrange flowers and string lights through the shrubs outside. Hanna had made Christmas seem magical, even for the maid's daughter.

"I'll do it. But I'm only asking Austin once. If he turns us down, then I'm done. That's it." She paused. "It really was beautiful back when Hanna was alive."

Sarah's face lit up. "Thank you! I think this can work."

"So do I," Mrs. Beabots agreed. "Now let's get some suitable pumpkins for your office, dear."

Katia pretended to be interested in the pumpkin selection, but she couldn't shake the feeling that she'd just been railroaded by the best saleswomen she'd ever met.

CHAPTER FOURTEEN

IT WAS POURING rain as Katia stood with Sarah and Mrs. Beabots outside Austin's front door, holding a huge umbrella above their heads. She couldn't believe she was this nervous about a silly fund-raising meeting. She was coming to care a great deal about Mrs. Beabots, and she was nurturing a friendship with Sarah. However, Katia didn't think Austin would agree to open his house to as many as three hundred people on a Sunday afternoon just so they could finally peer into his private abode.

Katia dropped her head. This was a bad move all around. Mrs. Beabots was going to be disheartened when they were turned down, and Sarah probably would keep trying to fix things, which would only frustrate Austin more.

Katia had been up most of the night thinking of pitches and a persuasive approach that would convince him to participate. That was the reason her new friends had come to her. They believed she was their closer.

Daisy answered the door with a strong-armed

whoosh and an ear-to-ear smile. "Ladies! Welcome. Come get out of the weather. Not fit for man or beast." Daisy gestured toward the living room. "Austin's on the phone, but he won't be long. I'll see to that. I have a fire going in there, so come on in."

Mrs. Beabots walked straight to the fireplace and held out her hands to warm them. "It's so cozy in here. I do love a real fire, don't you, Katia?"

"I do," Katia replied, surprised that Austin hadn't succumbed to the convenience of gas logs and electrical-switch starters. She knew it had taken thought and extra work to prepare the fire for them, and it hadn't been Daisy's doing. This was all Austin. When they were young, it had always been his job to build the fire before his father got home from work. This was a good sign, she concluded. Perhaps he would be open to this event after all.

Austin walked into the room wearing black pants, a navy cashmere sweater over a snow-white cotton shirt and a smile so charming he took Katia's breath away. "Good evening, ladies," he said, walking straight up to Mrs. Beabots and taking her hand in both of his. "It's great to see you again, Mrs. Beabots. You're looking marvelous, as always."

"Austin." She beamed and placed her other

hand over his. "I've missed seeing you, now that Hanna has been gone so long. I'm hoping this is the beginning of a renewed friendship for us."

He bent and kissed her cheek. "Thank you for thinking of my mother. I'd forgotten how involved she was in the community when she was alive. I guess the years have just gotten away from me." Then he turned to Sarah. "You're looking terrific, Sarah. Married life must agree with you."

"It truly does," Sarah replied with a smile. "Though, I had no idea taking care of two children could be so demanding."

Austin nodded. "If you do it right, it should be demanding."

Katia was standing next to Sarah, and she watched as Austin's eyes surreptitiously tracked back to her while he was speaking with her friends. When he moved toward her, she wasn't sure if he would be formal or if he would embrace her.

"Katia, I'm guessing they brought you along to persuade me."

"They did," she said as he moved back toward the fireplace. Oddly, she felt slighted. No handshake and no compliment. A tiny fissure of sadness crept through her, disturbing her just enough to make an impression. She didn't need

Austin's approval for anything, yet she wanted it. Why?

"Please, ladies, have a seat. I've got a fine Madeira port if you'd like…"

"I'd love one," Mrs. Beabots chimed in before Austin could finish.

He gave another charming smile and glanced at Sarah. "And you, as well?"

"Thank you," Sarah replied, taking a seat in a blue-and-white club chair across from the bergère chairs.

Mrs. Beabots sat on the sofa next to Katia. Austin went to a drop-leaf table in the corner of the room and poured four small glasses of port from a crystal decanter. He offered a glass to each of them just as Daisy entered the room with an enormous wooden tray filled with fresh fruits, cheeses, crackers and petit fours. She placed the tray on the coffee table and passed out pink linen cocktail napkins.

"These were your mother's," Katia said, smoothing out her napkin. "They were one of the first things I learned to iron when I was a little girl."

Mrs. Beabots reached over and patted Katia's hand. "You remember her fondly, then."

"Most of the time, yes," Katia replied. She couldn't help but recall that Hanna had often acted just as paranoid about Katia and Austin's relationship as Stephania had been.

Austin sat in a large blue leather wing chair, and after retrieving a strawberry and popping it into his mouth, he studied each of his guests for a long moment before his gaze moved on to Katia and lingered there. He sipped his wine cautiously, but didn't say a word.

Katia was as familiar with this move of his as she was with his backhand, though he had yet to set a real tennis date with her. He was waiting for her to start the discussion, and because he was letting her think he was going to be a hard sell, she knew he had something up his sleeve.

Austin had always liked to turn the tables on her, but she couldn't figure out why he'd do it now. If he didn't want to put his house on the tour, all he had to do was say no.

"Mrs. Beabots tells me you're familiar with the Heritage Foundation and the Christmas Candlelight Tour, Austin," Katia began.

"I am." He grabbed a piece of cheese and a couple of wheat crackers. He took his time nibbling them.

Katia continued, "And Sarah tells me that, though you've been invited to join in the tour, you never have before. And yet you've agreed to this meeting. I have to say that I don't believe for a minute that you were anxious to get our opinion about your port or to show off Daisy's culinary expertise. I think you want to help the foundation this year. I think you've finally realized what an asset the McCreary mansion would be on the tour. Mrs. Beabots believes they can double their donations with your participation."

AUSTIN DIDN'T TAKE his eyes off Katia as she spoke. When she had finished her spiel, he considered his words for a moment before launching into his reply.

"I'm flattered that you think I'm so interesting that people have enough morbid curiosity, or simply nosiness to actually pay money to find out some secret I might have. Makes me feel like a celebrity. Frankly, though, that's why I've shied away from this event in the past. This year is different."

"It's because of the museum, isn't it?" Katia asked.

"Yes. It is. As you all know, I'm deeply devoted to my parents and my ancestors and their creativity, talent and inventiveness. Their—" he steepled his fingers and pressed his lips against them "—pioneer visions. They were all more ambitious than I am. I would have been content being a car mechanic." He looked down at his loafers, not seeing them or even his small audience. "I'm still happiest under the hood." He chuckled to himself. "There's something about a boy's first car that strikes that pioneer chord in a great many men. We get our first adrenaline rush when we see a machine that can take us places, especially away from home, from demanding parents. Cars, for many young men, are an initiation into adulthood." He blinked, his guests coming into focus again. "I digress. The reason I'm thinking about the Candlelight Tour this year is because I'm building a shrine, in essence, to my male ancestors, but my mother is barely acknowledged in all this. My mother loved Christmas, and because of that, I think she would be quite proud to display this house on your tour."

"Austin!" Mrs. Beabots clapped her hands together. "You darling boy! Thank you."

"Yes," Sarah said. "Everyone on the committee will be very grateful."

KATIA STARED AT AUSTIN. She wasn't fooled for a minute. He wasn't done. There would be a proviso. There always was. Just like he wouldn't sign a straight deal with her for the construction insurance policy, she knew he'd want to negotiate bit further.

"So tell us, Austin. What's the stipulation?"

He tilted his head back and guffawed. "You

know me too well, Katia. I do have two things I want, or the deal is off."

"Off?" Sarah gulped, her eyes widening.

"On the brochure, I want a dedication to my mother, so that everyone understands I'm doing this in her honor."

"Done," Mrs. Beabots said emphatically.

Katia's eyes narrowed as he took a breath. "And the second stipulation?"

Austin met her gaze, as confident as a gambler with a winning hand. "I want Katia to do the decorating."

"Me? Why? I'm not part of the foundation. I was just helping Mrs. Beabots and Sarah—"

"So?" He shrugged. "It worked. You got me. I'll open my house, but you know how my mother used to decorate everything. I want it to look like it would if she were alive. You can have all the helpers you need, and I'll have Daisy at your beck and call. But you will spearhead the decoration. That's my deal. Take it or leave it."

Katia slung her gaze to Mrs. Beabots. "I don't know if I have time to help with something like this. I still don't have my office furnished." Her hands flew to her cheeks. "I can think of dozens of things I have to accomplish before December."

The turmoil in Katia's head reminded her

of frantic birds in a cage. Despite the mountain of work she needed to scale, the one thing that underscored her trepidation was the fact that Austin was setting this up so she would be forced to be in his house on a weekly basis from now until the first weekend of December. Katia knew exactly what Austin was expecting.

In the McCreary attic there were no less than fifty boxes and crates of ornaments, garlands, Christmas linens, dishes, glassware and silk florals. Katia remembered her mother talking about the standing orders for wreaths on every single window and the yards and yards of spruce and cedar garland she ordered from the tree farm. Austin would expect all of it to be an exact replica of Hanna's extravagant Christmas decor. She wouldn't put it past him to hire a photographer and put the pictures in his museum.

Katia knew Austin was tossing her a challenge, which was just fine with her. She was up to it.

But in a few short days, both Jack and his ironclad rules about client-agent relationships would be moving to Indian Lake.

Austin clearly had romance on his mind. If he didn't, then what was he doing with her?

There was the possibility that he was masking some kind of revenge scheme, and that he was trying to romance her only to dump her later, just as she'd done to him. She didn't think he was that devious; perhaps she'd underestimated his anger. Then again, what if his intentions were pure? What if he did still have feelings for her?

At the thought of romance with Austin, a zing went through Katia's heart. This wasn't an attack. It was an awakening. Could she trust those emotions? What if she lost him again and she had to relive that horrible heartache?

The worst thing for Katia at this point in her career and her life was to allow herself to fall back in love with Austin.

Handling Jack was going to be another matter. As far as her boss knew, Austin McCreary was nothing more to her than a client. She could never tell Jack the whole truth about her past with Austin, but there was the real possibility that he would hear it from just about anyone in town. It was too easy for Jack to become suspicious, especially if he ever saw the way Austin looked longingly at her, like he was doing now.

And if she spent too much time with Austin playing Christmas carols and decorating a tree, Jack could very well fire her with no questions asked.

Because she'd been so determined to land Austin's business over the past few weeks, she hadn't thought or planned much beyond getting him to sign the contract.

Suddenly, what had seemed like an innocent Christmas charity fund-raiser was now a threat to her career. Katia had unwittingly treaded onto a minefield of her own making.

She pressed her hand against her temple to hold her jumbled thoughts inside. She took a deep breath and smiled at Austin.

"I'll be happy to decorate the house for you."

CHAPTER FIFTEEN

JACK CARTER'S ARRIVAL in Indian Lake was a comedy of errors. Driving into town in his turbo-charged BMW, he got a speeding ticket for doing thirty-five in a twenty-five zone. The moving van he'd hired got lost on the interstate and took the wrong exit for Indian Lake, and Jack ended up spending more time relaying navigation instructions on his Bluetooth than talking with his client, whom he kept putting on hold. This caused Jack a great deal of frustration, which he carried with him right through the door of his new offices.

Katia was waiting by the entrance as he trudged up the stairs with a large cardboard box, grumbling incoherently.

"Welcome to your new home, Jack," Katia said brightly, her arms spread wide. She was proud to have gotten the office so ready for him, and couldn't wait to show off what she'd accomplished.

"Hi," he muttered, walking past her.

Luke Bosworth was in the last stages of hanging Jack's office door.

"Oh, Luke," Katia said, following her boss into the loft. "This is Jack Carter. The owner of Carter and Associates."

Luke swung the door closed, glanced at the shiny new brass hinges with satisfaction and turned to extend his hand to Jack. "Nice to finally meet you. I've heard a lot of good things about you from Katia."

Jack exhaled and returned Luke's smile. "Thanks for helping out so much. Katia says you're quite talented, and it looks as though she was dead on. I love the door."

"The design was all Katia. I just hung the thing."

"And put up the walls," Katia interjected. "Jack, the carpet installers should be here in half an hour, and then we can start moving your furniture in this afternoon."

"Terrific," he said, putting the box on the floor and taking in the walls filled with Isabelle's art work, the antique desks and chairs. He walked over to the coffee table, where Katia had made an arrangement of tiny hay bales and gourds. On the floor near the windows she'd arranged an assortment of pumpkins. "I like this," he said with a wide grin.

"Thanks," Katia replied. "I would have brought

up some cornstalks, but I thought that might be overkill."

"Oh, I don't know," Jack said. "The kid in me would have liked it, but I'm not sure our clients would."

Luke chuckled. "This is Indian Lake. They'd love it—believe me." He turned to Katia. "Well, I guess that's it for today. The door is up and once your carpet is in, you should be good to go. Give me a shout if you need anything else." Luke walked over to Jack and shook his hand again. "Listen, I know this is only your first few minutes in town, but I'd like to extend an invitation from my wife, Sarah, and me for dinner over the weekend. Sarah and Mrs. Beabots have turned Sunday dinner into an occasion." Luke glanced over at Katia. "They've even roped Katia into cooking. She makes a mean chicken potpie."

"I know Katia is a very good cook. I would appreciate that very much, Luke. I'll look forward to it."

"Five o'clock Sunday, then," Luke said, going back to his toolbox and putting the last of his tools away. "We live next door to Katia, so we're not hard to find. I hope you like kids and big dogs."

"Guard dog or hunting dog?"

"Terminally friendly dog. Golden retriever. I

haven't taken him hunting. He's too exhausting just playing with my kids."

"Sounds great. What can I bring? I have an incredible cabernet. Actually, it's from the vineyard here."

"Crenshaw's?"

"The same," Jack replied. "I guess everyone knows about their wine, huh?"

"If they don't, they should," Luke said as he went to the door. "See you both later." He waved and left.

"Nice guy." Jack said. He walked over to his office and inspected the work more closely. "And very, very good at his trade."

"I think so," Katia said. "Where are the movers?"

"Oh!" Jack slapped his forehead and yanked his cell phone from his pants' pocket. "They've gotten lost twice. They were great in the city whenever I needed them, but among the cornfields they're as fish-out-of-water as I am."

Jack gave the driver more explicit instructions and ended the call. "Ten minutes, max."

"Good. Want some coffee? I just started a pot. Come. I'll show you the break room."

Katia poured Jack a tall mug of coffee and offered him one of Maddie Strong's coconut-and-pineapple cupcakes. From the way he rolled his eyes, devoured the cupcake and then went after a second, she knew she'd made good choices for initiating him to Indian Lake. She could kiss Luke for his spur-of-the-moment dinner invitation. That couldn't have been more perfect if she'd planned it.

Before Jack had finished his coffee, his cell phone rang, and the movers announced their arrival.

For the next two hours, they unloaded all the office furniture, cartons of computer equipment, the phone system and nearly a hundred boxes of client files.

"I had no idea we had this much!" Katia moaned as she realized they would need to buy a second bank of filing cabinets.

"Frankly, neither did I. Barry and I agreed that all the physical paper should be in one location and not split between his house and this office. If he needs anything, we can fax it."

"By the way, where is the fax machine?"

"It was the first thing they loaded. It'll be the last off. Let's sit and strategize while the movers finish up. Did you hire the receptionist?"

"Melanie starts tomorrow. I thought you and I should try to get things relatively under control before she starts. The phone company will be here later today to get our phones and internet hooked up."

"Excellent. As soon as the guys finish here,

we'll head out to the lake to unload my stuff into my condo."

"Oh, I forgot to ask, have you seen it yet?"

"No. I came straight here. But I got a text from Cate Sullivan that she's going to meet me there..." He checked his watch. "In twenty minutes."

Just then, they heard a voice in the doorway. "Hello, there," Austin called across the loft.

Katia whirled around. "Austin?"

"Can I come in? Are you open for business?" He walked toward her with the sleek gait that had always been part of his allure. Half was due to his athleticism and prowess on the tennis court, and the other half was confidence.

Jack rose from his chair. "Who's this?" he whispered to Katia.

"Our first client." She rose and smiled softly at Austin, but before she could introduce the two men, Jack held out his hand. "I'm Jack Carter, and you must be Austin McCreary."

"I am," Austin replied, shaking Jack's hand. He peeked around Jack's shoulder to lock eyes with Katia. "I had no idea I'd be interrupting all this activity. I came by to give you my check."

"Of course!" Katia said. "Austin, you didn't need to do that. I could have stopped by the house."

"I had some banking down the block." He

looked around at the piles of moving boxes. "I was going to ask if you'd like to go to lunch, but clearly you have your work cut out for you today. I should have called first."

Katia walked up to the men and stood next to Jack. "You can say that again. I had no idea Jack was moving this much stuff. We'll be unpacking through Sunday."

"We'd better not be. I just got my first Sunday-dinner invitation," Jack said.

Katia turned to Austin. "That's right. Jack's only been here ten minutes, and he's going to dinner at Sarah and Luke's on Sunday. I'm sure Mrs. Beabots will bake her sugar pie. I'll make bruschetta."

Austin chuckled. "Well, I can't think of better people to introduce you to the town than Sarah and Mrs. Beabots. She's the town icon, you know."

"Didn't know that," Jack replied, shoving his hands into his jeans' pockets.

"Mrs. B is the best cook in town. I envy you that dinner," Austin said with a faint note of sadness that Katia thought only she could detect.

Jack smiled broadly. "I should be the one taking you out to dinner as thanks for your business, Austin. And I mean that. As soon as I get settled, with a bed to sleep in, how about I give you call and we do just that?"

"Great," Austin replied.

"Austin, do you want a receipt for the check? I have a receipt book around here somewhere…" Katia began, heading over to her cluttered desk.

"Don't bother. I'll have the cancelled check. I'm fine. Pleased, in fact." Austin met Katia's gaze, his eyes filled with more than just gratitude.

Jack stepped closer to Katia and laid a hand on her shoulder. "You couldn't have done any better than to do business with Katia, Austin. She's one of our finest agents. I went over her paperwork and the proposal, and I thought it was flawless."

Jack did not remove his hand instantly, as he usually did, and Katia saw a cloud descend over Austin's clear blue eyes. Something was wrong.

"I worked very hard to put together a comprehensive package for Austin," she said to Jack. When she turned back to Austin, his face had gone blank.

"You sure did," Jack said, smiling broadly. "Frankly, Austin, I don't know what I'd do without Katia. She's practically my right hand. Without her help, my move here would have been a disaster. I guess that comes from working together so well over the years."

Katia smiled up at Jack, feeling the glow of appreciation. Her eyes slid back to Austin, and there was no mistaking the flash of jealousy in his eyes and the tight set of his mouth.

Finally, Jack dropped his arm. "As for your policy, Austin, I doubt I could have done better myself."

Austin tore his eyes from Katia and gave Jack a perfunctory smile as he extended his hand. "Again, nice to meet you, Jack. I'm sure I'll be seeing you around town as well as doing business with you." He looked at Katia again. "I have to get back to the plant. You two apparently need your time together. Have a good day." Without a smile or another word, he turned and headed down the stairs.

Katia sensed that Austin had gotten the wrong impression about her and Jack, but there wasn't anything she could do about it right now. If she ran after him to explain things, Austin might believe that she was feeling guilty and trying to cover up something romantic between her and Jack. And what if Austin wasn't jealous at all? What if she'd read him wrong?

Then there was the matter of Jack. She didn't want him to think there was anything other than a business deal between her and Austin. She was only just beginning to understand the emotions that were resurfacing in her. As much as she wanted to trap them in a net and reel them in, she couldn't. She feared that one of these days, they would escape, and she would lose everything. She'd lose the respect she had earned from Jack and possibly the tenuous relationship she was building with Austin, which she wanted more than she'd realized. She felt as if she was walking a tightrope.

Jack watched Austin leave, then he turned to Katia. "I like him."

"Sure you do." She tilted her chin up. "He just agreed to a nearly six-figure deal with us."

Jack walked over to the window and surveyed the town. Katia followed him.

There were still golden leaves clinging to the trees, but a good rainstorm would wash the last holdouts away. The planters were overflowing with potato vines, black-eyed Susans, pink petunias and African grasses. No killing frost had yet come to blight their beauty. Down on the sidewalk a group of office workers dressed in Halloween costumes was crossing the street on their way to an early lunch. The courthouse windows were decorated with paper leaves and witches flying across a harvest moon. It was a cool day, but two convertibles pulled up to the stoplight with their tops down, the drivers dressed in warm jackets and enjoying the sunshine.

Jack turned to Katia with a grin. "This is so charming. I wasn't expecting that. It kind of reminds me of my childhood. Do the kids still trick-or-treat here?"

"Like you wouldn't believe. Mrs. Beabots says she expects over a thousand tonight. I told her I would help with passing out the candy. She made gingersnap cookies for us to munch on between ghosts and goblins."

"Wow, I want to come!"

She frowned. "You'll be unpacking your condo. Which—" She looked at her watch. "Your movers should be about ready to drive over there."

"Right! Cate Sullivan is going to meet me there with the keys," Jack replied brightly. "Let me see if there's anything left to bring up here. Once I get everything set up there, I can come back and help you in the office."

"Jack, just take care of the condo. We'll deal with this tomorrow. I'll get as much done as I can. See you in the morning."

"Great!" Jack said, slipping out the door.

Katia watched as Jack spoke to the movers. They climbed into their truck and he got into his car. They pulled away from the curb and headed north toward the lake.

As soon as Jack was out of sight, she picked up her cell phone and punched out Austin's cell

number, which she'd gleaned from his insurance
paperwork. He didn't pick up.

She left a message for him to call her back
when he had time. She purposefully kept her
tone light, reminding him that they needed to
plan the decorations for the Candlelight Tour.

Katia didn't understand why Austin had reacted the way he did, but she knew one thing
for certain. What she'd seen in Austin's eyes
was jealousy.

CHAPTER SIXTEEN

HALLOWEEN NIGHT BROUGHT an onslaught of children and preteens to Mrs. Beabots's front door, and Katia was exhausted just from handing out mini candy bars and bubble gum. Mrs. Beabots had made hot apple cider with cinnamon sticks and homemade doughnuts for Timmy, Annie, Luke and Sarah, who'd stopped by on their way up Maple Avenue. The children were anxious to get on with their "rounds," and though Sarah's housekeeper, Miss Milse, was on candy duty next door, the family didn't stay long.

It was nearly ten o'clock before the steady stream of children tapered off and the treats ran out.

Katia locked the front door and turned off the porch light, the signal to all trick-or-treaters that the candy was gone.

After wishing Mrs. Beabots a good night, Katia went upstairs to her apartment. She checked her cell phone before plugging it into the charger. She had three messages from Jack and one from

Melanie, who said she'd meet Katia at the office at seven-thirty the next morning.

There were no calls from Austin.

Katia put on her pajamas and turned out the light. She'd only just crawled into bed when her phone buzzed. She whipped the covers back and grabbed her phone from the dresser.

"Jack," she said, answering the call. "What's up?"

"I have no food. I mean none. I refuse to buy a breakfast burrito at a drive-through. And I can't find my juicer. I know I packed it." His words were laced with frustration.

"I've got fruit here. I can stop at the grocery—"

"No. No, I don't want you to do a thing. I just realized I don't know where the nearest grocery store is."

Chuckling, she gave him directions from his condo to the supermarket. "I made up a little map of all the stores and other places you'll need to know in town. You took off so quickly earlier that I forgot to give it to you. I also think we should plan a reception to introduce you and the company to Indian Lake."

"Superb idea. How soon can we put that together?"

"I'll work with Melanie on it. I want it before Thanksgiving. No more than two or three weeks."

"Great. Okay, I'll see you in the morning."

Katia hung up and checked her incoming calls again. There were no voice mails and no missed calls. *Austin, what is going on?*

She went to the window and peered out at the lamplight shining through the sparse amber leaves. She saw a couple walking down the street with a dog. By now, the neighborhood children would all be in bed, most likely with sugar rushes keeping them wide awake.

She peered down the block, but she couldn't see Austin's house from her vantage point. Her mind flashed back to Austin standing in her new office, looking at Jack with his hand on her shoulder. Austin thought they were a couple.

Because she'd betrayed him once, he would expect it again. She'd just laid solid ground for the two of them to stand on, and Jack's possessive gesture had undone her work in one fell swoop. She needed to explain to Austin that she and Jack were business associates and good friends—nothing more.

She looked down at her phone again, then tossed it onto the bed. This was a conversation she needed to have in person.

Katia went to the closet, took out a pair of black jeans, a cuddly rose mohair sweater and a long black peacoat. She shoved the phone into her pocket while simultaneously sticking her bare feet into a pair of flats.

Stealthily, she made her way down the stairs and let herself out the back door.

Katia walked to Austin's house, shuffling through piles of fallen leaves on the sidewalk. She stood across the street from his mansion and scanned all the windows. The only light burning was the one in his bedroom. She took out her phone and called his cell.

Just as she expected, she got his voice mail.

"Austin. I'm outside your house, across the street. I can see your window, and I know you're still up because your light is on. I need to talk to you. I think you have the wrong impression about me and Jack. Please call me back and stop playing this stupid game."

She punched the end-call button and waited.

In a few moments, Austin's silhouette appeared in the window, backlit by the bedroom lamp. His broad shoulders nearly filled the width of the pane. Then her phone rang. She answered it and kept her eyes on him.

"I was reading," Austin said.

"Liar. I bet you were on the internet looking at cars."

"Actually, I was talking to my friend Joe in Phoenix, finalizing my annual Christmas trip out there. We buy cars together sometimes. Do a little business," he said.

"Oh. Sorry. I thought you were trying to avoid me."

"Truthfully, I was. So…Jack. I suppose you're standing across the street to tell me Jack isn't your boyfriend."

"No, Austin. He's my boss. I like him, and I care about him and the survival of his business. He's my friend, but that's all."

There was a long pause on his end. "I just assumed—"

"You were wrong, Austin. You jump to conclusions too often. You always have. Anyway, that's what I wanted to tell you."

"Then, I take it you weren't planning to break into my house again?"

"Not tonight." She chuckled, glad the tension between them was gone. "By the way, did you change the locks now that you know I have a key?"

"No."

"Really?" She was surprised. She'd figured he or Daisy would have made certain she couldn't barge in again. What did that say?

"I've been too busy. I should get that done."

Austin placed his right hand against the window-pane, as if reaching out to touch her. It was a simple, unconscious movement on his part, she thought, but it spoke volumes to her. The Austin she remembered, the lonely, isolated young boy who had sought her out when everyone was too busy for him... He was doing it again.

Katia's heart softened, but then she felt the ground turn to quicksand. She'd signed Austin as a client. She told herself she didn't want anything more from him. Friendship, like the one she had with Jack, was all that was acceptable. But if that was truly all she wanted, what in the world was she doing standing here, in the cold, outside Austin's house? Explaining her connection with Jack wasn't part of her job, but it was in her best interest, professionally, to clear up Austin's misunderstanding. Still, was she here as his insurance agent, or was her heart making all the decisions?

If it was, she needed to rein it in fast. Antics like this could cost her everything she'd worked for.

"I have to get home, Austin," she finally said. "Thanks for taking my call. I just wanted to make sure you understood."

"I do," he replied. "Good night, Katia."

"Good night," she said, lifting her hand to wave to him as she moved out of the lamplight and into the shadows.

AUSTIN WATCHED AS Katia vanished into the night. He chewed his bottom lip and frowned. *It was only a street to cross and a door to open, Katia. And you would have been in my arms. That would have been more convincing.*

He turned and flopped down on his pillows. He shut off his iPad. Before Katia had appeared, he'd been searching for other insurance brokers to cover his museum and cars. But he'd been just as unsuccessful as he'd been before Katia moved to Indian Lake.

He had to agree with Jack that Katia was very, very good at her job. He was impressed with how she'd put all the pieces together to take care of his quite unusual needs.

Austin had spent a lot of years being angry and hurt after Katia had left, and now that she was back, he daydreamed about raging at her, but he couldn't do it. He'd learned a long time ago that negative actions led nowhere and accomplished nothing. Still, that didn't quell the roil in his gut he sometimes felt when he was with her.

Katia could protest all she wanted that she and Jack weren't involved, but he'd recognized the way Jack had looked at her. Maybe Jack didn't know his own feelings. That was a possibility. The other problem was that Jack and Katia were together all day, every day, building a relationship whether they knew it or not. Katia probably did things for Jack that most wives would do. Shopping, running errands, scheduling dentist appointments and listening to his worries and woes.

There was no question. Jack had the home-court advantage right now, and Austin didn't like it one bit.

The one and only solace Austin found was the fact that when he'd kissed her, Katia had kissed him back. She couldn't deny that.

Austin was still astounded that his long-buried feelings were so easily uncovered. It was as if the intervening years hadn't existed. He'd been so angry and heartbroken that he'd assumed he would go all his life despising Katia. But this was like a resurrection. He felt young again, filled with dreams and purpose.

True, he'd set his biggest dream into motion long before she showed up. The museum would be his life's imprint on Indian Lake. He might not be the designer and inventor that his great-grandfather had been, but he could certainly ensure that they would be remembered for generations to come.

Austin liked to think Katia was in sync with him about the museum. She'd grown up in this house, right by his side. Now that he knew the real reason for her vanishing act on his prom night, he understood things a lot better—and not just from Katia's perspective.

His mother had been a domineering force after his father's death. Though she hadn't worked at the plant, when Daniel died she'd made certain the plant had stayed solvent. Yet despite her good intentions and community involvement, Hanna was a snob. She hadn't believed Katia was suitable "wife material" for Austin, and she'd held no romantic ideals about teen love. Austin realized now that even if Stephania hadn't quit, Hanna would most likely have found a way to keep Austin and Katia apart.

Looking back on the past without his usual nostalgic filter, he understood that he and Katia would have parted ways eventually. In truth, she wasn't responsible for his broken heart. No one was. He'd been placing blame and wanting revenge for years, and it had eaten him up. He'd skewed his life into a solitary corner, almost becoming the recluse people in town accused him of being. He'd missed opportunities and skipped experiences all because he'd clung to his anger.

That same anger had shot to the forefront today when Jack, a stranger to him, had simply touched the shoulder of his top employee. It was an acceptable gesture for two coworkers, but Austin had overreacted. He'd dug up his anger and put it back on like a superhero cape. Except there was nothing heroic about his actions, or rather, nonactions.

He'd acted like a three-year-old. He'd pouted and ignored Katia's phone calls, even though he'd kept his cell phone in his pocket so he wouldn't miss a single one.

Then she'd shown up across the street. In the dark. Late at night. She had to have been worried about his reaction. He'd seen the expression in the Carter and Associates office. She'd recognized that he was upset, though he'd thought he'd covered himself in front of Jack. But Katia knew him too well.

She'd been concerned enough to walk down to his house and force him to take her call and listen to her explanation.

Tell me. Tell me, Katia. Do you care about me at all? Or is it just my business you want?

Austin flipped the duvet over himself and turned off the light.

CHAPTER SEVENTEEN

KATIA WAS EXHAUSTED after a full day of moving files, orienting Melanie and showing Jack around the most vital places in town—the post office, grocery store, hospital, office-supply store, men's shop, pharmacy and, of course, Cupcakes and Coffee.

Jack had lived in Chicago all his life, and Katia had been right to anticipate that moving to Indian Lake would be a huge culture shock.

"My condos don't have a spa," Jack groused. "Where am I supposed to work out?"

"The YMCA," Melanie offered as she took a stack of files from Katia's hands and placed them in a drawer. "It's not expensive, and the family plan—"

"I don't have a family," he interrupted. "I don't see a theater or bookstore or a barber anywhere."

Katia glared at him. "It's all in the list I gave you. Live theater is in an abandoned old church. The cineplex is just outside town, and your barber, because you want the best, works out of her own home. She's near the lake, as well."

"You're kidding."

"Judy is the best. I made an appointment for you in two weeks. Just a trim, right?"

Jack lifted his paper coffee cup and drained it. "Thanks. And I've gotta say, this is the best double cappuccino I've ever had."

"Told you," Katia said, moving out of the way of the carpet installers, who had just finished laying a dark brown embossed carpet in Jack's office. "Help me hook up Melanie's computer while the guys move your desk in there. Then you can get your work space arranged just like you want it."

Jack rubbed the back of his neck. "I must be missing something. I don't remember you running such a tight ship in Chicago."

"It's the country air here. Reminds me of my mother's work ethic."

"What's that?"

"Never put off until tomorrow that which you can do today." She grinned.

"Wise woman," Jack replied, moving the printer to the table next to Melanie's desk and plugging it in. "Once I figure out what the biggest account in this town would be—"

"That's easy," Melanie said, flipping her long copper braid away from her shoulder. "The largest employer in Indian Lake is the hospital, and the largest land holder and buildings' owner is the county itself."

Jack froze and stared at Melanie. "What did you say your past experience was?"

"I was an executive secretary to the owner of the Indian Lake Foundry. They laid me off."

"What were they, nuts?" Jack guffawed.

"No, bankrupt. The owner's son embezzled four million dollars and went to Brazil."

Jack pounded the printer table in excitement. "Their loss is our gain! That's just about the most brilliant advice I've been given—" he looked at Katia, who sent him a glare "—in at least a week."

"Thanks," Melanie said. "I've lived in Indian Lake all my life. I like to think I know my way around. And if I don't, my husband sure does."

Jack turned back to Katia. "Let's investigate the hospital. Then we'll go after the county. I'll call the hospital president."

"I'll dig around and see who I still know over there," Katia offered. "Together, we'll sell to them."

One of the main reasons Katia had hired Melanie was because of her expansive knowledge of Indian Lake and its residents. The fact that Jack liked her was a gold star for Katia.

Everything was working out just fine, Katia thought.

IT WAS WELL after six o'clock before Katia went home, though she felt as if it could easily be midnight. This was one time she'd wished she'd driven to work and not walked. By the time she trudged up the stairs, all she could think about was a hot bath with a lot of bath salts.

She flopped down on the bed, fully clothed. "I swear I will never move again," she moaned.

There was a knock at her door. She sat up slowly, and the knock persisted. "I'm coming," she called. She opened the door.

Mrs. Beabots was dressed in a vintage Chanel black wool suit with gold buttons. She wore half a dozen gold chain necklaces and plain black pumps, and she carried a quilted Chanel shoulder bag.

"You have to drive me, Katia."

"Drive you?"

"Our plans got all jumbled up. Sarah is already there because she promised to help with the food and decorations, and so when Luke came home, he picked up the kids and didn't know that I wasn't with Sarah. So he left without me. And I can't drive anymore. Could you take me?"

"Sure. But where are you going?"

"Why, to the elopement."

She must have misunderstood. "An elopement? By definition, wouldn't that mean no guests?"

"It's all hush-hush. Can't tell a soul. But..." She eyed Katia's jeans and the sweatshirt she'd worn all day for unpacking the office. "You'll need to change, of course."

"But I'll just be dropping you off."

"Oh, no! You're going to stay. Liz practically commanded me to invite you. So put on a nice outfit. Red would be lovely with your hair. Oh! And I have a fantastic new lipstick you can try." She started digging in her purse.

"Liz Crenshaw is getting married?"

"Why, yes, dear. I thought I'd mentioned that. She and Gabe. Tonight. In about an hour. Now, hurry. Here's the lipstick. I'll meet you downstairs."

Katia shut the door. "This is the craziest little town!"

FLICKERING LANTERNS LIT a winding path from the tasting room door and up the hill to the very spot inside the vineyard where, according to town legend, Liz had first leveled her shotgun on Gabe.

"We thought it was romantic," Gabe explained to Katia and Mrs. Beabots as he took the elderly woman's arm and led them both along the path.

"Shotguns are very romantic," Mrs. Beabots teased.

The area was illuminated with nearly a hundred votive candles inside jars, glasses and hollowed-out pumpkins, gourds and squash. Though it was evident that this had all been put together in a short period of time, the effect was magical.

The night sky was crystal clear, with a full moon and billions of stars shining down on the vineyard. The lights from the house and tasting room were blazing their welcome, and Katia could smell a real log fire burning somewhere.

Mrs. Beabots introduced Katia to Father Michael, who would be officiating the ceremony. Gabe then introduced her to his mother, Gina, and his brothers, Mica and Rafe. She already knew Louisa, Aurelio and Maria from her previous visits to Crenshaw's. Maddie and Nate walked up the path and greeted everyone with radiant smiles.

"We're the music," Maddie said, taking out her iPhone and scrolling through a playlist. Nate produced a portable wireless speaker, and soon Tony Bennett's "The Shadow of Your Smile" was playing quietly.

Sarah came up the path holding a bouquet of colorful fall flowers. Behind her, Annie tossed yellow rose petals and Timmy held a pillow.

Sam proudly escorted Liz toward the little group.

Liz wore a long-sleeved, cream-colored sweater dress that was banded on the hem and the cuffs with cream satin. She wore her burnished honey-blond hair long and full and had sprinkled it with rhinestone pins and picks. She carried a bouquet of orange and yellow roses with streamers of bronze, brown and gold. Liz was glowing with joy, and to Katia, she looked brighter than the moonlight.

Katia was covered in chills and felt her heart swell with emotion as Liz and Gabe gazed lovingly into each other's eyes and exchanged their own vows. Katia would never forget how they spoke and giggled and cried. Katia knew she was witnessing true love, and she felt an internal shift that altered her perspective. Liz's face held the same euphoria Katia had experienced when she was sixteen and in love with Austin. She was astounded at the magnitude of her happiness for Liz and Gabe. When Tina had announced her engagement, she'd mostly felt envy. But it seemed that each day she awoke in Indian Lake, her heart opened a little bit more.

Was it just last night she'd walked to Austin's on impulse? She hadn't even thought through what she would say or do when she got there. She just couldn't stand the idea that

Austin would be upset with her for something she hadn't done.

Being here with Liz and Gabe, Katia could only think of the look in Austin's eyes when he'd seen her with Jack. Part of her wanted to rush off to Austin and tell him she'd do anything not to feel the shame of letting him go all these years thinking the worst of her. That she was afraid that if she saw him, *she* would be the one who got hurt. Maybe she'd stayed away from Austin because loving him would have meant years of torturous waiting while he finished school, during which time he could have met someone else. Someone with a better background, a better education. Someone more worthy of the McCreary name.

Were those the real reasons she hadn't contacted him when she'd moved to Chicago? Was she that insecure? Had she actually bought into Hanna's prejudices and her mother's archaic beliefs?

Pressing a palm to her cheek, Katia realized she was sweating, even in the chilly night.

Suddenly, everyone was applauding, and the groom kissed the bride. There were cheers and hugs all around. Arms wrapped around her, and she found herself embracing everyone back.

Gabe shouted above the happy whoops and cheers, "Liz and I invite you to our wedding dinner in the tasting room." At that, he grabbed his wife's hand, and they raced down the lighted path.

Katia walked with Mrs. Beabots, who took a slower pace as everyone ran ahead of them. Katia turned to Mrs. Beabots. "Isn't Gabe's father here?"

"It's a sad thing. Angelo refused to come. He said that Gabe had shunned his family when he chose Liz and his new life as a vintner. You'd think with two perfectly capable sons to help him run that tomato patch, he'd be happy. But not Angelo. He just doesn't get it."

"That's terrible. They're so happy. Insanely happy, really," Katia said wistfully. "I've never seen anyone like them."

"Oh, I have," Mrs. Beabots replied. "My Raymond was much like Gabe and Nate, too. Headstrong. Serious. Determined. And very romantic."

Gina and Sam walked up behind them. Sam was holding Gina's hand as they took their time descending in the dark. Katia didn't need an interpreter to understand what was going on between the two of them.

"How are you tonight, Emma?" Sam asked.

"Divine," Mrs. Beabots said. "I don't know when I've seen a more beautiful and meaningful wedding."

"I wanted to give them a spring wedding at our villa, but they couldn't wait," Gina said. "Gabe told me two days ago they were going to elope to Kentucky. I called Sam, and together we stopped them and promised this impromptu little ceremony. I've been cooking ever since."

"Yeah. Gina made her ravioli," Sam said proudly. "It's my favorite."

"Really?" Mrs. Beabots cocked a curious eye toward Gina. "What's the secret?"

"Oh, Emma. You never give away your secrets, so why should I tell you mine?" Gina teased. "But seriously, it's in how I sear the paste."

Gina and Sam continued on ahead.

"Did you hear that?" Mrs. Beabots asked Katia. "She sears the tomato paste?"

Katia didn't know whether to laugh or cringe. She'd just seen Sam Crenshaw holding hands with a married woman—Gabe's mother, to boot—who was at least twenty years younger than him, and all Mrs. Beabots commented on was the tomato paste?

Katia held the door open for Mrs. Beabots as they went inside. In the corner of the tasting room were a classical guitarist and a violinist. Both were young, and it was Katia's guess that they'd been available on such short notice because they were students, not professionals.

A long table was set up with mounds of Italian bread, huge wooden salad bowls with two kinds of green salad and three casserole dishes of ravioli, cannelloni and penne pasta. In the far corner was a tall silver antique epergne filled with Maddie's cupcakes. On the top cupcake was a statue of a bride and groom.

Unexpected tears sprang to Katia's eyes. It was the sweetest and most endearing wedding dinner she'd ever seen. It had all been planned in forty-eight hours because Gabe was so anxious to make Liz his bride that he couldn't wait another day. Katia felt she was standing in the middle of a fairy tale. Someone else's fairy tale.

But it gave her hope that such miracles could happen.

CHAPTER EIGHTEEN

AUSTIN SHOVED HIS cold hands into the pockets of his battered, sheepskin-lined leather bomber jacket. His grandfather, David McCreary, had worn this coat in WWII as the pilot of a P-51D Mustang when he'd flown as a long-range, high-altitude escort for bombing campaigns against Germany with the 354th Pioneer Fighter Group.

Austin was watching the steel frame of his museum take shape, beams and girders creating the skeleton of the three-story building. Considering his grandfather's bomber jacket, he mused about the possibility of erecting an air museum someday. Second only to his cars was Austin's fascination with old airplanes. Combat airplanes, to be exact. He marveled over the kind of courage it took for men during the First World War to risk their lives in flimsy aircrafts. The untested, highly combustible engines were as great a threat to a pilot's life then as enemy bullets.

The inventors and designers of those first planes, as well as the first automobiles, were dead. Even their children were dead. Their exploits and triumphs would wane in the minds and imaginations of present and future generations. Their lessons would be lost, if not for...

"Lunatics like me," Austin said aloud, lifting a paper cup of Maddie Strong's cappuccino to his lips. The coffee warmed him.

Despite the cold, he wanted to stay out here long enough to give Hal further instructions before going back to the plant to check on the shipment of serpentine belts to his new corporate client. While he'd been consumed with planning and building the museum for months, the orders at the plant had continued to flow. They might never reach the peak levels he'd enjoyed before the crash of 2008, but still, his business was steady, he hadn't had to downsize his staff like other manufacturers in the area and his family's three-generation reputation for making good products was paying off. Austin had to admit, with a great deal of gratitude to God, that his life continued to float along on an even keel, slipping around dangerous obstacles and always sailing safely into port.

At least it had until Katia had returned to town.

Austin sipped his coffee again, but it had grown cold. He tossed the contents across the frost-covered ground. Lately, Austin had begun to feel as if he was sliding over the edge of a bottomless waterfall. Of all the sensations in the world Austin abhorred, it was a free fall. He had no bearings, no parachute... All he saw was Jack Carter's smug look as he gazed down at Katia.

Austin had never been a jealous person. He'd had nothing and no one to be jealous about. Except perhaps for that rash of raw envy he experienced every year when he watched Wimbledon, wishing he was the reigning world tennis champion. Maybe he hadn't taken enough risks in his life, which would have pitted him against foes and challenges. In most ways, he'd been flat-out lucky. Maybe the universe was saving up all his bad karma for one massive attack that would bring him down.

However, his every waking moment was consumed by this invasive, almost debilitating virus that forced him to focus on that instant when Jack had put his hand on Katia's shoulder and looked at her as if she was the only woman in the world. And he didn't have the first clue how to eradicate his system of the disease.

It was naive to think that Katia hadn't had some kind of love life after leaving Indian Lake. She was, hands down, the most beautiful woman he'd ever met. He'd had very short-term flings at car shows around the country, but he'd never been even remotely serious about anyone. Staying single had served him well. His life had been serene and pleasant. It had also grown stale and boring.

Deep down, he had to admit that he distrusted women because Katia had left him. At least that was how he'd explained his commitment phobia for the past eighteen years. The other problem was that Austin had never met a woman who measured up to the Katia he'd known. Austin didn't want a wife or someone to be the mother of his children. He wanted a friend and a companion. He wanted someone who understood his solitary ways and how to pry him out of his self-induced exiles. Austin wasn't looking for an adrenaline junkie or supermodel like the women he'd met at auto auctions.

"What I want is Katia," he said aloud, his words whipping away from him on an icy wind. The revelation was clear as glass.

But Katia had moved on. She'd built a life in Chicago, with Jack. He had no illusions now about why she'd moved her company to Indian Lake. She intended to capture a new market and new clients. Apparently, Austin had been at the top of her shopping list, and he'd fallen for her sales pitch. He'd signed the contract she needed to impress her boss.

In the darkest part of his mind, the realization

that Katia was using him crept out of its hole. If that was true, then he could never let himself trust her. And if he couldn't trust, his love was doomed to misery; perhaps even more misery than he'd already endured because of her.

Katia had said she and Jack were only friends, at most. She could very well not have any feelings for her boss at all, but that didn't automatically mean she cared for Austin.

And that was the meat of the problem. Austin really didn't know where he stood with Katia. It was sad, he thought. He'd been branded by a slow ring of fire the first time Katia had stepped foot in his house—and they'd only been children.

Even then, her cool blue-green eyes had seemed to look deep into his heart and read his every wish and fear. Austin didn't believe in soul mates, per se, but there had to be a reason that Katia had been part of his childhood and had returned at this juncture in his life, right when he thought he should be sitting on top of the world. But the fact was, there was a melancholy to building his museum. Sure, he was creating a testimony to his father and great-grandfather, but at the same time, he was finally facing a kind of grief he'd never experienced before.

All his life, he'd clung to the past and found

solace in history because it was irreversible. *He* was the future, and that brought both responsibility and dread.

Austin had always felt he didn't measure up. He hadn't founded a company, won a national trophy or garnered a title. He was just a guy whose laurel wreath had been put there by his parents. As he took stock of his life, he realized it wasn't a glass that was half-full. It was empty.

With each day and each rafter that the crews riveted to his museum, the project grew closer to its conclusion. It would be finished. *And then what, Austin?*

His passions would need refueling, if not a change of direction.

He glanced at his cell phone. There was a missed call from Katia, but his phone had not rung. She'd left a message.

He couldn't fight the smile that broke across his face as he hit the voice mail button.

"Hi, Austin. It's Katia. We need to get together soon. If I remember correctly, your attic is crammed with crates of Christmas decorations that I need to go through. How about Saturday morning?"

He hit the call-back button, and Katia answered on the first ring.

That was a good sign.

"Hey. I missed your call."

"Austin, I can barely hear you," she replied. "Are you in your car?"

"I'm at the job site. The wind is picking up. Listen, I can't do Saturday. Rafe and I have a handball game. Then a workout. How about Friday night? After work? Unless you have a date or something," he purposefully probed.

"A date?" she laughed. "Friday night would be great. I could bring over pizza."

Austin exhaled as the rancid taste of jealousy dissolved in his mouth. No date. No Jack. Austin had asked about Friday as a test to see how high Jack was on Katia's priority list. Jack had just arrived in town, and if they were serious about each other, Jack would have expected this first weekend from Katia. Friday was the end of the workweek, time to celebrate a job well done. A night to go out. Dance, maybe. Hit a club or two. That kind of thing was hard to do in Indian Lake, but for Jack? Austin bet he'd drive into Chicago on a fraction of a whim. Yes, Friday night would have been sacrosanct to a man like Jack. At least, it would have been to Austin if he'd had Katia in his life.

Feeling confident, Austin pressed Katia further. "You don't have to do that. I can have Daisy whip us up something. I was thinking angel-hair pasta and scallops."

Katia laughed. "Austin, it's barely past breakfast. You're thinking with your stomach, like you did when we were kids."

"What's wrong with that? The culinary arts are the one thing that lift our lives out of the mundane."

"Who said that?"

"I saw it in a movie, I think. It might have been Benjamin Franklin."

"You said that because you know I like to cook," she bantered.

"Oh, yeah? Prove it. You make the pasta and scallops, then. I'll give Daisy the night off."

"Deal. So Friday night, then. I can be there at six."

Austin hung up and listened to the Canada geese honking as they flew in huge flocks across the endless pearl-gray sky. This time of year had always depressed Austin, and he couldn't pack his bags fast enough to head to sunny Arizona where he would browse the car shows, meet with antique car collectors and pretend his life was full of excitement and purpose.

But in one phone call with Katia, his adrenaline had shot off the charts, and he couldn't stop smiling. Even his hands had warmed. He tried to warn himself that one Friday night wouldn't quiet all the alarm bells that had gone off when he'd seen Katia and Jack together. There was still the possibility that Katia had feelings for Jack.

Austin's strategy now was to find out if Katia had any of those old feelings for him.

KATIA WAS WEARING skinny jeans with a light sprinkling of rhinestones on the back pockets, a gray turtleneck sweater and gray suede boots when Austin opened the door for her. She carried her black peacoat over one arm, and held a yellow-striped bakery box of Maddie's cupcakes in the other. She offered the box to Austin.

"Maddie said these were your favorites. And there's a lemon one with lemon-curd filling for Daisy, which is her favorite."

"Really?" Austin asked, looking down at the box. "I didn't know that. Thanks." Then he met her eyes and felt his heart trip. Did she know she had that effect on him, and if she did, would she use it against him?

Katia's face filled with anticipation, as if this little gift for him meant something more than just a token of thanks. Austin sensed she wanted to please him in some way. He liked that.

"Come in," he said, taking her jacket. "It's getting cold out there."

She stepped over the threshold and rubbed her shoulders. "It doesn't bother me. In fact, I walked from my apartment. It was brisk, but really not all that bad." She glanced into the living room, where a fire was going. "It's cozy in here."

"I thought we'd need some cheering up after spending time in that dreary attic. Let me put these things in the kitchen, and then we can get to work. Are you really ready for this?"

She rubbed her hands together greedily. "I can't wait. I remember so many treasures up there. I hope they're still there."

His shoulders slumped as his eyes slid toward the staircase. "I haven't been to the attic since my mother died…"

Suddenly, she was at his side, her hand on his cheek, her deep green eyes peering deeply into his. Her expression was filled with sincerity and concern. "Oh, Austin. I didn't even think about that and what all this would mean to you. Maybe this whole tour thing isn't a good idea. We might resurrect the wrong ghosts, and I don't want to put you through any pain. That's the last thing I want."

Hoisting her jacket over his shoulder, he covered her hand with his. He wouldn't peel his eyes from hers for all the money in the world. "I didn't think about it, either, until just now, but if we do it together, I'll be okay."

"You sure?"

He lifted his chin. "You know, I forgot to thank you, Katia, for being there for me when

I was a child. There were so many rough spots, and you helped me through them."

"I loved you through them, Austin," she said. "I wish I'd known about Hanna's death. I would have come back for her funeral. For you."

He shook his head and pulled her hand away, though he didn't let go. "I don't think so. It was over ten years ago. I wouldn't have wanted to see you. I was still too angry. To intent on revenge."

She gently squeezed his fingers. "Do you still want revenge?"

Austin thought of a dozen things he wanted from Katia right now, right here, starting with a kiss. He wanted to hold her in front of the fire. He was curious about what kind of plans she'd made for her future, and mostly, he wanted to know just exactly where he fit into her world. Was he just a client? Just a former teenage crush? Could they ever be real friends again? He studied her face. "No, Katia. I don't want revenge. I've gotten past all that. Negative feelings are a waste of energy and time. For years, I put thoughts of you in a box and locked you away like the decorations in the attic. Now that you've explained why you left the way you did and why you didn't contact me, I understand. I guess."

A soft smile picked up the corners of her mouth. "But you're not sure."

"Not entirely sure, no," he said.

She slipped her arm around his neck and moved closer. Agonizingly close. "I bet I could remind you very quickly," she whispered.

Katia's voice filled Austin's mind with a fast-forward video of their youth. He remembered a thousand stolen moments, a thousand kisses and whispers. He was toast.

"Katia, if you're going to kiss me, you better do it, or I'm going to drop dead on the spot."

"I'm not," she said, and pulled away. "I just... can't get involved with you, Austin. Not that way."

"Why?"

"It's complicated, but basically I could damage my career. You're a client, Austin. It's against corporate policy."

"And is that all I am to you, Katia? Another set of figures to add to your sales quota?"

"Austin! I can't believe you're saying this."

"Well, believe it, because it sure looks like that to me. Sometimes I feel like you're fishing for reactions from me—emotional ones—and then the next minute, I get an icy chill from you. So what is it?"

"I'm trying very hard to negotiate these tricky waters I've found myself in, Austin. I didn't think there'd be anything between us now, after all this time apart."

"And is there? For you, I mean?"

Her eyes moved slowly across his face, causing an agonizing rumble in his chest that he wouldn't have missed for the world. At that moment, he didn't care how angry he'd been five minutes ago or what she would say five minutes from now. In this moment, he saw the Katia he knew and wanted to have faith in. Oh, how badly he wanted to believe that she still loved him.

"When I'm here with you, my mind is a jumble," she continued. "I can't think straight. And when I'm away from you, I think about you—a lot, actually. The truth is, you'll always be my friend, Austin. More than a friend, really. And isn't that enough? For now, I mean?"

Austin wasn't sure if she was leading him on or if she was truly this confused. But no matter what she said or did, he apparently couldn't control his heart's reaction to her.

"If that's how it is, then, that's what it is. Now let's go get those decorations."

KATIA AND AUSTIN spent an hour and a half in the attic, sorting through decorations in old cardboard boxes, plastic bins and enormous wooden crates. Though there was overhead lighting, Katia was thankful that Austin had brought up an orange extension cord and a utility work light, and he'd given her a legal pad and pen to make notes.

"I'd forgotten how enormous this place was," Katia said, staring up at the gabled roof.

"It's one of the reasons this house looks so much larger than the others on the avenue. I turned the third-floor ballroom into a home theater, bathroom and guest quarters. I don't know why I did that. I never have any out-of-town guests." He pulled an old sheet off an Oak Lake rocking chair. "Anyway, this fourth floor was used by household staff back when my great-grandfather built the house. I think the gardener and his wife lived up here."

"That's why the ceiling is finished out," Katia replied. "And those old ceiling fixtures seem to be art nouveau."

Austin looked up. "Wow. I missed that. You think they're the real thing?"

"Sure. Why not? They probably didn't think a thing of it back then."

"My mother changed a lot of the lighting on the first floor back in the nineties when she redecorated." He marched over to another wooden crate filled with packing straw and old corrugated cardboard. "But if she saved the original chandeliers..."

Katia rose and followed him. "You could put them in the museum?"

"Precisely," he said excitedly, yanking fistfuls of straw out of the crate. "Amazing! They're here!" He pulled a dark, wrought iron, twelve-candle electric chandelier from the crate. "Bring that work light. Let's see if there are any markings."

Katia brought the light and peered at the underside. "It says 'Paris, 1892.'"

"Fantastic. It's gorgeous," he said, scrutinizing the expertly crafted acanthus-leaf design that was so popular at that time.

"Austin, this is a really precious antique. What if something happened to it? What if it was stolen?"

He chuckled. "But, Katia, I have insurance."

"Funny. Seriously, Austin, we should put this in the dining room here at the house, where it used to be. This is a work of art. It's irreplaceable. Sure, you can get reimbursed for stolen art, but you can't get it back."

Austin carefully put the chandelier back into the crate. "You told me I'd be covered. I'm about to put irreplaceable cars in my museum. You assured me I would have the best policy. I do, don't I?"

"Yes," she replied, nodding a bit too forcefully. "Absolutely." Katia was confident in the products she had assembled for Austin, not just the best deals but the most extensive coverage he could possibly get. Insuring the building itself was a walk in the park. But the cars were another matter. As she looked down at the one-of-a-kind chandelier, she realized that these precious extractions from the past, these puzzle pieces of history, could never be insured completely. There were too many vagaries in life. Too many opportunities for the wheel of fortune to turn in the wrong direction. Just as she couldn't guarantee that Austin would never again seek revenge against her, she could not tell him that his cars would ever be perfectly safe. Nothing in the world was perfectly safe.

Not possessions, not people. Not love.

"I have to know the cars have the best insurance, Katia," he said firmly. "They mean a great deal to me."

"Austin, I, of all people, know that. That's why I've worked so hard to get you what you want and need. But think about it—you have half your cars stored in these old carriage houses here on your property. How safe are they? Those buildings haven't been refurbished in years."

Putting his hands on his hips, he glared at her with eyes of blue steel. "You don't honestly think I keep my cars here, do you?"

Katia gaped. "What? But you gave me a list."

"I did. Which is ever changing. Most of my cars are in Scottsdale, Arizona, where they won't rust or be impaired by the freezes."

"And when were you going to tell me this?" She asked. "I'm your insurance agent."

"When we got closer to the finish date. Besides, I'll be going to Arizona over the holidays, and that's when I usually sell a car or two. Perhaps pick up something new. So the list will change. There's a Cord 812 Phaeton I've been trying to trade up to for years."

Katia frowned. Was he telling her that he didn't trust her? He would have every reason not to trust her. But this was business. Still, Katia could see that she was going to have to keep selling Austin.

It occurred to her that he might be testing her. She had to admit, she felt a bit shaky. The prime cut of Austin's deal was yet to be realized. Was he dangling that fact in front of her like a carrot? Or did he have genuine concerns?

"This Cord Phaeton that you want. How much are we talking?"

"To buy it or insure it?"

"Just the part that involves me."

"At auction, it would go for one-hundred-and-eighty-five-thousand dollars. The seller has never let it out of his hands, which makes me wonder if it isn't really the Sultan of Brunei who owns it. Anyway, I could trade my Bugatti for it."

"The blue Bugatti that I love?" She gasped.

"Oh, you like that car?"

"You know I do." She willed him to remember.

The Bugatti was where she'd found him on Valentine's Day all those years ago, crying over his father's death. She'd made him a Valentine... But he'd obviously forgotten.

"Yeah," he said bending down to pack straw around the chandelier. "I like that car too much. I'll trade something else. The Cord Phaeton is just a dream car. It's out of my league."

"Well, if you change things up, buy other cars, you have to let me know immediately, Austin."

"Of course. I can't buy them without providing the insurance."

"Remember we're doing a floater policy. No driving them up to Indiana from Arizona because you want to see the bluebonnets in Texas."

Austin laughed. "How do you know I'd do that?"

"Lucky guess," she replied quickly, wondering how and why she would remember a statement he'd made nearly twenty years ago one dismal March day. They'd driven out to the beach in his father's Cadillac. After hours of kisses and promises to love each other forever, they'd mused about the future.

"If I could take you anywhere right now," Austin had said, "it would be Texas. The bluebonnets are blooming. Oceans of blue up and down all the highways. My father used to drive that route from Arizona to Indiana in the winter to avoid the freezing rain in Kansas and Oklahoma. It takes a day longer, but it was worth it. Those were my favorite spring breaks when I was a kid. Just to see the flowers. It made me smile."

Katia remembered more and more slices of their past each time she was around Austin. This attic and these old decorations triggered memories of her own mother, too. Inexplicably, waves of nostalgia and longing for the mother and the Austin she used to know snaked around her ankles and pulled her under like a riptide.

Katia was unsure of everything in her life. She'd moved here so quickly, without time to consider the ramifications of her actions. She'd been threatened with the loss of her job and the looming stress that Jack's company could dissolve. The move had seemed like their only option. However, in all her calculations, Katia hadn't given enough thought to what it would be like to see Austin again; much less be with him.

Sure, she'd known she needed to apologize

and she'd hoped her shame and guilt would be assuaged. But moments like this were like opening Pandora's box. She recalled days filled with laughter and innocent yearning for a boy she'd given her heart to the first day she met him. Austin had been her world, and she'd been so certain of his love for her that she'd planned for no other future than the one with Austin in it.

She'd loved him so deeply, so completely, she'd only believed that as long as they were together, somehow their world would be made right.

Now she knew better. Austin was just part of her youth. She'd sewn up her broken heart the way her mother had taught her to do and embraced her new life. Until this moment, Katia had believed that she'd analyzed, mourned and coped with her past.

She was wrong.

Being within arm's reach of Austin, happiness radiating from his face, she realized all those youthful dreams were simply sleeping, waiting to be awakened with a kiss. Or just the right word.

Suddenly, Katia couldn't breathe. In her present life, constantly lurking in the wings, there was this internal assailant that crushed her lungs and heart like tightening steel bands.

Not now! she chided her body. Not here in

front of Austin when she was trying desperately to win his confidence. Win his business.

In the end, it didn't matter what Katia used to feel for Austin or that her head was filled with far too many thoughts about him. It didn't even matter that several times a day, she relived his most recent kiss. She had to keep him at a distance. If Jack ever got a whiff of any personal involvement between her and their biggest client, she'd be fired.

Katia's airway became more constricted, as if malevolent hands were tightening screws in her lungs. She felt a burning in her chest, and sweat broke out across her forehead.

From the back of her brain she swore she heard a voice telling her to run.

"I need to go, Austin," she said abruptly.

"What? But we haven't had dinner."

"You know, I forgot I told Mrs. Beabots I would help her with, um, some of the food for Thanksgiving. I have to run to the store for her."

"Oh," he replied disappointedly. "That's nice of you to help."

She rushed on. "Mrs. Beabots is having a huge dinner with Sarah and all her family. I suppose you have big plans?"

Austin bent down to pick up the pad, pen, utility light and extension cord. "I usually go out of town." He followed her as she led the way to the attic stairs. He placed his hand on the small of her back and guided her around a stack of books that was placed perilously close to the first step.

"Watch that," he said.

Katia thought her heart was going to pound right out of her chest. This was the worst panic attack yet. If she could only get outside and breathe some fresh air. Or get away from Austin and the familiarity of his touch.

"And you're not going away this year?" she asked, barely stringing the words together.

"No. I'll be here," he said as they started down the steps. "By the way, when are you going to start decorating?"

"The day after Thanksgiving," she managed.

Katia practically raced to the main staircase. The front door appeared ahead. She was nearly free.

"I'll call you," she said extending her hand to him.

Austin just stared back at her for a prolonged, silent moment. "So you'll be at Mrs. Beabots's for Thanksgiving?"

Katia got the impression he was probing for more information, but she didn't know what.

"Yes," she replied, taking her hand from his and putting it on the door handle. She glanced back at him. "Why don't you join us? There will be plenty of food. I'm doing half the cooking. I don't think Mrs. Beabots will mind."

Austin's face instantly shone with happiness and she realized that her invitation meant a lot to him.

"I'd love it. You clear it with Mrs. B. Okay?"

"Sure. I'll call you."

Katia opened the blessed door. Once outside, she nearly ran down the sidewalk, taking in gulps of air. She held her hand over her heart and felt it return to normal by the time she'd walked a half a block. She was safe once again.

CHAPTER NINETEEN

Katia threw worries and concern along with fresh grated nutmeg and cinnamon into her baked sweet-potato casserole. She added brown sugar and butter and turned on the mixer to blend the ingredients. She sprayed a ceramic casserole dish with nonstick spray and then turned to Mrs. Beabots, who was stuffing a huge turkey with quartered apples, onion, carrot, celery and orange.

"I'll put this casserole in the oven after I take out the broccoli soufflé. For now, the soufflé demands a very even heat," Katia said, glancing toward the lit oven interior.

She could feel a frown burrow into her forehead with the force of a farmer's plow. She should never have suggested that Austin join them for dinner today. Mrs. Beabots had quickly picked up the phone to graciously invite him when Katia had mentioned it. Based on her last encounter with Austin, Katia now believed there was something deeper than guilt that caused her to react so anxiously when she was around him.

She just wished she knew what it was.

"Did you cut the sage from the garden for me?" Mrs. Beabots asked as she peeled the breast skin away from the turkey meat with her fingers.

"I did." Katia went to the refrigerator and took out a paper towel with the sage and some thyme and parsley she'd previously washed. "I have it all here for you."

"Thank you, dear. Would you mind picking off the prettiest sage leaves and handing them to me while I butter the insides?"

Katia chose long, elegant sage leaves and watched as Mrs. Beabots artistically arranged them between the turkey breast meat and the skin to form a pattern across the top of the turkey. Then she brushed the top skin with melted clarified butter.

"That's gorgeous," Katia said. "I've never seen that done."

Mrs. Beabots smiled. "I put more sage in the cavity, along with parsley, and it's just delicious. Once this bakes and turns golden, it'll be worthy of a magazine cover."

"I'll bet," Katia replied, and went back to the squash. She poured it into the dish. "Thank you for inviting Austin. I just assumed he would have made plans."

"Hmm. He's always been out of town, from

what I understood. Thanksgiving. Christmas. New Year's. He's never been around. That's another reason Sarah and I have had trouble getting him to participate in our Christmas Tour. I've noticed that he's changing a bit."

"Changing?"

"Why, there's no question, dear." Mrs. Beabots walked around the island and went to the sink to wash her hands. "If you hadn't been part of the equation, he would never have agreed to the Candlelight Tour. And it doesn't take a detective to figure out that you're also the reason he's not running off to Arizona for the holiday."

Katia nearly dropped the mixer beater. "That's not true."

Mrs. Beabots pinned her blue eyes on Katia. "Are you so career minded that you can't see the obvious? Even in your own life?"

"What on earth are you talking about?"

"I wasn't absolutely certain until I saw the two of you together when we went to Austin's house. Actually, Sarah said she'd picked up little clues that something was different about Austin. Maddie had told her that suddenly Austin didn't want his Friday-morning cupcakes delivered anymore. He actually went to the café to pick up his order. For years, Austin, who was Maddie's sole investor, had never set foot in her café. Suddenly, you come to town and he's stopping by on a nearly regular basis for a latte before work. Then he agreed to open his house for the tour. That was more than a milestone. It was close to a miracle—in my book anyway. Now he's coming to my house for Thanksgiving. I invited him for years after Hanna died, and he always turned me down." She tapped the side of her cheek with her forefinger thoughtfully. "Deductions have always been a strong suit of mine. Believe me, I think I'm right. Austin is still in love with you."

"He is *not*!" Katia's response was much too quick and emphatic. "He…is a client and a friend," she said, dialing down her voice.

Mrs. Beabots gave Katia a cool, scrutinizing stare that could rival the best interrogators. The octogenarian's keen observations sat much too firmly in Katia's head. She hadn't met the Austin that most of the people of Indian Lake knew. She hadn't seen the man who had shut himself off from others, chained to his family's business and escaping to another state or car show when holidays rolled around.

Katia had thought Austin had only been testing the waters when he kissed her. Perhaps he wanted to see how angry he still was. But love? *There's no way.*

Logically, Katia didn't believe she deserved anything more from Austin than forgiveness.

That had been a major hurdle for them. She was still only learning the extent to which she'd hurt him and, in the process, had damaged her own self-esteem.

Was her guilt the cause of her anxiety attacks? Or was there something more? For years, she'd convinced herself that her life in Chicago and her challenging career were all she needed. She was happy; her life was filled with art gallery openings, after-theater parties, dinners with friends and shopping.

On holidays, Katia always had more than one invitation from friends and either had to choose between them or do double duty and attend two dinners in one day. Her friends adored her. Their children loved her, especially when she showed up with toys and candies. She was the "special aunt" to dozens of her friends' children.

Now, as she remembered those days, she felt a new feeling deep inside, and it was hollow. For the first time Katia realized there was something missing in that life that she now could name.

I don't have a family.

She grabbed the edge of the island with both hands as a wave of breathlessness overtook her. She took tiny sips of air as if savoring a fine wine. The panic left her.

"Are you all right, dear?" Mrs. Beabots asked as she quickly came to Katia's side and pressed her small hand against Katia's forehead. "You're perspiring."

"It happens," Katia replied. "Usually when I think too much."

"I hope I haven't upset you. I want this to be your best Thanksgiving ever," Mrs. Beabots said earnestly.

Katia took her hand and held it. "I'm sorry. I didn't mean to frighten you. Frankly, you've helped me already. I see things more clearly now. Even myself. And that's very good."

IN THE LARGE formal dining room, Katia held hands with Austin, who was seated to her left, and Annie, dressed as a pilgrim girl, on her right. Down the center of the table, Mrs. Beabots had placed a dozen taper candles amongst a plethora of minipumpkins, gourds and tiny ears of Indian corn. Annie and Timmy had made pinecone-and-construction-paper-turkey place cards for each guest. Mrs. Beabots sat proudly at the head of the table, and Luke sat at the other end. Timmy, who was also dressed as a pilgrim, sat next to Sarah, across from Katia and Austin.

After the Thanksgiving prayer, Luke raised his glass of wine. "A toast to our wonderful hostess and to all the lovely cooks who prepared our meal."

"To your good health," Austin said and clinked glasses with Katia.

Timmy piped up. "You're supposed to say, 'God bless us, every one.'"

Annie immediately corrected him. "That's for Christmas. Right, Dad?"

"I'm afraid she's right, son. But I think it's good for both Thanksgiving and Christmas," Luke replied as he picked up the carving set and went to work on the turkey.

Timmy's frown instantly turned to a wide grin. "Good. I like it for all holidays."

"Me, too," Sarah said. "Now, what do you want? White or dark meat?"

"I'll take the whole leg." Timmy grinned, eyeing the huge turkey leg his father had just cut off the bird. "I bet pirates used to eat turkey legs like that. How come we don't have a pirates' holiday?"

Austin laughed into his napkin. "And would you wear a pirate costume?"

Timmy beamed. "Sure would! I was a pilgrim last year for Halloween, but this year I was a pirate."

"I remember," Austin replied. "I think you got extra candy at my house."

"We both did," Annie said. "Thank you very much."

"You're welcome," Austin said and then whispered to Katia, "Daisy told me who they were."

"Ah!" She nodded. "So what's your favorite holiday, Timmy?"

"Halloween. Obviously!"

"Mine's Christmas," Annie interjected as she stuck her fork in the fruit piled prettily on her salad plate.

"I like Valentine's," Austin said in a low voice that only Katia heard.

When she glanced at him, his eyes were locked on her face.

Katia felt her heart skip a beat and her face warm. This time she didn't feel panic or anxiety. There was no tightening in her chest, only a comforting glow that made her smile ever so slightly. She knew exactly the Valentine's Day he was remembering, and of all the holidays in her life, she had to admit it was the one that haunted her with her most cherished memories. Though it had been the day of Austin's father's funeral, it also marked the beginning of his feelings for her. Maybe even his love for her. She hadn't been a pest or his shadow anymore; she'd become his confidante. His friend. He'd been at his lowest. She had been the one to pull him out of that valley.

"What's yours, Katia?" Sarah asked, taking Timmy's plate and adding a dollop of mashed potatoes and some butternut squash.

Suddenly, all eyes were on Katia, and she felt like a butterfly being inspected by a lepidopterist. If she gave Austin the answer he clearly wanted to hear, he would know that she remembered the same day as he did. He might even read something into her answer that she didn't intend.

Katia was only beginning to understand her own psyche. She was experiencing panic attacks that had everything to do with her personal life—or lack of it—and nothing to do with her career, which was where she should have placed all her priorities. But if she didn't give Austin enough encouragement, he might retreat into his shell, and no one, especially her, would get him out.

The children were looking at her with more interest and anticipation than she'd imagined a child could muster. To them, her answer mattered a great deal, though she didn't know why. Was this their way of deciding if they liked her or not? Or was it just part of the way kids measured life, in spoonfuls of information?

"I like them all," Katia replied diplomatically.

"That's not right," Timmy howled. "You have to have a favorite. Everybody has a favorite!"

Katia's smile was impish. "Holidays are better than workdays, right? And all holidays mean that I don't have to work, and I can do whatever I want. Today, I chose to be with all of you." She turned to Austin.

Austin's entire expression softened. Gone was the reservation that held his shoulders in a rigid line and the tense crease that formed between his brows each time he talked about his business. He was surprisingly relaxed amid the children's banter and joined in their conversation about school, the upcoming Christmas pageant play and Annie's starring role as the angel.

Katia was surprised by her own mood, as well. As they all talked about seemingly mundane activities and the usual holiday chores of putting up lights, shopping and baking, Katia felt happy. This time of year usually produced a great deal of anxiety for her. She was often overwhelmed by trying to get everything done, going to parties and dealing with the overload of work as her clients rushed to alter their policies for the new year.

Something was different this year, and though she tried to analyze the factors, she couldn't put her finger on it. Katia had changed drastically since she'd moved to Indian Lake. She wished she knew the cause.

It always amazed Katia how fast the much-anticipated and laboriously prepared Thanksgiving dinner was consumed. Austin and Luke both had seconds on meat and stuffing, but the children kept reminding everyone to save room for pie.

"I knew we'd all be stuffed after dinner, so I purposefully decided to serve dessert at five when Maddie and Nate and Liz, Gabe and Sam can join us. Liz said she's bringing a surprise," Mrs. Beabots said.

"Mmm. I hope it's dessert wine," Luke said, rising to help clear plates.

Sarah joined him and took Timmy's plate.

"We have to wait for pie?" the little boy asked.

"Only half an hour," Sarah reminded him. "Besides, I still have to whip the cream. Don't worry, there are four pies this year. Pumpkin, apple, pecan and, of course, Mrs. Beabots's sugar pie."

"I want some of all of them," Annie announced. "But no whipped cream."

Austin laughed. "No whipped cream? Are you kidding? What's pie without whipped cream? Especially the real kind."

Annie smoothed the white pinafore of her pilgrim costume. "I think you're right, Mr. McCreary. I should have whipped cream on all my pies."

Austin laughed again and rose to help with the dishes.

After the table was cleared and the leftover food was carefully covered and put away in the refrigerator, the doorbell rang, announcing the rest of Mrs. Beabots's guests.

Katia accompanied her to the front door.

"Happy Thanksgiving!" Maddie exclaimed as everyone hugged Mrs. Beabots. "And, Katia. I'm so glad to see you. How are you?"

"Wonderful," Katia answered honestly.

"Are you settling in to our little town yet? It's a radical change from Chicago, isn't it? I know when I go into the city I'm already counting the hours until I come back here. I can't believe I once thought I wanted to live there. I have the best of both worlds now."

"I think I know what you mean. I'm not missing the city as much as I expected to."

Austin walked up behind Katia and shook Nate's hand. "Good to see you again," he said.

"Mrs. Beabots told us you were invited," Nate said to Austin. "Glad you could make it."

"I'd forgotten what a great cook Mrs. Beabots was. I've had a great time," Austin said, smiling broadly.

Nate turned to Mrs. Beabots and handed her a bouquet of fall-colored roses. "These are for you."

Maddie gave her a yellow-and-white-striped bakery box of cupcakes tied with her signature brown ribbon. "We just came from Nate's parents' house."

Mrs. Beabots smiled. "I know Gina had a lovely dinner for you all."

"She did, but it seemed strange to be there for Thanksgiving and not here with you."

"Well, having you here at all is a treat," Mrs. Beabots said. "Thanksgiving dessert will be our new tradition."

"I like that already," Maddie replied, giving Mrs. Beabots another hug. "Don't you just love the holidays?"

"I do. And I have to admit that Thanksgiving is my favorite."

The doorbell rang again. "That'll be Liz and Gabe," Maddie said excitedly.

Liz, Gabe and Sam arrived with two bottles of ice wine. In the dining room, Sarah had set out the pies, plates, forks and whipped cream. Hot coffee filled a silver urn on the hunt board and there was cold milk for the children. Everyone chose their favorite pie and made themselves comfortable in the front parlor.

Gabe turned to Mrs. Beabots. "Could I ask you for some dessert wineglasses?"

"I have just the thing," Mrs. Beabots replied. "They were my mother's. Come with me."

Gabe followed her to the kitchen and returned with a tray filled with tiny etched-crystal sherry glasses.

Katia, who sat next to Liz on the Victorian settee, noticed that Gabe didn't offer any wine to Liz. But Gabe was so busy talking to everyone and making certain they all had a glass that Katia let the slight pass.

"Does everyone have a glass?" Gabe asked, setting down the tray and raising his glass.

"Yes," the guests shouted.

"Good." He looked at Liz and smiled broadly. "Then, Liz and I want you, our best friends in Indian Lake, to know that next summer we, er, uh—there will be an addition to our group." He laughed as he stumbled through his announcement. "Sorry. I didn't think this would be so difficult."

Katia whirled around to look at Liz. Sure enough, Liz was beaming radiantly at Gabe.

"A baby?" Katia nearly gasped.

Liz only nodded, never taking her eyes off Gabe. She mouthed the words *I love you.*

"I love you, darling," Gabe said.

"This is so fast!" Katia said to Liz. "I feel as though I've still got the rice from your wedding in my hair."

Liz blushed. "That's how I feel," she whispered. "It's just so…"

"Ideal?"

"Yes, Katia." Liz squeezed her arm affectionately. "I wish every woman in the world could feel what I feel."

Katia lowered her eyes as she drank in Liz's joy, which was almost tangible. "So do I."

Luke slapped Gabe on the back. "I'm really happy for you, man."

Annie tugged on Sarah's sleeve. "Are they going to have a baby for real?"

"Yes, sweetheart. For real. Isn't it delightful?" Sarah smiled and hugged Annie.

Mrs. Beabots clapped her hands together. "What a Thanksgiving present this is!"

Austin stood and shook Gabe's hand. "Congratulations. That's terrific news, Gabe. Since you were at your parents' house for dinner, I assume you just told them, as well?"

"We did. My mother is over the moon, as you can imagine. I think she's almost forgiven us for not having a big wedding."

"Well, this should make her happy," Austin replied.

Timmy sank his fork into the apple pie and took a big bite. Chewing thoughtfully, he finally said, "I hope it's a boy so I can play with him."

Liz leaned toward Timmy, who was sitting on the floor at Sarah's feet. "As soon as we find out, I'll call Sarah and tell her, okay?"

Timmy's eyes filled his face. "We'll be the first to know?"

"After Gabe, yes. I promise." Liz winked at Sarah.

Katia felt Austin's eyes on her. She knew he was watching her and registering her reaction to all this. A few months ago, one of her best girlfriends had announced her pregnancy, and though Katia was thrilled for her, she'd felt sad. In a very selfish way, it meant her friend would have less time for her. Less shopping. Less theater. Less camaraderie.

How was it possible that in Indian Lake, everything felt different? Instead of feeling hurt, she was daydreaming about what it would be like to hold Liz's baby. She thought of the shower she would plan with Mrs. Beabots and Sarah. Of the fun she would have visiting Liz and watching the little one grow. Quickly, she said a prayer that the baby would be healthy.

Katia felt something click in her brain, as if the train of her life had just switched tracks again. The rails she'd been riding weren't taking her where she wanted or needed to go any longer. She was headed in a new direction, though she didn't remember making any conscious decision to change course.

She met Austin's eyes and smiled. He returned her smile and tipped his glass toward her. The excited voices around them dimmed to a subtle hum in the background. For just a second, Katia felt as if she was back in that glittering bubble she'd occupied when she was young and her world had been centered on Austin. She'd been truly happy then, though she hadn't realized it until just now.

Mrs. Beabots had suggested that Austin might still be in love with her.

It wasn't until this moment that Katia realized she was in love with Austin.

A tide of emotions swept over and under her, as if she was a surfer who'd just snagged the wrong tip of a curl. She floundered, choking on the revelation. Before it filled her lungs and suffocated her, she reached for the light and broke the surface.

She was in love with Austin. Not the Austin of the past, but the Austin she knew now. She loved the sensitive, committed man he had become. The man who'd grabbed hold of his responsibilities to his father's business and never complained; the man who generously helped his employees and cared about his community; the man who'd invested in a young Maddie Strong when she'd had no hope for financial aid. She knew that loving him meant accepting his flaws and his reclusive tendencies. She understood that many of his behaviors likely stemmed from a fear of commitment, an avoidance of romantic relationships.

Katia knew all about that. There was a reason she didn't have a ring on her left hand. She had no wedding planned and there was absolutely no room in her head for thoughts about babies or a family of her own.

In a split second, Katia felt her airway close off as if it had been cauterized. Her hand flew to her throat, but this time, she let her eyes settle on Austin's smiling face. He didn't know what was going on with her as she struggled to remain calm.

She matched his smile with one of hers. The terror abated. She took a deep breath.

I'm in love with Austin.

As she said the words over and over in her head, she felt the tension ease, and her breathing return to normal. Then she realized that her heart had been trying to tell her that what she really wanted was not just a family of her own, but a life with Austin. A family with Austin.

Fantastic, Katia. And for you, there's not a more perfect recipe for disaster than to fall in love with a client.

CHAPTER TWENTY

KATIA NOTICED THAT Mrs. Beabots was getting tired as the guests said their good-nights. Only she and Austin remained, and there was at least two hours' worth of cleanup yet to do, so Katia quickly volunteered.

"You stay in the parlor and rest. I'll get you some chamomile tea, and I'll take care of the kitchen for you."

"I'll help," Austin said cheerily.

Katia eyed him. "You are going to wash dishes? Are you sure you know how?"

He feigned insult with his fist over his heart. "You really know how to hurt a guy. I've had kitchen detail plenty of times."

"Like when? You have Daisy."

"She has Saturday and Sunday nights off. What kind of boss do you think I am?"

Mrs. Beabots smiled. "I have to say, this is one Thanksgiving when I wouldn't say no to two dishwashers."

"I didn't know a holiday could be this, well, fun. And delicious," Austin said.

"Oh, Austin." Mrs. Beabots gave him her best pooh-pooh look. "Your mother was a wonderful cook and your Thanksgivings had to be fun. You just don't remember."

Austin didn't take his eyes from Katia. "I remember some of them."

Mrs. Beabots placed her chin in her hand and smiled. "I'm glad I could make this holiday a good one for you."

"Memories are important to me," Austin said. "But I guess you all have figured that out by now."

"Ah. The museum," Mrs. Beabots mused. "You're doing an admirable job preserving your father's car collection, Austin. You're to be commended for that."

"It's more than just that," he explained. "I want it to be a real historical gathering place. I want to preserve not just the cars but all the amazing and creative things my great-grandfather did when he worked at Duesenberg in Indianapolis."

"Oh, I think that's so lovely," Mrs. Beabots said ecstatically. "Especially since my husband's grandfather worked there, as well. Right alongside your great-grandfather, as I recall."

Austin opened his mouth to speak and shut it instantly. He tilted his head and peered at his hostess. "Raymond's grandfather? I don't know about him. But I do remember your husband quite well. He was a real character. You two were always off to a different foreign country every winter."

Mrs. Beabots smiled wistfully. "That was Raymond. Always looking for another adventure—or at least another business to invest in. Most of them were preposterous schemes. He was so easily bamboozled by a good sales pitch. Raymond liked to believe that he had his grandfather's knack for invention, but he didn't, poor thing," she said with a shake of her head.

"Invention?" Austin asked with a clip in his voice that put Katia on edge. Something was wrong.

"Why, yes. When Fred and August Duesenberg first began hand building their automobiles back in 1913, they lived in St. Paul. Raymond's grandfather, Joe Beabots, was not much more than a kid then, but he was just as much a self-taught engineer as they were. They hired him on, and he worked for through their bankruptcy in 1922 until 1937, when they had to close. Then Errett Lobban-Cord bought the Duesenberg company and their engineering skills, and they took Joe along with the deal. That's how the Beabots came to live in Indianapolis."

"I'm very curious as to what Joe invented, exactly," Austin said.

"Between you and me, not much, I wouldn't think. Whatever it was, I'm sure it wasn't anything momentous. Fred was the genius of the Duesenberg family. At least that's what Joe said, but Joe was always a modest man. There's a pile of old newspaper clippings in a scrapbook somewhere. I could try to find them for you, if it's important."

Katia watched Austin's jaw clench and shift as if he was biting back words. He'd shoved his hands into his pockets as he used to do when he was angry, but she didn't have the slightest idea why he'd be upset about Mrs. Beabots sharing her family's history with him. Frankly, it was generous of her landlord to draw Austin into her circle, include him in her holiday plans and even share her stories. Apparently, Austin was reading everything the wrong way.

"My father told me that my great-grandfather was responsible for those first dual overhead cams and that he even had significant input on the first hydraulic brakes ever offered on a passenger car."

"Ah! That was the Model A!" Mrs. Beabots exclaimed with a bright smile. "I remember now. They had such hopes for that car. It's interesting that you say that, though, because from what Joe always said, I got the impression that Fred and Augie didn't listen much to others' ideas. I think Joe was happy he got to hold the screwdrivers and wrenches, so to speak." She smiled up at Austin.

He pensively chewed his bottom lip.

"Austin, is something wrong?" Katia finally asked.

He rubbed his cheek with his palm. "I'm just a bit baffled because the stories I heard from my father were so different."

"How?" Katia pressed.

Austin's eyes clouded over and turned from blue to steel gray, as they did when he shut out the world and retreated inward. It was a look Katia didn't like at all.

"I always understood somehow that my great-grandfather was almost like a consultant to them. That Fred looked to him for ideas and input. Specifically, my father told me that it was my great-grandfather who created the lion's share of both those inventions, which were implemented in cars for a hundred years. If what Mrs. Beabots is saying is true, then Fred and August ran the show. They had underlings and apprentices, obviously, like Joe and my great-grandfather, but that was all. Certainly not co-inventors."

Mrs. Beabots's eyes were filled with empathy and concern. "I'm sorry if I crossed a line, Austin. I didn't mean to cause you any consternation.

On the contrary, I thought it was endearing that Joe and your great-grandfather might have shared experiences."

Austin squeezed her hand. "It's nothing to worry about. How could you know?"

"The truth is that none of us can really say what happened back then at all," Mrs. Beabots said. "I have hand-me-down stories from my husband's side of the family, and it's hard to tell how much they might have embellished the truth. I do know that when World War One came around and the Duesenbergs were building aviation and naval machines in Elizabeth, New Jersey, Joe was there. He was single then and practically a roustabout. He went wherever they went, tagging along like a lovesick puppy."

Austin's smile was thin. "I'm sure he was a great guy. And I'm sure there's truth behind the family history I was given, too."

"I'm sure there is, Austin," Katia agreed. "Maybe up in those old trunks in the attic you might find the documentation you need. I can't believe Hanna would ever have thrown away anything that important."

Austin released Mrs. Beabots's hand and glanced at Katia. "I think I should help you get to those dishes."

She could plainly see that his mind was miles away and a century back in time. "Forget the dishes. I can handle them myself. You have work to do, right?"

"Yes, I do," he replied, taking her hint. "Thank you for a delicious meal and a wonderful holiday, Mrs. Beabots."

"You're most welcome, Austin."

He turned to Katia. "Thanks. I guess I'll be seeing you."

Katia walked him to the door. Just as he stepped outside, she asked, "Are you all right?"

He shook his head. "I've just been told that my family history is a hoax. My museum is a theater of pure foolishness, and the dream I've held my entire adult life is now some kind of cosmic joke. No, Katia. I'm not all right, and I would ask that you keep all of this under the heading of 'client privilege.'"

"I'm not going to gossip about you, Austin."

"Great. That will make one person in Indian Lake."

She grabbed his arm and pulled him close to her. "I'm your friend, Austin. Not your enemy. When are you going to realize that?"

"Really? I thought you were my insurance agent."

He pulled his arm back and rushed down the steps to his car.

In the blink of an eye, Austin had sped away into the night shadows.

KATIA FINISHED THE dishes, dried the pots and
pans and put away the crystal. She brewed a
fresh cup of tea for Mrs. Beabots, who was doz-
ing in the tufted Victorian chair in the front
parlor.

"I made you some tea," Katia whispered,
wondering if she should wake her friend.

Mrs. Beabots opened her eyes. "I feel just terrible," she announced with a frown.

Katia was worried about Austin, but her heart
was filled with just as much empathy for Mrs.
Beabots, who had stumbled into a hornets' nest
of generations' old tales and legends. None of
this mess was her fault, and the worst part was
that Mrs. Beabots had thought she'd won back
Austin's friendship.

"What can I get you? What can I do?" Katia
asked.

Mrs. Beabots gestured for Katia to sit next to
her. "It's just heartsickness. I feel awful about
what I said to Austin. I have always made it a
habit not to meddle into other people's lives.
Goodness knows that I had plenty of people telling me what to do when I was young. I wouldn't
have hurt Austin's feelings for the world." She
rested her cheek against her palm and stared
up at Katia.

"You can't blame yourself. You were simply sharing your story. You had no idea that

he's been living under false pretenses all these years," Katia said heavily.

Mrs. Beabots slapped her thigh. "I'm ashamed of Hanna and Daniel for these…myths they've filled Austin's head with."

"What if it wasn't their fault, either?"

"What do you mean, Katia?"

"I lived in that house most of my childhood. Neither of them ever impressed me as duplicitous. What if the source of the problem goes all the way back to Austin's great-grandfather? Perhaps he created these stories to aggrandize himself in the eyes of the townspeople. When he came to Indian Lake, initially, after the Duesenberg plant shut down in 1937, he wasn't rich. I heard Daniel tell Austin that several times. Austin's great-grandfather, Ambrose, established the family business with his son, David, who was only about fifteen then."

"I see your point. The real truth is probably long buried with the past."

Katia nodded solemnly and looked down at her hands. "Austin has spent his whole life revering the past. He's come to believe all of his ancestors were better, smarter, more creative, more influential than he is. He doesn't understand his own worth."

Mrs. Beabots leaned forward and touched Katia's arm. "I have always believed that everything in this life happens for a reason. Even when we don't understand that reason at the exact moment we're seeking answers, we will understand eventually. I believe you came back to Indian Lake to save more than your boss's company, Katia. I believe there is a young man out there who has been floundering a bit too long. Mostly, I believe that we all have to save ourselves, but sometimes we can do that by helping others."

"You think I should go see Austin?"

"I do. And the sooner the better. He was very upset when he left."

Katia rose, leaned down and kissed Mrs. Beabots's forehead. "I know just where to find him."

A GENTLE SNOW had begun to fall outside, decorating the rooftops and bare tree branches.

Katia parked outside the McCreary mansion and walked to the back of the property. Not a single light was on in the house, which she'd expected.

She followed the curve of the driveway to the gate that led to the carriage houses. The entire backyard, tennis court and two of the carriage houses were pitch-dark. But the third carriage house was ablaze with lights.

Katia had learned to unlatch the gate long

ago, and tonight it opened easily for her. She knew Austin had left it unlocked on purpose. He was hoping she would come after him. She tried the carriage house door. It, too, was unlocked.

Rather than barge in, she knocked. One soft rap. Then three hard ones.

There was no answer. Katia took a deep breath for courage and opened the door.

"Austin?" She went inside, closed the door and looked around the garage.

Austin was bent over the engine of the blue Bugatti. His hands were covered with grease, and he wore an old pair of work overalls. He used to wear those overalls in high school, whenever he retreated to his sanctuary—just as he was doing now. She'd teased him then that the overalls were his armor against his parents, who wanted him to aspire to become head of the McCreary business and not just be a mechanic.

"Do you know that it was this Bugatti engine that caused the Duesenbergs to radically change nearly all their engineering ideas?" Austin said without taking his eyes off his work. "Sure, the First World War was coming about, but this straight-eight engine was actually two straight-four engines mounted in a series on an everyday crankcase with two flat crankshafts, which were both linked at ninety degrees to form a single shaft. The competition back then was crushing. The world was changing because of the war. They had to innovate to stay in the game. They landed an American contract to produce the engine for the French government, which would be used for war vehicles of all sorts." Austin stood and leveled his gaze at her.

He obviously wasn't surprised to see her. He acted as if her coming to him late at night was a habit. Something they'd been doing for years. "And that's the history of how the famous Duesenberg straight-eight engine came to be."

"Fascinating," she said, folding her arms across her chest, her head tilted to the right. "Do you mind telling me what any of that has got to do with your anger and your parting shots at me earlier this evening?"

He picked up a rag and wiped his hands. "History, Katia, is in its purest form the retelling of facts."

She harrumphed. "We both know that's not true. History is the filtered legends and myths of politicos who want to be remembered for things they did or didn't do."

"You are so jaded."

"And you, my friend, are being naive," she bantered back. This wasn't the time to assuage Austin's pain, but to set him straight. Though she had only just realized she was still in love with him, she couldn't allow her emotions to alter good judgment. In her opinion, Austin was off base in trying to give accolades and honors to his great-grandfather when it was possible that the man didn't deserve them at all. Why couldn't he see that *he* was a worthy person, perhaps even more so than Ambrose or his father? Austin had never manipulated the truth to aggrandize himself. She believed he was the best of all the McCrearys.

"Katia, the museum walls were finished this week. The masons will be bricking through most of December, if it doesn't get much colder. I'm very serious about my position in all of this."

"I know you are, Austin. I'm not telling you to abandon the museum."

"Then, what are you saying?"

"Simply that I want you to broaden your scope. Let's just say that your great-grandfather didn't actually design anything. But he was there, Austin. He chose to work with inventors, trying to build cars that could race in the Indianapolis 500. Only the visionaries of the day would risk their lives and futures on a couple of immigrants who clearly were not businessmen, who went bankrupt, who were always scrambling for investors. Frankly, it's your great-grandfather's loyalty that I see. He never gave up on them until they closed down for good. Isn't that right?"

"Yes," he said quietly, slipping the rag into the back pocket of his overalls. "Like I said, that's when he moved his family here."

"And what did he do here?"

"He built his auto-parts company."

Nodding, Katia took another step forward. "That's right. I bet he started with no more than a secretary and an associate or two at first."

"My grandmother did the accounting, typing, answered the phones."

"Ah." Katia's eyes brightened. "So there's another unsung hero in your story."

Austin held up his hand to stop her. "Where are you going with this?"

"I'm trying to show you that heroes aren't only the guys who go through a war with guns blazing or whip out a scalpel and save lives. Many heroes—the ones who built this country—are quiet men. Men like Ambrose, who believed in their mentors. Believed that what little they could do or were allowed to do in their jobs mattered. A hundred years ago, men risked their lives every day to build skyscrapers. I worked for a decade in a skyscraper in Chicago, and every single day I thanked those men, long dead now, who worked so hard so that I had a nice place to do my job. And that made me think of my father, a Russian immigrant like many of those workers, who made so many sacrifices for me."

Austin remained silent, but she could tell from the intensity in his eyes that he was listening to her. Really listening.

She continued, "I've never been a gossip, Austin, and to my knowledge neither is Mrs. Beabots. Apparently, she keeps secrets better than anyone I've ever met. She didn't intend to hurt you, and I have her word to you that she will never say anything that you don't want said about your family. Her own family history is her business. She only wanted to share it with you. She thought it would bring you closer together, not split you apart."

"I understand that, Katia. I'm not blaming her. I've always liked her a lot. Sometimes I even thought she empathized with me when my parents were giving me a hard time."

Katia's voice softened. "She told me she was always fond of you."

"I guess I felt that."

"Austin…" Katia moved very close and put her hand on his cheek. "I hope you understand what I'm saying. I think you're one of those silent heroes. I think what you've done, taking over the family business and running it all these years, even though you would rather have been playing tennis or making a living trading in antique cars, is worthy of admiration and respect. You didn't close the plant, and you could have. You're loyal to your workers. Because of you, I met Melanie, and she's probably one of the best assistants I've ever had. Jack and I talking about making her a sales associate. So you see? Even if your great-grandfather didn't actually invent some part of the Duesenberg engine—or even a headlight—that doesn't diminish what he did. He was there. He stayed right to the very end."

Austin placed his hand over hers and removed it from his cheek. He attempted a smile, but it fell quickly from his face.

"Thanks. But the problem is that even on the brochures I printed up for the presentation, which you attended—"

"Crashed," she interjected lightly, hoping to brighten his dour mood.

He ignored her joke. "On that brochure, I made a point that my great-grandfather was instrumental in several breakthroughs that helped to create the Model J supercar."

Katia thought for a long moment. "Did your father ever tell you what he did specifically for that car?"

"The chassis and suspension were conventional. Nothing new there. But the SJ had a forced induction that raised the power and helped increase the speed from 116 miles per hour to 129. That was an enormous breakthrough back then."

"And so when your father said that, you understood that it was your great-grandfather who'd been responsible, not Fred."

"I did," he replied glumly. He shoved his hands into his pockets. "So you see? I was right. People will think I'm an idiot."

"Stop saying that! You're making me nuts. Okay?"

"Look, this isn't your problem. It's my family and my mistake."

Katia felt dismissed, just like she used to when Hanna wanted her out of the way. Katia despised this feeling, and she'd learned over time to beat it back with fiery anger.

"Get over yourself, Austin. Don't come at me with your retreat taps blowing. It's simple. You dig through all those papers in the attic and find what facts you can. Then you mount the best ones and display them. I know you've got old photos of your great-grandfather standing with Fred and August Duesenberg next to one of their racing cars. Play down everything except what you can substantiate.

"You told me you wanted a museum here to preserve history. Let it be just that. Make a room in the museum that allows other families to present information about their own heritage, their family or associates who did noteworthy things. You could have one room dedicated to local sports alone. Use your brain, Austin."

Suddenly, Austin was smiling broadly.

"What?"

"I forgot about the fire you carry around in that belly of yours. You really come alive when there's a fight, don't you?"

Katia exhaled through her nose, her inner heat dissipating. "That's true."

"See? That's what I envy about you. You're so passionate, Katia. You fight for your job and your clients, but you're also willing to take on challenges for me. Why is that?" He moved closer to her so that they were only a breath apart.

His eyes searched hers.

"Because I don't want to see you hurt anymore, Austin. Maybe it's my way of making up for the past when I was the one who did the hurting."

"Maybe."

She couldn't tear her eyes from his face. For years, she and Austin had lived in a world where this was all that existed. They'd practically thought each other's thoughts. Now things were different.

"So you're just balancing out the karma, coming to my aid like this."

"I guess."

"You don't know?"

She could tell him that she was falling in love with him again, but then she'd be throwing away her career. Katia felt as if she was being sliced in two. Either choice left her with a half-life. She wanted it all.

And what of Austin? He was a man consumed with his family's past. His attention to his car collection teetered on obsession. How would she fit into that world? Austin remembered the young girl she'd been, but did he care to get to know the person she'd become? And if he did, could he ever really commit to her, especially since he apparently didn't completely trust her? They were adults now, not naive children. Did he feel anything for her that was true and real?

Katia believed in insurance against risk. She preached it every day, but this gamble was much too precarious.

"I've always been your friend, Austin. Even when I left and hurt you so badly, in the end, it was the right thing to do. I would have ruined your life."

His steady gaze wavered as he tilted his head back slightly. "I don't know about that."

"Well, I'm sure. Waiting around for you to

finish school would have made me even more needy and clingy than I already was. I couldn't stand being away from you. We would have ended up married—think how young we were! Our mothers would have been livid. We would never have had a chance to grow as individuals. One or both of us would have had to give something up—education, our careers—to stay together. You would have resented me, and knowing my temper, I would have picked fights with you daily. I would have destroyed us."

Austin stepped back. "Well, that's really bleak."

"It's the truth."

"I've always liked my version better," he replied longingly.

Rolling her eyes and clucking her tongue, she said, "Maybe that's the real fissure between us, Austin. I deal with facts. Stats. Charts and graphs. You reminisce. You fantasize about the not quite real. Then you live there...or here." She gestured toward the house. "Alone."

Austin retreated from her as if she'd thrown ice water into his face. He took his hands out of his pockets, turned away and closed the Bugatti hood. "I'm done," he said.

"That didn't come out right. I'm sorry. I just meant—"

"Oh, you said it fine," he replied. "But it's nearly midnight. You'd better go."

"Happily," she shot back, taking a pair of gloves out of her coat pocket. "Looks to me like my assessment was dead-on. Tell you what, Austin. If you ever want a real friend, call me. Maybe you don't like what I'm saying, but that's what friends are for. Happy Thanksgiving."

Katia let herself out. The snow was coming down in large, fluffy flakes that clung to her hair. She lifted the gate latch and walked down the driveway, her boots leaving clear prints in the snow. There was no wind to disturb the still, cold night, but Katia's angry heat dispelled the chill.

Driving away, she realized that she was just as guilty of retreat as Austin was.

But in all wars, especially those waged in the name of love, there was time to regroup. Katia could only hope this was just that time.

CHAPTER TWENTY-ONE

BLACK FRIDAY CAME and went without Katia visiting a single retail store. Saturday dragged on without a call from Austin and no answers to her texts or emails. She'd tried to be light and funny in her messages, but he was pulling his turtle act again.

On Sunday, after church services at St. Mark's, Katia drove Mrs. Beabots, Timmy and Annie back home while Sarah and Luke remained at the church to help organize the Christmas decoration committee.

Mrs. Beabots promised to watch Timmy and Annie for a half hour until Sarah came back home. "I suppose we could start by decorating my Christmas tree," Mrs. Beabots said to the children.

"You have a tree already?" Annie asked.

"It's being delivered by the Indian Lake nursery. They put in a tree stand for me and put it up in the big window in the living room."

"How big?" Timmy asked.

"Oh, the usual. Ten feet," Mrs. Beabots said proudly.

Katia's mouth fell open. "You have a ten-foot tree every year?"

Both children were clapping their hands and high-fiving each other.

"It's gonna be so cool!" Timmy said.

"I thought that this year we would make gingerbread men and put yarn through their heads and hang them on the tree," Mrs. Beabots said.

"That's sounds lovely," Katia offered, thinking wistfully of the small tree her mother had decorated for the two of them and put in their room at the McCreary house. "And you decorate this tree by yourself? No offense, but you must need a tall ladder."

"Oh, good heavens, no, dear. Lester MacDougal comes over and puts all the lights and ornaments on. I'll let the children hang the cookies and some candy canes. They'll love that."

"Oh, yes!" The children said in unison.

Katia pulled into Mrs. Beabots's driveway. The snow had all melted, and the sun had warmed the chrysanthemum blossoms. She turned off the car and everyone climbed out.

"So what kind of tree does Sarah have for you?" Katia asked the kids.

Mrs. Beabots laughed. "I don't know why they get so excited about *my* tree. Sarah's tree was fourteen feet tall last year, and it was a mass of all her old ornaments, Luke's ornaments and cookies the children made. It was a vision. She told me she had over two thousand lights on that tree."

"Two thousand!" Katia's eyes grew wide.

Mrs. Beabots led the way to the back door and they all filed inside, shucking their coats. Mrs. Beabots had put a pot roast, onions, carrots, celery and potatoes in a roaster and had started the oven before they left for church. The aroma of the cooking dinner was heavenly as they entered the warm, cozy kitchen.

Timmy spotted a glass-domed cake plate filled with cupcakes. "Are those from Miss Maddie?"

"Yes, they are, Timmy. Would you like one?"

"Yes, please!"

Annie frowned. "He's not supposed to have treats before Sunday dinner. Me, neither."

Katia watched as light faded from Timmy's face. "What if you two split the cupcake and drank a glass of milk with it? They're small, and I don't think your mom would be too upset about that."

Annie calculated the proposition for a long moment. "We're having chicken and peas. And I'm hungry for both. So I guess a half a cupcake would be okay."

"Yes!" Timmy shouted. "Can we have the chocolate one?"

"Absolutely," Mrs. Beabots replied, taking the dome off the plate.

"I'll get the milk," Katia said. She took out two plates and two small glasses from the cupboard.

Mrs. Beabots got the children settled at the small kitchen table near the back window so they could watch for Luke's truck.

She turned to Katia. "I saw that mind of yours whirling a minute ago. What are you scheming?"

"We have to get Austin's house decorated for the Candlelight Tour next weekend. Right?"

"Well, yes."

"When I spoke with Daisy, she said Wednesday would be best. Austin will be at work, and she can help us. Sarah will have half a day off. Between the four of us, we can get the downstairs decorated in one afternoon. But I didn't plan for the tree. Hanna used to have a lovely tree in the living room window."

"I remember. And Austin hasn't put up a tree since she died."

"That's because he's never here over the holidays."

"Is he going to be home this year?" Mrs. Beabots asked.

After my last argument with him? Probably not. "He hasn't said. But I'm thinking that it's time he makes some changes. Starting with a live Christmas tree. Do you have the number for the nursery?"

KATIA CALLED AUSTIN'S house and got his voice mail, which she expected. She hoped he was only pouting and not so angry with her that they couldn't get back to being friends.

Or more.

Don't even go there, Katia. Don't make trouble you can't handle. One thing at a time. One day at a time.

"Austin. If you don't answer me, I'll break into your house again. That is, assuming you haven't changed the locks. So look. Cops or no cops, I'm coming over. I have a surprise for you."

The Indian Lake Nursery delivery truck pulled up to Austin's house just as Katia turned into his driveway in her newly purchased silver Buick sedan. She supposed Austin would sneer at such an ordinary car, but it was only two years old and had low mileage. She purposefully didn't park on the street; if Austin attempted a getaway, she wanted to block him in.

"Hey, guys!" She waved to the driver and his

helper as she withdrew several shopping bags from her car trunk. "I'll be right with you."

She walked quickly to the door and pressed the bell twice. The melodious and preposterous tune played loud enough to be heard outside. "He needs to change this thing," she muttered, rubbing her chilled hands together.

The door swung open. Austin was wearing tan wool dress pants and a navy V-neck pullover with a white shirt underneath. Though his mouth was set, his eyes were welcoming.

She took that as a good sign. "Hi. You got my message."

"Why must you insist on giving me no choice about seeing you?"

"Did you change the locks?" she asked pointedly.

"No."

"Then, you want to see me. I'm here on community business."

"Excuse me?"

She hooked her thumb back over her shoulder. "They're here to deliver your Christmas tree."

"I don't want a tree."

"Sorry. You committed to this. I have exactly one week to get this house ready for the Candlelight Tour." She smiled at his blank expression. "You forgot."

"I did. I didn't. I mean, I didn't forget about the tour, just that it's coming up so fast."

"Right." She waved the guy in, then she turned back to Austin. "I know where it goes. You and I have furniture to move. Let's get to it."

Katia barged past Austin and headed straight to the living room. She placed her shopping bags on the floor, took off her coat and flung it over a wing chair. Then she grabbed the framed pictures off the end table that sat between two French chairs in the middle of the window.

She looked back at Austin. "Don't just stand there. Move these chairs to that far corner, where your mother used to put them at Christmas."

Austin shook his head, chuckling to himself, and easily hoisted the chair. Then he moved the brass and glass lamp and the end table.

The space was cleared just in time for the deliverymen to bring in the tree. Austin grabbed two black garbage bags from the kitchen to protect the wood floor, and Katia positioned the stand she'd bought on top of them. The guys from the nursery cut the jute ties around the branches, fluffed out the limbs and spun the tree until the fullest side was facing the room.

"If you have lights, we can string them for you," the taller of the two men said.

"I'll put the lights on," Austin said before Katia had a chance to reply. "Thanks anyway." He took out his wallet and handed the men a tip. "Thanks for your help. It's a great tree."

Austin walked the men to the door while Katia began digging boxes of lights out of her shopping bags.

"What's all this? We have lights."

She cocked her head. "Oh, really? And you think that after a decade plus they'll still work? Fat chance. I bought clear lights just like your mother used to have."

"I like the colored ones," he countered.

"I thought you might. I bought ten strings of those, too."

"You did not," he bantered. He peered into the bag.

"I also got a step-touch surge protector so that the lights are easy to turn off and on." She held up a small square box. "If that's too much trouble for you, though, here's a timer that will turn them on at dusk and off at ten."

"You thought of everything," he said appreciatively.

"I tried to." She smiled at him as she stood and handed him a strand of lights. "If we do this together, we should have the tree lit in less than an hour. Then we can get the boxes from the attic."

Austin plugged the surge protector into the wall and attached the first string of lights from the box. "Look at that, would you?"

"What?"

"The lights are so…well, merry. Pardon the pun. And I'd forgotten how uplifting the smell of a fresh pine tree can be. Reminds me of…"

"When we were kids?"

"Yeah, it does." He looked away from her and back to his work.

KATIA WAS BUSY unraveling the lights and chattering away about the things she remembered from her childhood Christmases in this house. Austin was only half listening; Katia's voice was a familiar sound that had always comforted and befriended him.

Ever since Thanksgiving, he'd been acting like a spoiled brat. Arrogant and selfish. At the time, he didn't care if he hurt Katia's feelings. He rationalized that he was licking his wounds.

But Katia had overlooked all his bad behavior. She'd called, texted and emailed him. He'd read all her messages, despite the long hours he'd spent on his cars, trying to kill the sense of betrayal he felt from his own family.

Maybe Katia was right. Maybe he was guilty of focusing on the wrong things. A true bene-factor only cared that the lives of the people receiving his gifts were elevated, illuminated or educated. In the end, it probably didn't matter to anyone but Austin if his great-grandfather was an inventor or not. He'd started a business in Indian Lake that had employed people for generations. That was fact.

Though Austin's mind whirled with thoughts about his ancestors, it was the sound of Katia's voice that broke through and brought him back to the present.

"I like to bring the lights deeper into the tree on the big branches, so the tree is lit from within," she was saying.

Together, they worked their way up the tree, stringing lights and changing an ordinary spruce into something magical. Austin hadn't decorated a Christmas tree since his mother died. In fact, he didn't remember decorating one since the last Christmas that Katia had lived in this house.

Katia had told him she wanted to be his friend. She was doing what a real friend would do. He knew she hadn't needed to go to all this trouble to buy precisely the kind of Norwegian spruce his mother always loved. She'd remembered that he liked colored lights, not the designer white ones that usually graced his family tree. And she'd come here tonight, after allowing him a couple days to cool down and think about everything she'd said.

Katia had some kind of sixth sense when it came to him. He would have been creeped out if anyone else knew him so well, but since it was Katia, Austin didn't mind in the least. He liked the way she read his moods and always appeared to come at his problems from a new perspective. She was logical and saw things without the "family filter" he used much too often.

Maybe Katia had been right when she'd accused him of retreating from his problems too often. He'd done that ever since Katia had left town. But that was a kid's reaction to life's problems. It wasn't what adults did. Katia had proved that to him. The more he slid back into his cave, the more she showed up at the door. Or broke in.

He was lucky to be able to count Katia as a real friend. She was good for him.

But was he good for her? He knew she needed his business. That was obvious. She'd also needed him to forgive her. She'd told him that she wanted to move forward with her life, and she couldn't do that without his forgiveness. Though they'd crossed that bridge, he wondered if lingering guilt caused Katia to be this attentive to him.

And if it was just residual guilt, then the relationship they had was based on need, not want.

"Austin, did you hear anything I just said?"

"Sorry, I was concentrating on the lights. What?"

"I asked if you wanted to do something different with your tree. We could string popcorn and cranberries and decorate it with candy canes and gingerbread men instead of your mother's priceless ornaments. I bet Daisy wouldn't mind making some cookies and putting yarn through them for us."

"That's…really old-fashioned. Do people even do that anymore?"

"Mrs. Beabots said she does a bit of that for Annie and Timmy. It got me thinking. Maybe we should make a childhood tree." She looked up at the dainty multicolored lights. "Something for both of us," she whispered as if she hadn't meant for him to hear it.

But he had.

Suddenly, Austin realized that the tree was a symbol of new beginnings for both of them. Perhaps Katia could put all her guilt aside. He had a houseful of ghosts, and he'd lived with them forever. Maybe it was time for him to do what Katia had suggested and start asking if he wanted more for himself than to build monuments to the past.

"We'll call it a sugarplum tree, and it will be perfect," Austin replied.

CHAPTER TWENTY-TWO

FOR THE REST of the week, Katia held meetings with potential clients, interviewed a new sales associate that Barry had recommended and continued to decorate the McCreary mansion. She even hired a trio of trumpeters to wear Edwardian costumes and stand on Austin's front lawn under a lamppost and play carols during the Candlelight Tour.

She'd strung all the crystal lights she'd bought in the shrubbery around the front door. Sarah had made a garland with battery-operated lights for the elegant staircase banister, which Katia wired into place. Mrs. Beabots had proudly decorated a fresh spruce wreath with red velvet ribbon, red silk roses and gold glass balls. Katia hung it on Austin's front door.

By the time Sunday afternoon arrived, Katia had discarded six outfits before finally settling on a black skirt and a red cowl-neck angora sweater. She wore her hair tumbling down her back.

Just the way Austin likes it.

Katia studied her reflection in the bathroom mirror and wondered if there was truth to that saying about magic at the holidays.

It only comes to those who believe.

For the first time since she'd left Indian Lake, Katia believed in a lot of things she'd packed away along with her youth. Somehow, all those hopes and dreams seemed appropriate in this town. They seemed to come alive here, as if there was something about Indian Lake that let them come true.

It was the holidays. Things happened at the holidays that couldn't always be explained. Authors wrote about these things in novels. Movies were made about mystical situations that defied all reason. People were nicer and went out of their way to help others at this time of year. So there had to be some truth to it all.

Was it too much for Katia to hope that Austin would see that she was in love with him? Would he ever get past the pain she'd caused him when they were young? Was that why he held back from her? Was it possible that he could put all his other priorities aside long enough to reach into his heart and realize that she was the woman for him?

Was it just make-believe that caused her to think that she'd figure out a way to convince Jack to change company policy?

Though Katia's head swam with misgivings and fear, there was no panic. Her heart was steady. Her breathing was normal. Katia was ready for the tour.

THE CANDLELIGHT TOUR was nothing that Austin had expected. He'd planned to put on his poker face, endure the night, meet total strangers whose faces he'd never remember. And when it was over, he hoped he could share a port by the fire with Katia.

Instead, he was greeted by people he hadn't seen since his mother died. Others, he hadn't seen since his father's funeral. Old employees, canes in hand, hobbled into the house, not to see decorations, but to use the opportunity to pay their respects to Austin and to thank him and his family for the years of employment they enjoyed. The men told stories of the early years when they were teenagers coming to work at the McCreary plant.

"There are few plants in the world that do what you do, Mr. McCreary," one rheumy-eyed ninety-year-old said as he leaned on his son's arm. "I always took pride in that. You're one in a million."

Austin was shocked at how much the older man's words meant to him. It was all he could do to keep the rumble of emotion out of his throat. Then it hit him. Austin had lived a solitary life for so long that he hadn't made the same kinds of social connections other people had. When he was at the plant, he was the employer. His employees didn't consider him their friend. They didn't meet him on the same court, like Rafe. Or Katia.

"I'm looking forward to the museum opening," a middle-aged woman said. "I have two sons who love antique cars. They're counting the days. Will you still open on St. Patrick's Day?"

"My contractor assures me we're on schedule," Austin replied proudly.

"It's a great service to the community," a tall, gangly man in his fifties said to Austin as he shook his hand. "Thank you for all you're doing for us."

The rest of the afternoon proceeded in much the same manner. A steady stream of visitors came to the house, complimented Austin on the museum and asked Katia about the Christmas tree, which they had dubbed the sugar-plum tree. She was quick to give credit to Mrs. Beabots, who'd taught her how to make marzipan fruits dusted with sugar. She'd hung them on the tree with nearly one hundred cookies in the shapes of snowflakes, stars, Santas, mittens and snowmen.

Daisy stood at the dining room table and served up plastic cups of homemade wassail, complete with floating baked apples for the guests. As the night grew darker and the crowds dwindled, Austin almost felt sad that the tour was winding down.

Katia left the living room and came to stand next to Austin at the front door. "It's been going really well, I think."

Austin smiled. "I've loved it," he said, turning to kiss Katia's cheek. He put his arm around the back of her waist and leaned into her. "Thank you for all you did, Katia. I had no idea how much fun I would have. I've seen friends of my father's I haven't seen for twenty years. And my mother's old friends, too. I can't believe I lost track of them."

"I'm glad you're happy, Austin."

"Me, too, Katia."

The moment was broken by the sound of someone clearing his throat.

Standing in the doorway, wearing a black wool coat and a very dark scowl, was Jack Carter.

IF JACK HAD blown in on the north wind, his presence couldn't have been more chilling.

Katia was quick to notice that Jack's gaze was fixed on Austin's hand at her waist. She hadn't noticed his hand, only his comforting arm around her back. Still, she was standing in the circle of Austin's embrace, as loose as it was.

Katia felt like a little kid caught stealing from the candy jar.

"Hi, Jack! How good of you to come and support the Indian Lake Heritage Foundation," she said brightly, trying to wrench away from Austin.

The flash of anger in Austin's eyes looked like lightning.

Katia remembered that expression. She'd seen it plenty of times when they were kids.

As she beamed at Jack, she felt the heat of Austin's eyes on her, but she pretended to ignore him and his foul mood.

Jack walked forward and extended his hand to Austin. "Glad to be here," he said in a clipped tone. Katia knew that the smile he offered to Austin was forced.

Katia figured there were at least a dozen words Jack would have liked to use at that moment, but he was much too polished to do so.

"Have you enjoyed the tour so far?" Austin asked with an equally forced smile.

He slipped his hand back around Katia's waist and actually tried to pull her closer to him.

There was no way Jack could miss the gesture, and sure enough, he was staring at the negligible space between them.

What was Austin thinking? He knew that Jack frowned on any kind of intimacy between agents and clients. Was Austin throwing Jack a gauntlet? And why would he put her in such a tenuous position? He knew that her career meant everything to her. She didn't believe for a minute that Austin was being arrogant. But possessive? Absolutely.

Though she knew she was walking that same tightrope again between Austin and her career, she felt her anger rise to an inferno. She'd always had self-control, nearly to a fault, and tonight she needed every bit of it to beat back her emotions.

Feeling the pressure of Austin's hand against her waist, it hit Katia that perhaps this wasn't about Jack at all. What if the Christmas spirit and the ambiance of the night had whisked Austin back to the past when she had been his and his alone? What if he was subconsciously displaying his true feelings for her?

What do you feel for me, Austin? Do you care about me still? And if you do, why can't you just say so?

The sound of Austin's voice broke through her thoughts as he carried on a polite conversation with Jack.

"I just got back into town, so this is the only one I'll have time to visit," Jack replied. "Judging by the music outside and how inviting you've made this, I should have returned earlier."

Austin turned to Katia with a dazzling smile. "It was all Katia, believe me," he said. "She had really great ideas. Wait till you see her sugar-plum tree in the living room. It's—"

"Right through this doorway," Katia interjected quickly, moving away from Austin and gesturing to the living room. Another couple and two children walked in the front door behind Jack, and Austin turned his attention to them.

"Curt and Sherry! How great to see you. Come in!"

Jack paused next to Katia before entering the living room. "I'll see you at the office in the morning," he whispered.

"I have an eight-o'clock meeting. I should be finished by nine-thirty."

"That's fine," he said coldly.

Katia swallowed the lump of nerves that threatened to choke her. She had to figure out how to handle this. She couldn't deny what Jack had seen. Meanwhile, she'd only recently won back Austin's trust, but not once had he said anything that led her to believe there was anything between them but friendship. That was why his possessiveness tonight didn't ring true to her. Maybe Austin was simply trying to show up Jack, as if she was some kind of trophy in a game. If so, then this wasn't the same Austin she'd known long ago. Of course, people changed; she certainly had. But she hoped she was wrong.

Katia was stupefied by the irony of her situation. Just a few months ago, when she'd moved here, she'd asked only that Austin would forgive her for the past, and that he'd consider her business deal. Now she was only a few months away from his signature on the remaining contracts that would make him her largest client ever.

She'd gotten precisely what she'd asked for, and she'd never been so unhappy. All these years, she'd never guessed that she was still in love with Austin or that she would fall in love with him all over again.

Tonight she'd managed to anger both Austin and Jack. There was a real possibility she could lose everything.

CHAPTER TWENTY-THREE

KATIA KNEW THAT if one was about to face down a foe, it was best to enter the battlefield with plenty of ammunition and, at the very least, diversionary tactics.

Jack was in his office with the door shut when Katia arrived after meeting with a potential new client. She took off her coat and hung it up, then went immediately to Melanie's desk.

"I told Jack I'd meet with him at nine-thirty. I hear voices. Is he on the phone?"

Melanie shook her head. "He's interviewing a new associate."

Katia's eyes grew wide with disbelief. She hadn't had a chance to tell her side of the story yet and Jack was already replacing her? Obviously, he was very serious about his policy against dating clients.

"Do you know anything about him?" Katia asked.

Melanie lifted a sheet of paper. "*She* is from South Bend. She brings clients with her, and she's willing to move to town rather than commute." Melanie handed the resume to Katia.

One glance told Katia that Claire Ebberhart had a BA from St. Mary's College and she'd worked a variety of jobs in accounting and banking before settling into the insurance world. "If she's even halfway personable, I'd hire her," Katia said. "She looks very good on paper."

"They've been in there for over an hour. That's a rather long interview, isn't it?"

"Jack hired me in less than twenty minutes. He prides himself on going with his gut."

Katia went to her desk, checked her phone messages, turned on her computer and glanced at her emails. She was just returning a quick text to Sarah when Jack walked out of his office with Claire.

"Thank you for taking so much time with me, Jack," the dark-haired, slender woman said.

Jack shook Claire's hand. "I'll be in touch. Melanie has all your contact information. Have a safe drive back home."

"I will," Claire said, extending her hand to him.

Katia couldn't tell if Jack was ignoring her or if he simply hadn't seen her. It wasn't like him not to introduce her to a potential employee. Not unless he considered Katia an ex-employee.

This was no time to fade into the background. Katia stood up and walked around her desk. "Hello, I'm Katia Stanislaus. You must be Claire Ebberhart." Katia held out her hand.

Jack's eyes tracked from Claire to Katia. "I didn't see you, Katia. Just get in, did you?" he asked pointedly.

If that's how Jack wanted to play this, Katia was ready for him. "Yes, I did," Katia replied, gracing Claire with a bright smile. "I had a breakfast meeting with a large client this morning and just got that contract signed. Most corporate clients expect to meet on their turf. Accommodating them is key to winning their business."

"Oh, I absolutely agree," Claire confirmed.

Jack instantly dropped his acerbic expression. "I'll be in touch, Claire."

"Thanks," she replied, heading out the door.

Jack gestured toward his office. "I believe we have a meeting scheduled, Katia."

"We do."

"Hold all our calls, Melanie."

"Done," Melanie said as she plucked the ringing phone off the hook.

Jack sat in his chair and placed his hands on the arms with a firm grasp. He looked as if he was holding himself down, and Katia wondered if he was trying not to jump across the desk at her. "Mind telling me what the heck is going on between you and Austin McCreary?"

"I don't know what you're talking about."

"Sure you do. I walked in last night, and you two appeared awfully chummy for a business relationship. He had his arm around you with half the town traipsing in and out of that house. How many people saw you like that? A hundred?"

"Four hundred and ten, I'm told," Katia replied. "Sarah said ours was the most viewed house on the tour."

"Ours?"

"I meant my committee's project house. Sarah Bosworth, Mrs. Beabots and I did all the decorating. Most of the afternoon, I was in the living room explaining the sugarplum tree to the visitors."

Jack pursed his lips and rubbed his forehead. "I'm not talking about the decorations. I'm talking about the way you looked at him. As though he was your dream guy."

Katia kept her tone light and nearly flippant. If she even hinted that Austin actually was the most important man in her life, Jack would replace her with Claire Ebberhart before the morning was through. Katia had worked too long and too hard to lose her position with this company. If she had to start over someplace else, she'd have to prove herself all over again.

Until Jack had seen her standing with Austin, Katia had known exactly where she stood with Carter and Associates. She had no idea where she ranked with Austin on his romance meter. Weighing those two facts, she chose to keep her job.

"Austin is an old friend, and he's the biggest single client this firm has ever seen. If it weren't for me, you wouldn't have his business. In addition, I just came from the Indian Lake Hospital president's office," she said more forcefully than she'd planned. But given the circumstances, she felt the power play was warranted. "A few weeks ago, we agreed that going after the hospital and the county's business were the most prudent next steps for us."

"Yes. Yes. We talked about this. I remember."

"I presented our package to him, and this morning he signed with us."

Jack's mouth fell open. "He told me three weeks ago that corporate wouldn't switch from their current provider. How'd you do that?"

"Emory Wills has been the hospital president since I was in high school. He's a friend of Austin's. I went to Emory and asked for a donation for the Heritage Foundation. I told him about the Candlelight Tour. One thing led to another, and we talked business. Real business. Next year, they're expanding the hospital again. He'll need a policy for the new wing. I talked him into coming over to us for the entire campus. He agreed. Remember when I told you I was looking into insuring just the hospital equipment? It's an area we've never worked before. But Emory wants to go with us on that policy, as well." Katia leaned back in her chair while Jack absorbed everything.

"I couldn't get that guy to budge an inch. Now I feel as if I'm losing my edge," Jack said glumly.

"Not in the least. It's just that I have history here, Jack. A lot of people remember me and my mother. I'd forgotten how many friends I had here. And how much I missed them. It's been a revelation."

Jack rapped his fingers on the desk. "All the more reason that it's imperative you stick to my rules. No dating. Not Austin or any other client."

Katia stared at him for a long moment. This was the time to push her agenda. She was in the driver's seat with Emory's signed contract. "Business in Indian Lake is a bit different than other places, Jack. Companies here want to work with people they know and trust. Being friendly and social with them is expected. That makes it even more difficult to keep the two worlds apart. Maybe you should rethink that rule…"

Jack shot to his feet. "Absolutely not! Most corporations have a no-dating policy. It's there for a reason. I learned that the hard way. Do you know why I adopted it?"

"I have a feeling I'm about to find out."

"When I first started in this business, I worked for a good-size firm. I was a real hot-shot, or so I thought. In six months, I was leading in sales. My boss threw me a big bone. He wanted me to sign up a new women's softball team. Sports-injury insurance. I was so sure I was on my way to a whole new career. I saw myself working with major-league teams. I was going to meet legends in basketball, football and baseball. Oh, I had stars in my eyes all right. The owner of the softball team was a real lioness. She knew she had some talented women on her team. Olympic material. I got her the best policy at a really good price. But she wanted more. She wanted me. We dated for several months. When she became coldhearted and vindictive, I broke it off.

"She went to my boss and not only cancelled the contract, but told him all kinds of lies about me. She was very well connected. She told other sports-management people I had been dealing with that I had romanced my way to my contracts. She told them I couldn't be trusted. They believed her. I got fired." Jack took a deep breath. "I won't have that happen to me again, Katia. My firm will never be accused of garnering clients that way. What you do, or any of my employees does, reflects on me. It's imperative to me that my reputation and this company's remain pristine."

"I understand, Jack" was all Katia could say.

"I'm not an idiot and I'm not blind. You have feelings for Austin. It's written all over your face. So unless you're engaged to the guy or you want to work someplace else, it stops here."

"I've worked alongside you for too long to just walk away, Jack. I'm doing my absolute best to bring this company back to life. It was my idea to move here, and we've already saved thousands of dollars. I've got half a dozen contracts that will sign before the year is out. By March 1, when Austin starts moving the rest of his cars here, he'll be signed up for the remainder of his contract, as well. I couldn't be any more on board, Jack, unless I owned this company myself."

Jack considered what she'd said. "So Austin is just a client."

"A friend and a client," she corrected. "I imagine he'll introduce both of us to even more clients in the future."

"I hope that happens."

"I don't see why not. All I have to do is ask."

Jack nodded. "Well, I think we have a very clear understanding now," he said, dismissing her.

Katia stood and walked to the door. "Oh, what about Claire?"

Jack's expression was granite, and his eyes were as hard as steel. "I'm hiring her. She could be a real asset."

Katia felt the blood drain from her face. Jack didn't believe her explanations about Austin in the least. "Good decision," she said, and closed the door.

DECEMBER HAD ALWAYS meant long workdays and weekends filled with holiday preparations for Katia. This year, because she felt Jack scrutinizing every move she made, Katia came to work early and left late. She set up meetings and pitched her product with her usual competence and thoroughness. She made a point not to return to the office until she had the contract signed.

Katia ordered all her gifts online and had them shipped to her friends in Chicago. She told Mrs. Beabots to expect daily deliveries for her. Katia didn't know when she'd have time to wrap gifts, much less see her friends.

In an email, Katia told Austin that she was working double time. He asked her to join him for dinner at an Italian restaurant in town.

Katia's internal alarm system kicked in immediately. She'd just smoothed things over with Jack, and she had at least a semblance of solid ground beneath her feet, despite the new hire. Yet she wanted to see Austin.

To make sure no one in town saw them together, she'd suggested that they meet at his house. He'd agreed, and that was the reason she was now sitting next to him at his dining room table.

The center of the table was covered with spruce, pine and cedar greens and small silver bowls holding lush, crimson amaryllis blooms. Red votive candles flickered merrily. Daisy had prepared roast pork loin, garlic mashed potatoes and Brussels sprouts. For a cold winter night, the meal was perfect.

Unfortunately, nothing Katia said to Austin seemed to lighten his dark mood. They were halfway through their meal when his fork clattered on his plate. Katia jumped, which told her she was sitting on far too many pins and needles around Austin.

"What is it?" she asked.

"What are we doing, Katia?"

She closed her eyes for a moment. She'd wanted

to be with him, but now she realized she'd made a mistake. "Besides the obvious of sharing a meal, as friends, I wanted to see you."

"Why?" He shoved his chair away from the table and tossed his napkin down.

"Because I…"

He snorted. "Hard to say it, isn't it?"

"I don't know what you mean."

"Okay. Then, let me say it for you. You want to see me, but you don't want to be seen *with* me. That's why you declined dinner downtown where Jack could see us together. And God forbid I should try to hold you or kiss you. That would be really going too far, wouldn't it? I might jeopardize everything you want. That about sum it up?"

"Austin, it's really complicated for me, and I'm trying to put everything into perspective here—"

He cut her off with a wave of his hand. "Forget it. I've heard all your explanations. I don't know why I asked you out tonight."

She ground her jaw, feeling anger, frustration and confusion fill her brain. She couldn't think. "Me, either."

"The truth is, Katia, I wanted to see you, too. I like being with you when you're not tied up in knots about your job and your boss. I keep thinking that if you spend more time with me, you'll see that I might be as important to you as those things are. Apparently not. You frustrate me to death! I still get the feeling that you're leading me on—"

"That's not true."

"No? Right now you're sitting there looking at me with the same love-filled eyes I've remembered for years. I've always been pretty good at reading faces, and yours is the easiest. But each time you pull this 'hide in the shadows' bit, as if you're ashamed of me, I'm sucked back to when you left Indian Lake and didn't contact me. I feel abandoned and hopeless. I keep telling myself that, no, that's not what Katia wants—"

"It's not," she said forcefully, leaning forward.

He shook his head. "Maybe not directly, but that's how it comes across to me. And it's not good."

"Austin, the last thing in the world I want is for you to feel those awful things again. I couldn't bear it if I caused that."

He peered into her eyes. "Then, you should leave, Katia."

"Maybe if you would start being my friend and try to see my side in all this, we could figure it out."

He rose and looked down at her. "I'll work on that." His tone held a finality that told her there was no more room for discussion.

Katia scooted her chair out and walked to the hall closet where he'd hung her coat. She reached into the side pocket of her purse.

"Here," she said.

"What's this?"

She put his old house key in his hand. "A Christmas present. I won't be needing it anymore."

When she walked out of the house, it was snowing, and the wind kicked around the trees with a vengeance. The brittle, frigid night matched Katia's broken heart.

THREE DAYS BEFORE CHRISTMAS, Katia was at her desk, Melanie was answering the phones and Jack was in his office with Claire Ebberhart, who had joined the firm the week before. Katia's cell phone rang. *Austin.*

"Hi," she said in a near whisper, and turned her chair around so Melanie couldn't hear her conversation.

"I called to say goodbye," Austin said, though there was so much noise in the background, Katia wasn't quite sure she'd heard him right.

"Where are you? And what are you doing?"

"I'm at O'Hare. I'm off to Phoenix."

Katia shot to her feet. "Just like that? You didn't tell me."

"Sure I did. I shut down the plant for two

weeks every year while I go to Phoenix for the holidays. You've been more than a little busy lately anyway." He spoke loudly over the noise.

"I know. It couldn't be helped. We're new here, and it's been a lot more work than I expected."

"So you said. Well, I just wanted to say merry Christmas and happy New Year."

"Happy New Year to you, too, Austin." Katia felt the words cut through her heart like glass. She wouldn't be seeing Austin at all over the holidays.

She'd been so intent on saving her career that she'd had to assess every aspect of her life. That meant purposefully doing everything she could not to think about Austin, let alone see him or call him. What a fool she'd been to believe she could make her feelings for Austin go away. Austin wasn't a right click, delete on a computer. He was Austin.

He filled her life, mind and heart like he had when they were teens. She wished there was some way to eradicate her need to be with him, but the only effective distraction she'd found had been work. Hours and hours of mind-numbing work.

Every night she'd fallen into bed so drained and exhausted she hadn't thought about anything. She'd managed to speak to Austin in snippets over the past three weeks, but that was all.

Apparently, he'd felt the slight.

Or had he?

He'd just said that he closed the plant and went away every year. This was his normal routine. Katia hadn't been in his life for a very long time, and she was the one trying to keep him at arm's length. She had to accept the consequences of that.

"Have a great time in Arizona," she said with a hollow feeling in her chest. "When will you be back?"

She dropped into her chair and put her forehead in her hand. She wasn't doing very well with this balancing act between her heart and her career.

"I'm not sure. It depends on the car shows and how long it takes to get the cars lined up. The museum is coming along nicely. Hal will send me photos every day. If I have to stay in Phoenix, Tom can run the plant after the first of the year. He's done it before."

Katia felt more than a little deflated. She was crushed. She realized she'd conjured some fantasies about spending time with Austin over the holidays. Jack would be in Chicago, and she'd be able to see Austin without looking over her shoulder for fear of losing her job. But those had been daydreams. They had nothing to do with reality. Austin was her client and nothing more. She told herself this was how it had to be, for her survival. This was what she'd asked him for, but everything about her decision felt wrong. Yet she didn't know how to change any of it.

Austin had made it crystal clear that he wouldn't be in her life in half measures. Still, Katia couldn't help wondering why Austin was so upset with her decision when he hadn't made any mention of a permanent relationship with her. He'd never said that he loved her. He'd never gone the limit and gotten down on one knee. She couldn't fault him for respecting her decision, but at the same time, he hadn't swept her off her feet, and that hurt.

"Have a safe trip, Austin," she said and hung up, wondering if he would care if he knew he held her heart in his hands.

CHAPTER TWENTY-FOUR

KATIA SAT IN the front row at St. Mark's Church with Mrs. Beabots, who was apparently the most honored guest at Maddie's wedding. Because Maddie had little or no family in attendance, Mrs. Beabots served as the mother of the bride and was the last one seated before the processional began. She wore a raw silk champagne dress and a jacket with beaded cuffs and collar. She winked at Katia and took her hand as the guests stood.

"Wait till you see Maddie. She's just beautiful," Mrs. Beabots whispered with joyous tears in her eyes.

As the children's choir began and the music swelled to fill the church, Katia looked at Nate, who stood at the altar with his brothers. The Barzonni men were dressed alike in midnight-black tuxedos and snow-white shirts. Katia couldn't imagine anyone radiating more happiness than Nate at that moment. She noticed that he shifted his weight, whispered to Rafe and then fidgeted with his jacket lapels. He looked as if he was corralled in a paddock and ready to race down the aisle, grab Maddie and start the ceremony.

As Katia watched Nate smiling and joking with his brothers and Scott Abbott, the local bookstore owner and stringer for the Indian Lake newspaper, she wondered what that would be like to have a man in her life, a man who was so anxious to be with her that his eyes filled with anticipation just at the thought of seeing her. She certainly didn't have that with Austin. Oh, there was a time when she remembered his face looking as though the sun had risen behind his eyes, but they had been young. She chalked it up to naïveté. She and Austin had lost that kind of innocence when she'd betrayed him.

Regret stung Katia's eyes as she realized that Austin didn't trust her and never would. No matter how much he protested to the contrary, he would always hold her accountable, and the grudge he carried would keep them apart.

Katia had never felt so alone in all her life. Not after leaving Indian Lake at sixteen and not even after her mother's death.

Though she'd suffered when she'd moved to Chicago, this was the first time Katia could fully put herself in Austin's shoes. He'd had no warning or explanation as to why she'd left. Standing in LaGuardia, he'd been prepared for the girl he loved to come to his prom. Austin had told her that he'd thought about marriage then. His plans for their future together had been shattered. How devastated and bereft he must have been.

That was exactly how she felt right now.

After their last dinner together, Austin had made it clear that he didn't trust her, and even though he had thought he'd wanted to see her, the reality of their being together was too painful. Katia felt as if her heart was being ripped to shreds with talons. Tears filled her eyes. This wasn't a panic attack. This pain was worse than anything she'd ever experienced. This was the pain Austin had felt when she'd abandoned him.

Her heart went out to him, and she wished there was some way she could make it up to him.

Her fatal mistake had been falling in love with him, and there was no doubt in her mind that she truly loved Austin. She missed talking to him about his cars and the progress of the museum. She'd actually looked forward to learning how to play handball and racquetball with him this winter. She'd come to enjoy cooking in the big kitchen with Daisy, like they had for the Candlelight Tour. But now there were huge empty spaces in her days and evenings that for weeks had been filled with Austin. She had plugged those gaps with her own musings and worry about what could have been and what they should have said to each other. In the end, Katia could never be certain if anything between them would ever change, whether she'd been brave enough to tell him that she loved him or not. In her worst moments, she believed it wouldn't have made any difference at all.

Now Austin was on his way to Phoenix, and he'd be gone for weeks. She didn't care that he "always" went to Arizona for the holidays. She didn't care that he was arranging for the transport of his cars as well as the purchase and trading of other vehicles. She knew what he was doing. He was showing her that she didn't exist for him.

He didn't want her.

"Aren't they lovely?" Mrs. Beabots tugged on Katia's arm and tilted her head toward the aisle as Olivia, Liz and Isabelle walked to the front of the church. They were dressed alike in winter-white straight velvet skirts and sparkling ivory cardigans. They carried bouquets of white roses with sprigs of dancing rhinestones that glittered in the evening candlelight.

Next was little Annie, dressed in a long white satin dress with a blush-pink sash around her waist, her red hair crowned with white tea roses and rhinestones.

Maddie wore a white *peau de soie* gown with an A-line skirt. Around the hem were aurora borealis crystals, seed pearls and rhinestones. With each movement, she looked as if she was walking among glittering stars. She wore a fingertip veil that was banded in white satin ribbons, and carried a bouquet of holly, white and blush roses and matching satin streamers that fell nearly to her knees. But it was Maddie's smile as she walked toward Nate that broke through Katia's bleak thoughts.

Maddie had no family here, no parent to walk her down the aisle. But she didn't appear to be letting that darken her mood. Maddie's face was filled with expectation, love and so much happiness that Katia imagined reaching out and grabbing a handful of it to put into her pocket for safekeeping. Maddie's joy was so profound that Katia felt as if something was changing inside her.

She wasn't quite sure, but it felt like hope.

AUSTIN WATCHED FIREWORKS illuminate the crystal clear night sky above Camelback Mountain. From his vantage point at the terrace bar at the newly refurbished Camelback Inn, he had a panoramic view of the mountains and the desert beyond. He'd finished a lobster dinner with friends, listened to a small band play

"Auld Lang Syne" and now they were all hugging each other to ring in the New Year.

Joe Collier had been Austin's friend since they'd met at York. They'd always shared a love of traditional values, tennis and of course, antique cars. Joe was an investment banker by profession, but once he'd met his wife, Vicki, a Scottsdale native, two years after college graduation, Joe had moved to Arizona, where he'd immersed himself in high-tech communications and become a venture capitalist. He funded start-up companies run by brainiac kids. Joe had a knack for finding pearls in the oceans of new technology, and he kept up a yearly crusade to get Austin to move to Arizona to be his partner.

"I understand that you're loyal to your employees back there in Indian Lake, and what I'm suggesting would be a radical change. But, Austin, people move every day. They grow. They expand their horizons. Think out of the box here with me for a second. You could do this. Maybe we could work something out so you could be part-time," Joe said excitedly, shoving the sleeves of his black cashmere sweater up to his elbows.

"There's no such thing as part-time in a successful business, Joe. We both know that," Austin replied staunchly, leaning back in the deeply cushioned patio chair. "My plant is shut down, and I'm still on the internet and phone with my clients. It may be the holidays, but in two days, it's business as usual. So why don't you tell me the real reason you want me working for you. I'm not such a genius with any of these new gadgets you're investing in."

"Quit calling it that. This is revolutionary. We're developing a waterproof, readable, high-resolution, unbreakable screen for cell phones, ereaders and tablets."

Austin paused while lifting a glass of port to his lips. "Waterproof."

"Sweatproof, swimproof, showerproof. You name it."

Vicki smiled broadly. "As deep as two hundred feet."

Austin's eyes tracked from Joe to Vicki. "Why do you look as if you're gloating?"

"Because I found the genius who thinks he's invented this screen and the airtight casings around it," Vicki said. "I pushed Joe to invest with him, and I hope we get to be at the opening bell on Wall Street the day they launch their IPO."

Joe chuckled. "Vic thinks big." He grabbed a handful of nuts. "Seriously, Austin, I'm offering you a chance to get in on the ground floor here. I know how much you revere inventors, being from a family of them, and even though I don't know my shoelaces from my loafers, this is exciting stuff. I need a guy who can do operations. There's nobody better than you. You've been running that manufacturing plant for a long time. You understand employees, production timelines, shipping, suppliers and, ultimately, making the client happy. That's not my area. Plus, the guys who came up with the idea are good at dreaming and working inside their heads, but they don't understand the first thing about practical day-to-day stuff. These two kids I've invested in, college dropouts, can barely order lunch. I had to hire an assistant for each of them to run their lives. Can you believe that? How in the world would they understand sales meetings or deal with truckers? They can't even pay utility bills on time. When the news of this invention hits the wires and gets tweeted from here to kingdom come, it's going to be massive. That's where you come in again. You know how to handle success like that. Frankly, it's that kind of huge, instantaneous demand that closes down most of these start-ups before they clock six months on the job."

"I just don't know—" Austin started to say.

"This is the future, Austin. I need a guy I can trust, and I want to share this with you."

"The future," Austin mused, swirling his

port. Katia had talked to him about the future, but he hadn't really been listening. What had she been trying to say to him? "I guess I'm guilty of not putting my future first."

Joe threw his head back. "Oh, man. I never thought I'd hear you admit it."

"You know this about me? I'm only surprised because an old friend back home recently brought it up."

Vicki cocked an eyebrow. "You're serious? This is a new revelation?"

Austin leaned forward and put his glass on the table. "To say I've been in a fog…for quite some time…is stating the obvious. How come you guys didn't tell me this before?"

Joe put his hand on Austin's shoulder. "We did. Every year. You weren't listening. Does this mean you might consider my offer?"

"It might," Austin replied without thinking. He was amazed at how fast the words came out. Then he thought of the ramifications. Working with Joe would mean moving to Arizona. Possibly on a permanent basis. Austin's parents had laid out his life for him as if they were putting out his clothes for Sunday school, and until now, he'd never really questioned it. Sure, he'd had other dreams, other passions. But he'd gone to the schools they'd chosen. Ran the business his father had preserved for him. Very little had been asked of him in return, except that he "carry on."

Austin had never truly chosen for himself.

This opportunity was like an atomic explosion inside him. If he chose this new life, even his daily commute, his routines, would be different. The weather would be different. He could play tennis every week of the year in Arizona. He would make new friends in the place of old ones.

He could start everything from scratch. He could be an entirely different person if he chose to be.

Leave Indian Lake. Could I actually do that?

Would he sell the plant? Sell the family home? He wasn't even finished with the museum, and already he was considering abandoning it.

Of course, he'd always planned to donate the building to the city as a monument to his ancestors. Now that he knew they probably didn't deserve his "trophy house," his interest in the project had dimmed. He'd never started a venture he hadn't finished, so he knew he would find the enthusiasm to see the museum to fruition. He could only imagine what people would say about him if he didn't. Especially if he moved to another state.

Who am I kidding? The only reason I'm even

talking to Joe about working with him is because of Katia.

On the face of it, Katia had never purported to be anything more than his insurance agent and his friend. He believed she didn't have a romantic relationship with Jack, if what he'd observed and what she'd told him was accurate. As far as Austin could tell, there wasn't another man in Katia's life.

And that was the point.

Austin wasn't in her life, either.

Katia had proved that she was his friend, but each time they'd moved one ministep beyond that, she'd put on the brakes. She'd jumped back from him faster than an Arizona jackrabbit. During the preparations for the Candlelight Tour, and on that very night, Austin had thought that they were moving to a new level. He could have sworn that when she looked into his eyes when they were standing together at the front door that she was on the verge of telling him she loved him.

He'd seen that open, vulnerable look of love in her eyes long ago. She was the Katia of their youth, full of life and love that she wanted to give to him alone. His heart had responded by practically pounding its way out of his chest. He'd held his breath, waiting for her to say the words. He could still feel his arm around her.

Smell the perfume she wore when he'd placed his lips close to her ear.

And then it had happened.

Her eyes had turned to ice. Her muscles had stiffened, and she'd pushed his hand away as if he was contagious. He'd felt unwanted. Unloved.

Being the glutton for punishment that he was obviously becoming, he'd invited her to dinner. What a disaster that had been. If he'd had any doubt that Katia didn't want him in her life, that conversation had nailed it. She'd even given him his key back. It was over.

Austin had stared at her in disbelief as she'd walked out the door. He felt just as he had when she'd abandoned him once before. He'd vowed he would never put himself in such a precarious position again. He would never believe again. He would never allow anyone to hurt him like Katia had.

This time it had been Katia, once more, who had inflicted the pain.

Austin hated feeling like an idiot. Since the only person who'd made him feel this way—twice—was Katia, the answer was to erase her from his life.

But she lived on the same street as he did and worked nearly as close, her friends were his friends and Indian Lake was a small place. He was bound to see her far too often. Moving out of town was a clear choice. He could still honor the insurance contracts. He wouldn't take that away from her. She'd worked hard, and her coverage was the best deal he could find.

The more Austin thought about his situation, the more he realized that Katia, Joe and Vicki were right. It was time for Austin to make his own mark on the world and accomplish something that he could be proud of. In truth, he'd probably done everything he could in Indian Lake. He'd hit his own glass ceiling.

He needed new challenges and new adventures. Even if he were to find out that Katia still had feelings for him, what could he offer her, really? A man who was still searching for himself?

Then he thought of Thanksgiving at Mrs. Beabots. Of course Katia could not commit to him. He'd been living in the shadow of the past more than he'd realized.

Thanksgiving night, Gabe and Liz had announced they were going to have a baby. Liz's face had been filled with love, and he'd immediately compared her expression to Katia's, when he'd seen unconditional love in her eyes. At that moment, Austin had realized that he wanted a family of his own. But he only wanted children with Katia. He only wanted to be with Katia.

But what could he teach his children when he didn't understand very much about himself? How could he teach them to reach for their dreams when he hadn't done it himself?

Perhaps all these upheavals he'd experienced since Katia had returned to Indian Lake were showing him that he'd come to a new fork in the road. It was time to take the path less taken. The tracks his father and grandfathers had laid for him were worn.

Taking a deep breath of desert air, Austin felt vibrant and more alive than he had in years. He picked up his glass of port and held it up to Joe. "Let's toast. To new beginnings."

"What?" Joe was incredulous. "You mean you're actually going to do this?"

Vicki's delight was tangible. "This is truly the best New Year's ever! I'm so happy."

"So am I," Austin said truthfully. "I'll figure out a way to make it work, but you have no idea how thrilled I am right now."

CHAPTER TWENTY-FIVE

BRILLIANT AZURE SKIES and a radiant sun melted the snow from the sidewalks as Katia walked to work. It was only mid-February, but the mild weather teased the promise of an early spring. It had been over a month since Katia had received a text from Austin telling her he would be remaining in Arizona most of the winter. He'd given no explanation other than that he was "working remotely." She'd answered with a text probing for more information, but his only reply was to ask that all his insurance paperwork be scanned and emailed to him.

Katia had paced the floor late at night, going over dozens of scenarios and reasons why Austin would act so out of character. She knew Mrs. Beabots's revelation about his great-grandfather's lack of contribution to the Duesenberg automobiles had been a substantial blow. She just hadn't realized it had been enough to change the course of Austin's life—and her own.

She'd gone to Austin's house to interrogate

Daisy, but as pleasant and as fun as Daisy was, she had nothing to add to the puzzle. Austin had told his housekeeper that he was working on a "new deal" and had asked her to ship him a box of clothing and his new tennis shoes. Other than that, everything about his disappearance from Indian Lake was a mystery.

Daisy had told Katia that Austin had asked her to keep the house running as usual, and there was no discussion about how long he would be gone. She'd also said that in all the years she'd worked for Austin, he'd never been this unpredictable. He was a man of regimen, schedules and dependability.

Austin didn't do mystery.

This time, Austin was the one to leave Indian Lake with no warning, and Katia was the one to feel rejected. Being friends with Austin would never be enough for her. She wished she'd done something to make him understand just how much she loved him. In her mind, she was all in, but in actuality, she was far from it. Her choice had hurt them both, and she was to blame—again.

Katia's angst and confusion caused a near paralysis in her personal life, and her work had never been so difficult. Coming up with original ideas to garner new business for Jack was like pulling teeth. Somehow she managed to do well enough that neither her clients nor her coworkers noticed that she was going through the motions.

Her obsession with Austin was like a mental disorder, and she had no choice but to try to treat it. She'd worked up a list of reasons as to why she chose her work over Austin and recited them in the morning like mantras, hoping they would obliterate the growing unease she felt as she crossed off the days on her calendar. She had no idea when or even if Austin would return to Indian Lake. Once again, she felt that fate had rightly put her in Austin's shoes. Had he felt like this when she'd left for Chicago? Had he wondered if she'd ever come back to him, if she'd ever try to make amends?

Weeks passed, each day lonelier than the last. Katia told herself that once she'd made her choice, she couldn't go back on her word.

Yet as the weeks rambled by with little word from Austin, she spun dreams of having enough courage to fly out to Phoenix and confront him. There were times when she'd nearly convinced herself that if he rejected her, she'd be able to live through it.

But she knew she couldn't. The only thing holding her together was the fantasy that someday she would see Austin again, that eventually he would have to come home. She could only hope that, by then, she would have figured out how to put all the pieces of her shattered life back together.

Flinging her arms around herself to ward off a chill that came from her memories and not the winter air, Katia tried not to think about what she knew in her heart to be true: that she'd lost Austin forever.

By THE MIDDLE of the most blustery March in Indian Lake's history, Katia had begun watching the Weather Channel on the flat-screen television Jack had installed in the reception area, on her computer and on her cell phone app.

The weather announcer was describing yet another severe band of thunderstorms, flash floods and tornados that had touched down in Kansas and Iowa and were headed toward Indiana when Katia's office phone rang.

"Katia Stanislaus," she answered, not taking her eyes off the weather map.

"Katia. It's Austin."

Katia hit the mute button on the remote and sank into her desk chair. Though she'd received a dozen and a half emails from him, she hadn't actually spoken to him in weeks. Just the sound of his voice set her heart racing and caused her hands to tremble.

"Austin," she said breathlessly, no doubt

sounding unprofessional. She didn't care. She was happy to hear from him. She cradled the receiver in both hands and spun her chair around to face the back wall so that nothing would distract her. "Is everything okay?"

"It will be if you can help me," he replied.

His voice was even and controlled. He didn't seem as if he was as close to flipping out as she was. She wanted to jump through the phone, but she pulled out her best acting to date and smoothly said, "What can I do for you?"

"This is so not what I should be asking my insurance agent for, but I'm going crazy here. My event planner for the museum opening is apparently double booked and has bailed on me. Daisy practically went postal when I asked her to take over. Olivia is all booked up at the deli. I don't know what to do."

Katia cringed when he referred to her as his "agent," but as he continued, she felt a warm glow spiral through her body. He needed her. Granted, it wasn't much of a request, but it would keep her in contact with him a few times a day.

"The opening is next week."

"You don't have to tell me," he groaned. "I know it's a lot to ask—"

"I'll do it," she blurted. "I mean, I'll help you. It's going to take some real planning." She turned her chair around to grab a pen and saw the tracking of the storm on the screen. "Austin. I think we should order an enclosed canvas walkway from the parking lot to the museum entrance. We could have some bad weather next week. I think it's best to be prepared for rain."

"Fine with me. Any other ideas off the top of your head?"

"I'll call Maddie and see if she can cater. We don't need much. Just sandwiches, soda and water...and her cupcakes would be a real hit."

"I like it," he replied, sounding pleased. "Oh, and by the way, I called Debra La Pointe. She's got that theater just south of town. She's hired actors and tour guides for the opening. Could you call her and double-check that everything is still on schedule with her people?"

"Sure," she replied, and finally asked the big question. "When are you coming home? Back to Indian Lake?"

"I don't know. My work here with Joe is non-stop. I must be putting in fourteen-hour days and most of the weekends, and I love it. I don't know when I've been this excited about anything."

"Not even the museum?"

"Well, maybe in the beginning, but actually, no. Not really."

"What about the plant?"

"It's doing great. I promoted Tom to plant manager this morning, and he's got the place working like a fine-tuned Swiss clock."

"I don't suppose you'd want to share what you're working on?" she coaxed.

"I vowed to my partner I wouldn't disclose any details."

Katia felt her heart sink even lower. A partner. Was it a woman? Was this really about his business? Or had she truly shoved Austin away with both hands this time? "I take it this new venture has nothing to do with cars."

Austin chuckled. "I adore your curiosity, Katia. No, it's so far from antique cars, you wouldn't believe it," he said excitedly. "All I can tell you is that Joe and I have very high hopes."

Katia realized she was smiling. "I'm thrilled for you, Austin. You sound so…happy," she said sincerely. Considering how much she missed him, she was surprised at her own reaction. She was genuinely glad that he was doing well. Perhaps that was a sign of how deep her love for him ran. Even though she was miserable without him, she felt joy for him.

Austin reminded her that Hal had agreed to stay on after the last of the construction was completed and that he would handle the placement of the antique cars in Austin's absence.

Most of the cars from Austin's carriage

houses had been moved, but only three antique cars had arrived from Arizona: a 1957 Thunderbird convertible, a 1943 Cadillac sedan and a 1960 British MG. She knew these weren't Austin's most prestigious or expensive cars. Austin told her he would be shipping one car a month, each more rare and valuable to the museum, as a marketing ploy to keep interest high and to bring visitors back to see the new arrivals. Katia thought the plan was a good one.

"I'll adjust the policies to reflect the reduced initial inventory. You don't need to pay insurance on something that isn't there yet."

"I appreciate that, Katia," he said. "Listen, I have to run. Let me know the details of the opening as you finalize things. And don't forget to keep track of your hours and any expenses you incur. I'll be more than happy to pay you what I was going to pay the event planner, plus a bonus for bailing me out. Oh, and if you call and I don't pick up, just text me. I can read a text even when I'm in a meeting. I know you'll make it lovely."

"Thanks, but you don't need to pay me. I'm happy to do it."

"No way. I insist."

"Austin, isn't there any way you can be here? This is your creation. The newspapers and bloggers are going to be here, and they'll all want to interview you."

"Will Jack let you off for the day so you can oversee things?"

"Sure he will."

There was a long pause. "I hope so. Anyway, you can handle it. You knew my parents and grew up in their house. You have lots of stories you can give them."

Katia drummed her fingers on the desk, trying to decide if she should ask the obvious. They were actually talking, and she didn't want to crank up his anger, but she had to know. Was she the reason he wasn't coming back?

"Austin, I have to ask you—"

"What?"

Katia's courage slid away and she asked the second most important question. "Is the reason you're not going to be here because you don't want to face the press?"

"No, Katia," he answered very quickly. "I'm very busy here. I have to go. Bye."

Katia hung up and slumped back in her chair. Austin still had not told her the nature of his new business in Phoenix. He still didn't trust her.

Perhaps they had too much history to make a new life together now. Perhaps both of them had tried to blame their shared past for their current disquietude with their lives.

She'd been ashamed and guilt ridden. Austin hadn't told her in so many words, but he *must* still hold a grudge against her for leaving. He'd been nursing a broken heart for a long time. If this was a lesson he was trying to force upon her, she deserved it. But it didn't feel like that. This was different, as if Austin was searching for something that she couldn't give him.

Whatever it was, it made him happy, and it kept him away from her.

OVER THE NEXT WEEK, Katia pulled together everything Austin needed for the museum opening, right down to the parking valet service, which she found in Valparaiso. She hired off-duty police for security, emailed every reporter and blogger in the area and, with Maddie's help, the food was taken care of. She was amazed at what she'd accomplished in five days.

Katia was just closing up her desk for the night when her cell phone rang. Her smile felt good, stretching from ear to ear.

"Austin."

"I'm coming home," Austin said. "Tonight, on the last plane out of here. I want to beat the storm."

A thrill went through her body. "Tonight," she

repeated. She'd hinted for days about how important it was for him to be in town for the gala, but he'd shied away from any commitment. His reply had always been the same. He'd told her he was swamped. He'd told her he would "try." But in the end, he'd left her hanging.

Katia still believed that Austin was ashamed of the flaws in his family legend. She guessed he was afraid to face the media. Austin was the kind of man who would answer their questions truthfully, no matter how much pain they caused him. So she'd figured he would avoid putting himself in that position at all costs.

A hundred different declarations came to Katia's mind. *I can't wait to see you. I want to hold you. I love you.* But she bit back the words. "Good," she finally said. "Everyone will be glad to see you."

There was a long pause on his end that caused Katia to hold her breath. She thought that her heart had stopped beating. *Please say you want to see me, too.*

"I should be back in enough time to catch the shuttle to the train station. I've arranged for Daisy to pick me up and take me home."

Katia felt her heart sink. He hadn't asked for her help. He didn't need her. This was precisely what she'd told herself she'd wanted. She'd chosen her career over him. She'd done the right thing for them both.

Oh, yeah? Then, why do I feel so awful...so lost?

She couldn't falter now. She had to be strong. Funny—she'd never realized that strength could taste so bitter.

"That's great," she replied, her mouth going dry. "Listen, Austin. I need to get these final contract papers to you for a signature."

"Which ones are these?"

"Just for the cars. Remember, I reduced the policy since all the cars aren't there yet?"

"Oh, right. Well, I'll be at the museum most of tomorrow, but I can come by your office if that's easier."

"Either way. I'll touch base tomorrow," she replied as a tear slipped from her eye. She wiped it away with her finger. *I've missed you, Austin.* "I'll see you tomorrow, then?"

"Sure, but, Katia, just in case I'm too swamped, you can always scan them and email them. No worries."

A burning lump swelled in her throat. She couldn't talk or breathe. This feeling was worse than any anxiety attack she'd ever had. What was even more disheartening was the fact that she knew only Austin could put out the fire. "Fine."

"I'll be in touch," he said and hung up.

Katia flung her head back, willing her tears not to fall. Instead, they seeped into her temples and dampened her hair.

Melanie walked over to Katia's desk. "Hey, you okay?"

Katia swiped her face with both hands. "Sure." She sat up straight. "I just finished out the biggest deal of my life."

"You don't look joyous," Melanie offered. "So I'm guessing this is about Austin?"

Katia glanced toward Jack's office, but the door was shut since he was in conference with a new client. She kept her voice low anyway. "It's that obvious?"

Melanie put her hand on her hip. "My husband has worked for the man for nearly fifteen years. I've only worked with you for a few months. You're not a complicated person. I have to say, the both of you have been acting strangely since the holidays. I hope you figure it out."

"Well, I certainly have. I made my choice."

Melanie's eyes narrowed. "Is that right? Well, whatever it was, it was the wrong one."

Katia's eyes widened. "What makes you say that?"

"You're miserable. Before Christmas, you were the happiest person I'd ever met. You came in here singing every morning. Or whistling. Do you know that? I'm always grumpy until I've had two mugs of coffee. Or a cappuccino. At least. But you, you lifted everyone's spirits. Then everything changed. I get the winter blues every year, but, sweetie, you're practically purple. I think it's because Austin moved away."

"Well, he's coming back tonight," Katia said. She looked down at Austin's contract, which was sitting on her desk. "But he doesn't want to see me."

Melanie's mouth dropped open. "I don't believe that for a second. Austin is constantly asking Tom if he knows how you are."

"What? You never told me that!"

Melanie shrugged. "It all seemed part of their guy talk, really. I was always making dinner or helping the kids with homework. Not until this minute did I read anything into it. I guess Austin thought I would have told Tom anything unusual that happened here. So as long as the report was always the same, that you were working hard and closing deals, it seemed innocent to me."

"But then…that means maybe Austin *didn't* move away because of me."

"Why would he have done that?"

Katia fidgeted with the pens on her desk. "Because Austin and I have history. Big-time history. I broke his heart back when we were in high school."

Melanie's face was instantly empathetic. She sank into the chair opposite Katia's desk. "That explains why he seemed so changed this fall. Tom must have commented on it a dozen times."

"He did?" Katia's interest was piqued.

"Yes. And then just as strangely, Austin became introverted again right after Thanksgiving. Then he went to Phoenix, and we haven't seen him since. He calls Tom daily with instructions and that kind of thing, but Austin has never, ever stayed away from Indian Lake this long."

"I think he's trying to teach me a lesson."

Melanie shook her head. "Austin's not like that. If he loved you, he wouldn't do that."

"He doesn't love me anymore," Katia assured her.

"Are you sure about that? Would you stake your life on it?"

"What are you saying?"

"That if I were fighting for the man I loved, I'd be in his face, pleading my case and making very sure he knew what he was missing before I gave it all up."

Katia was thoughtful for a long moment. "He's supposed to sign his contracts. He's coming here tomorrow." She looked pointedly at Melanie. "What else would you do?"

"If Austin's coming home, I'd meet him on his own turf—certainly not here. All the way around, I'd go for broke."

Risk everything? Could I do that?

Melanie was right. Katia's life was tangled up with Austin's and probably always had been. She'd been driven to succeed in business, but when she was a kid, she had been motivated by trying to make the McCrearys proud of her. She wanted Austin's respect as an equal. Deep down, Katia had always questioned whether Austin truly loved her. She was guilty of believing her mother's insecurities about being born to a lesser class. But Austin's family had come to this country with nothing, too, and they had all worked hard for their success.

If she really loved him, she would do anything to keep him. That meant she had to be more courageous than she'd ever been.

And he was worth it.

"That's right," Katia finally said. "If I've lost him already, there's nothing left to lose."

THE WEATHER REPORT was changing just about every half hour, Austin noticed as he drove to Katia's office. The storms were approaching Indian Lake. Rain was one thing. High winds were an entirely different matter, and he didn't like the report that two tornadoes had touched down in western Illinois. Though it was the middle of the afternoon, ink-black clouds were moving in from the west in a ragged line above the bare trees. The air felt abnormally warm and moist. Most of the snow had melted, leaving only patches of dirty ice by the curbs, and Austin was thankful for the dry streets as he parked his blue Bugatti outside Carter and Associates.

He climbed the stairs and entered the office. Melanie looked up and smiled.

"Austin! How good to see you." She rose and gave him a quick hug. "How did you find everything at the plant?"

"Excellent. Tom has done a remarkable job. I always knew he was capable, but this really proves it. For him to take over after I dumped everything in his lap was one thing, and I'm so thankful for that, but he's really excelled."

"He's a good man, Austin," she said. "And so are you. I suppose you're here to see Katia."

"I am."

"She's not here. Actually, she quit her job today."

"She *what*?" The shock caused him to take a step back.

"She handed in her resignation to Jack this morning."

"But this job was the world to her." He couldn't believe it. Was she leaving Indian Lake? Going back to Chicago?

"She's been unhappy for quite some time," Melanie explained. "I thought you would have sensed that."

"She was?" Austin was confused. This made no sense to him. Katia had told her she liked— no, loved—being back in Indian Lake. She'd told him she was committed to Jack and to helping his company make a go of it here. She adored her new friends. How in the world did she expect to pry herself away from Mrs. Beabots, who clearly saw her as a daughter? "She would never quit," he stated resolutely, as if saying the words would change the reality of the situation.

"Apparently, that's not true. But don't worry. Her last corporate act was to get your papers to you. She went out to your museum. Give her a call."

"Not good enough. I need to talk to her," Austin said. "I'm on my way."

"But, Austin, there are tornado warnings. Wait till the danger has passed."

"I can't. She just resigned. I have to talk to her before she makes any more crazy decisions."

"Be careful," Melanie called as Austin flew down the stairs and out the door.

By the time Austin had covered the few paces

to his car, the wind had kicked up to what felt like a gale force. The sky was whirling with dark clouds that dipped in funnels across a strange, sandy-pink backdrop. Austin had to strain to open the car door. As he climbed inside, it slammed shut in the wind.

The radio was just as antique as the car itself and could only pick up AM signals, but it still worked. For years, Austin had kept the radio set to the local station, though he hardly ever bothered to tune in. Today, he was thankful that his old habits died hard. The announcer's voice crackled, but Austin distinctly heard the warning. "A tornado has touched down in Porter County and is headed east. All Indian Lake residents are requested to remain indoors and to seek shelter."

Austin checked the traffic, which was stopped at the light. He edged away from the curb, made a U-turn and headed south toward his museum.

As he sped through the yellow light at the next corner, Austin heard the air-alert siren go off across the Indian Lake Golf Course. The siren had been installed during World War II, and since then, it had been used to alert the townspeople to incoming tornadoes.

Austin floored the accelerator. He turned up the volume on the radio, hoping for an updated report.

If Katia had gone to the museum, he hoped she and all his personnel would have sought shelter in the underground rooms. Because the building wasn't officially open, he feared there hadn't been time to devise emergency drills. He would just have to pray that Katia knew what to do.

Austin was speeding twenty miles over the limit when he heard the terrifying sound.

Like a freight train barreling down from the sky, the funnel cloud spun and swooped across the cornfields to the right and just ahead of him. Austin put on the emergency brake and pulled over to the side of the highway. He fiddled with the radio again, but the announcer said nothing about this tornado spiraling out of the sky and touching down only a quarter of mile away.

The sound was deafening. It was bone-chilling and eerie, as if death walked with the wind. He saw flashes of lightning in the black curtain of sky, but there was no rain. Then he heard a pounding as the funnel hit the earth and sucked up rows of early-spring soil. A tree was uprooted and then plunked down several yards away. The world closed in as twigs, dirt and sand pelted his windshield. Austin feared the top would be ripped off, so he cranked both windows a crack to allow air to pass through. The top was pelted with debris that caused a slight rip near the center. As the funnel continued to pass, he prayed he would be safe. Apparently, the tornado hadn't damaged any homes yet, as there were no boards, vehicles, glass or even animals spinning in the storm.

He grabbed his cell phone and dialed Katia's cell. It rang once.

"Come on. Come on!" he muttered.

It rang three times before the voice mail picked up.

"Katia! Get to the basement! Tell everyone to get to the basement. I hope you can hear this! The tornado is here!"

He tossed the phone on the passenger seat and watched as the tornado shot across the highway, scorching the earth and ripping up concrete and asphalt, making a new trail from west to east. Then, in the blink of an eye, the impossible happened.

The tornado spun straight for Austin's museum.

He shouted in fear and shifted the car into gear. Without a thought for his own safety, he hit the gas pedal and drove.

The sounds of the siren blaring against the roar of the wind assaulted Austin's ears. He couldn't drive fast enough.

If anything happens to her...

"Katia! Katia!" he yelled, pounding the steering wheel and feeling as if the blood had drained out of him.

He was numb. All he could see ahead was the malicious, uncaring force of nature as it tore up half of the newly paved stoned drive to his museum and then sliced off the right south side of the building as if it was serving up a piece of cake.

It carried the section of his building away with it, like a mother snatching a newborn from its crib, possessive and wholly controlling.

Windows were broken and bricks stuck out of the wall at jagged angles. Wires hung loose from the second and third floors and flapped in the breeze. The gutters looked like long arms reaching out toward him.

Austin drove over the gritty chunks of asphalt and concrete. There was destruction all around him, but he didn't think about his building or even the cars inside. He saw only one face.

Katia.

When he couldn't get the car any closer, he skidded to a halt and bolted out.

"Katia! Where are you?"

The tornado winds died quickly. The air was silent and still, and the sky cleared. Austin felt the hairs on the back of his neck stand on end. He had the feeling that the world had just come to an end, and he was the only person left alive.

He had an awful feeling that something terrible had happened to Katia. Regret filled his heart. He should never have stayed away so long. He should have told her why he didn't come home after the holidays. If she was all right and they'd get a second chance, he vowed to always, always tell her everything in his heart.

Austin picked his way over timbers, tree limbs and uprooted shrubs. Pave stones from the driveway had been tossed along the walk leading to the front door.

The amputated building horrified Austin. What if Katia hadn't made it to the shelter? What if there were live wires inside?

"Katia!" Austin shouted again, and just as he was nearing the door, Katia appeared, along with Hal and three others.

Austin raced toward her.

"Austin!" she called joyously.

He threw his arms around her, holding her close, his palm on the back of her head, pressing her into his shoulder. "I thought I'd lost you."

He breathed a sigh of relief. She really was still alive. He'd nearly lost her, but she'd survived. And he'd gotten his second chance.

KATIA CLUNG TO AUSTIN, feeling safe, but more than that, she was buoyed by his presence.

"You're crazy, you know that? Driving into a tornado? You could have been killed." She pulled back and scowled at him. Huge tears filled her eyes.

"I was worried about you. Melanie told me you were here. Then I heard the sirens and the tornado warning. I was terrified." He squeezed her arms. "You didn't break anything, did you?"

"No. I'm fine, honestly. We're all fine." She gestured at Hal, the security guard and two women in janitor uniforms and rubber cleaning gloves inspecting the damage. "We heard the warning on the radio. It was hard to miss it. Thank goodness. We all rushed down to the basement. I knew not to take the elevator in case the electricity shut off and we'd be stranded."

"Good thinking," he said. Then he glanced over at the severed museum wing. "The entire south wall is gone…the driveway is a shambles, and the landscaping uprooted. This will take months to repair."

She placed her hand on his cheek and turned his face back to her. "And you'll do that. The insurance will cover it. This can be fixed, Austin. Luckily, most of the museum is intact. The majority of the damage seems to be to the grounds. We'll work on it together."

He closed his eyes for a long moment and

took a deep breath. "It's a lot to take in. But d
you promise? You'll work with me?"

"Yes, Austin. Together we can do anything."

He threaded his fingers into the hair at he
temples. He locked eyes with her. "You're sur
you're all right?"

"Shaken up, but I'm fine." She blinked. "Wai
a minute. You said you went to my office an
then you drove through the storm? You coul
have been killed! You...did that for me?"

"I did," he confessed.

"Are you crazy? I could have lost you, too
Don't ever do that again," she said angrily.

"I had to talk to you. Melanie told me tha
you quit your job. I was shocked. This job is..
everything to you."

"Not everything, Austin. I found that out th
hard way."

"Oh, Katia," he said. Then he kissed her
"Katia," he said again, his lips only a breatl
away from hers. "I love you. I always have."

"But you left me. I thought you were tryin
to teach me a lesson. Show me how it felt when
I left you. Trust me, it worked. I've been mis
erable."

"I'm sorry, Katia. You pushed me away s
many times because you valued your job, and
felt unwanted. I discovered a lot of things whil
I was away." He smiled and kissed her cheek

'If I had my way, I'd keep you right here in my arms forever."

"I thought you went away to get revenge on me," she said, placing her hands over his and forcing him to look into her eyes once more. "Austin, please, forgive me for the past."

"I have. I do," he whispered. "I didn't go away to get rid of you. I left to get you back. The right way."

She closed her eyes, trying to dispel the fog he'd created in her head. Maybe it was the adrenaline and shock from the tornado, but nothing, especially not Austin, was making sense to her right now. "I really, really don't understand."

"The more I thought about us and what you'd said, the more I realized you were right. I *have* been living in the past. But my life isn't about the past. It's about what I can make happen in the future. When I was in Arizona, I found an opportunity to do that. I also learned that I can never leave Indian Lake. This is my home. It's your home."

"But you sounded so excited about this new venture…"

Austin kissed both her palms and held her hands. "That's the really great part. I'm bringing all the manufacturing here. I'll have to expand my plant, refit some of the equipment and buy a lot of new machines, but what I have here is just what Joe needs. It made no sense for Joe to invest in an entirely new plant down there when I had nearly everything, employees included, right here in my own backyard."

"Austin, this is great news! You're going to be a hero to so many families."

He nodded. "*Hero* is a bit strong, but we'll be increasing the workforce here in Indian Lake. That's for sure." He put his arms around her again. His voice was filled with sincerity. "Katia, I want you to know that all these weeks away were torture for me—not seeing you. The business was exciting, but it was hollow." He put his forehead against hers. "I didn't have you."

"But you said you had friends there—"

He flung his head back and laughed. "I did say that, didn't I? This has all been my fault. I led you to believe that all I wanted was friendship from you. But I don't. I want more. More than what we had even when we were young. I want you with me every day of my life, Katia. I want to have our own family. We both deserve that. I think we've both been so lonely for so long that we've lost sight of what we could have if we just—"

She kissed him to stop him from talking. "I love you, Austin. I know now that I never stopped loving you. That's why there's never been anyone else for me. There never could be."

He kissed the tip of her nose. "A long time ago, I was the loneliest little boy on earth, and heaven sent you to me. It was like magic. One day you were just *there*. And you loved me from that first instant. I'm the luckiest man alive."

"Oh, Austin, we're both lucky," she replied, and this time she let her kiss linger.

Katia realized that they'd been so lost in so many ways over the years. But this time, they'd finally been found—by each other.

* * * * *

LARGER-PRINT BOOKS!

GET 2 FREE
LARGER-PRINT NOVELS
PLUS 2 FREE
MYSTERY GIFTS

Love Inspired®

SUSPENSE
RIVETING INSPIRATIONAL ROMANCE

Larger-print novels are now available...